Pat Eden stood
at the kitchen window

As she watched, her husband finished loading rocking horses into his truck. Even after all these years, her heart filled with love. Noel was a fine man, and they'd lived a good life, though very different from what might have been.

She waited, knowing he'd come into the house and ask her the question she'd been expecting since Laurel had called requesting they come to Michigan to see her new shop. But only Noel was leaving in the morning.

She heard his boots on the porch, then the door opened.

"All set?" she asked.

Noel's eyes sought hers, but she couldn't bear the recrimination she read there and turned her face. She didn't want to hear what he was going to say.

"Please come with me tomorrow. Your daughter wants you to."

"I can't. Don't ask me again. It's too much."

With a resigned sigh, he stepped away. "I'll tell Laurel you send your love."

"Yes, do that," Pat said, feeling ice penetrate every bone in her body. The ice that had first formed on that awful afternoon so many years ago.

Dear Reader,

I am often asked where I get the ideas for my stories. In the case of *A Summer Place*, I can pinpoint the exact source of my inspiration—Grand Beach, Michigan. When my paternal grandmother was widowed, my parents sent me there to spend the summers of my sixth and seventh years with her at the family cottage. My homesickness lasted one evening, because the next day I made an important discovery: despite living in landlocked Kansas City, I was at heart a fish! My first collision with a breaking wave began what has been a lifelong affinity for water.

Sages say you can't go home again, but I have. In the summer of 1977 I revisited the family cottage, which my grandmother had previously sold. The owner greeted me warmly. I can't tell you what a thrill it was to gaze over the same lake view that had captivated me as a child. Then in 2000, in preparation for writing this book, I returned once more and had the incredible experience of finding the current owners (relatives of the 1977 owner) at home. They graciously invited me into the house and, unbelievably, almost everything was exactly as I remembered it, including the linoleum in the hallway and, best of all, the little pull-down desk in the corner of the tiny bedroom that had been mine so many years before. Memories swept over me—eating huckleberries warm off the bush, rinsing my sand-encrusted body with the garden hose, snuggling in bed with my grandmother listening to the Chicago Symphony on the radio, the tangy odor of her cigarettes and the taste of her special dessert treat—ice-cold Milky Way bars.

Although fictional Belleporte is *not* Grand Beach, I hope it will draw you to its magic as it does my heroine, Laurel Eden. When Laurel decides to settle in Belleporte, little does she suspect that the move will alter her life by unlocking a shocking family secret and introducing her to Ben Nolan, the kind of hero capable of a "forever" commitment. I invite you to share with me the breathtaking sweep of Lake Michigan and Laurel's heartwarming experience of love and reconciliation.

Sincerely,

Laura Abbot

P.S. I would love to hear from you. You can write me at either LauraAbbot@msn.com or P.O. Box 2105 Eureka Springs, AR 72632. Please check out the Superromance Web site at www.superauthors.com.

A Summer Place
Laura Abbot

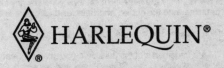

HARLEQUIN®

TORONTO • NEW YORK • LONDON
AMSTERDAM • PARIS • SYDNEY • HAMBURG
STOCKHOLM • ATHENS • TOKYO • MILAN • MADRID
PRAGUE • WARSAW • BUDAPEST • AUCKLAND

ISBN 0-373-71101-8

A SUMMER PLACE

This edition published by arrangement with Harlequin Books S.A.

® and TM are trademarks of the publisher. Trademarks indicated with
® are registered in the United States Patent and Trademark Office, the
Canadian Trade Marks Office and in other countries.

Visit us at www.eHarlequin.com

Printed in U.S.A.

Every family needs a "rock."
Thanks, Larry, for being ours.

CHAPTER ONE

ONLY FOUR DAYS REMAINED of her vacation.

Half listening to the TV meteorologist promising balmy days and cool nights along the Michigan coast, Laurel Eden fluffed the pillows behind her back and, with a sigh, selected several more of the brochures she'd requested from the state tourism department. She hadn't expended all this time and effort to face a dead end.

Somewhere in this blizzard of information was the answer. The ideal site for her gift store. She'd budgeted carefully and wisely invested her lump sum divorce settlement. She'd made the necessary contacts, done her research. Yet despite all her preparation, the right location continued to elude her.

Adding to her frustration was pressure from her parents to settle in the mountains of West Virginia, where they lived, instead of in Michigan. Without hurting their feelings, she'd patiently explained that, with her failed marriage finally behind her, she needed to make a success of something all her own.

As a sales rep for a cooperative of Appalachian artisans and craftsmen, of which her parents were members, she'd traveled throughout the North Central states, but it was western Michigan—and the lake—that drew her with an elemental pull. Once she'd decided to settle here, she'd assumed picking a site would be a simple matter. Wrong.

She turned to the sole remaining brochure. A small resort community on Lake Michigan, near Lake City. A viable weekend destination for Chicagoans. So far so good. She unfolded the glossy paper and studied the photographic spread.

Her breathing slowed.

A quaint lakeside gazebo, surrounded by tulip beds. In the distance, blue-green foam-tipped breakers.

A shiver of anticipation ratcheted down her spine. She couldn't ignore the hope that filled her. Besides, she had nothing to lose by going to Belleporte, which wasn't that far out of her way.

Even the name of the town seemed a positive omen. After all, *belle* meant beautiful.

ARRIVING IN BELLEPORTE late the next morning, Laurel was immediately captivated by the diverse architecture of the residences—a Cape Cod, a charming faux-Tudor, a boarding-house box of a home with a huge wraparound front porch. Winding roads curled away from the core of the town through thick woods and on toward the dunes and lakeside beach cottages—although in her judgment, "cottage" hardly did justice to the high-priced dwellings.

By midafternoon she'd checked into Primrose House, one of several local bed-and-breakfasts, and explored the business district. Though small, there were a few shops as well as a law office, a real estate agency and a branch banking facility. The owner of the sandwich shop where she stopped for lunch was a longtime resident and filled Laurel in on the town's history.

Founded in the 1920s as a summer retreat for wealthy Chicagoans, Belleporte had always been a family-oriented community. Although the town's population more than doubled in the summer months, over half of the homes were now permanently occupied, and many had passed from the original families.

Late in the afternoon, Laurel strolled along the beach, considering her options. The repetitive sound of the waves beating against the sand helped ground her runaway enthusiasm. Was Belleporte the place? Or was she merely frustrated by her fruitless search and impatient to make a decision?

If she decided on Belleporte, The Gift Horse would have to fill a specialized niche, attracting both locals and visitors, and be profitable enough to support her during the off-season.

When the wind freshened, she plunged her hands into her jacket pockets and lowered her head, lost in thought. Business considerations aside, she also had to be realistic about her personal motives. She needed to be sure about Belleporte. After all, she would be giving up a lucrative job to pursue this dream. She could hardly afford another impetuous mistake like her doomed marriage to Curt Vanover. It had taken her four years to get out of that situation, reclaim her maiden name and forge a new life for herself.

She paused and looked around. Whether it was the homey cottages perched on the dunes, the cry of gulls or the gathering clouds scudding across the sinking sun, she was hooked. Taking a deep breath, she reversed direction. Okay. Tomorrow she would look for property.

A persistent, mournful clanging intruded on her thoughts. She glanced up at a large brown-shingled house perched on the edge of the dunes. In the side yard, a metal cable knocked against a flagpole with a hollow, forlorn sound. Squinting, she studied the house. Stone chimneys dominated either end, and tall, curtained, second-story windows, set in gables, resembled eyes forever fixed on the horizon. A sun-bleached deck. Playground equipment.

A faint memory, like a wind-driven mist, swept over her, and for reasons she couldn't explain, she found herself mounting the wooden steps leading from the beach to the house. An eerily familiar house. But that couldn't be. She'd never been to Belleporte before.

When she reached the deck, she clutched the railing, exulting in the magnificent lake view. It was easy to picture a summer sun setting on the blue, blue lake, while adults gathered on the deck for cocktails and conversation and children exchanged playful shouts in the yard. This had to be one of those cottages where family members returned year after year, each generation enjoying it anew.

Beneath her fingers, in the weathered wood of the railing, were indentations, carved initials and dates, the earliest from 1929. "KL" and "FS," then "JK" and others she couldn't quite make out. She smiled to herself, imagining a family rite of claiming one's territory.

Once, she, too, had envisioned herself at the center of this kind of family. Once she'd thought she would have a happy, enduring marriage, lots of children and a rich legacy of rituals and traditions. Momentarily, bitter memories threatened her peace of mind, but she shook them off.

The covered deck furniture, drawn curtains and smokeless chimneys all suggested the house had been closed for the winter. Surely it wouldn't hurt if she walked around it. Viewing it from the front, maybe she'd remember what other home it reminded her of.

What could it hurt to satisfy her curiosity?

BEN NOLAN SHUT his briefcase, checked his calendar for the next day, shrugged into a windbreaker and walked out of his office.

"What's up? You're leaving early." Janet Kerns, his plain-spoken receptionist, secretary, legal assistant and gofer, swiveled from the file cabinet to face him.

"My buddy Jay Kelley phoned earlier from Chicago to ask if I'd check on the Sullivan place. His grandmother was concerned after the vandalism last week at Maxwells'. Besides that, Mom called. It's Mikey again. I don't know why that brother of mine can't keep himself out of trouble."

"He's a teenager, counselor." Janet arched her eyebrows. "And if memory serves, the rest of you Nolan boys weren't angels, either."

"You've hit on one of the drawbacks of working in the town where you grew up. You can't escape your past." He glanced at his watch. "I'll run by Summer Haven first, then double back by Mom's. After that, I can retreat to my lonely bachelor pad, nuke a pizza and tackle the Pendleton brief."

"You're breaking my heart."

He grinned. "I was just seeing if I could get a little sympathy around here."

"Was that in the job description?" Janet scooped up a stack of folders. "Anything you need me to do before I leave?"

Ben shrugged. "Maybe flush a few clients out of the woodwork."

The older woman shook her finger. "None of that talk. Building a new law practice, especially in a small community like this, takes time."

"Now I remember another reason I hired you, besides, of course, those sparingly rendered doses of sympathy. You're one helluva cheerleader." Smiling, he turned to leave. "See you in the morning."

"Have a good evening, Ben," she said softly.

A good evening. He hoped so. Despite his joking, he desperately needed to complete the brief, but he also needed to see what was going on with his brother. It hadn't been easy on any of them when their dad had died last spring. The older siblings, Bess, Brian, and, to some extent, Terry, were out on their own like Ben. But that left Megan and Mikey at home, and his mother worried about their not having a father. Although he was doing what he could to help, Ben feared he sometimes came across more as an interfering parent figure than a concerned big brother. He didn't worry so much about Megan, who was a high school senior and a pretty responsible kid, but fifteen-year-old Mikey was a different story, and Ben didn't enjoy his role as the heavy.

He tossed the briefcase onto the back seat of his Honda and eased away from the curb. It shouldn't take long to check the beach house, and it was a small

enough favor to do for his friend Jay, whose grandmother Sullivan's family had built Summer Haven
well over half a century ago. Without the legal business Jay, his father John and Mrs. Sullivan had thrown
his way, Ben would never have been in a position to
return to Belleporte and open his practice. Although
Jay insisted the family sought out Ben because he was
a talented attorney, Ben suspected their friendship, begun on the beach when they were boys, had played a
major role.

He drove along the nearly deserted serpentine road
that led to a cluster of exclusive beach houses, then
pulled to a stop in the Sullivans' driveway. Stepping
out of the car, he paused, listening to the crashing
waves. Earlier the weather had been mild, but now a
gust of chilling November wind caught him, and he
turned up the collar of his jacket.

From the front of the house, all appeared ship-
shape, but as he rounded the corner to check the rest
of the property, he was startled to discover a small
figure in a red jacket peering in the French doors off
the patio.

"What do you think you're doing?"

The kid spun around, a startled expression on his—
Hold it. This was no kid. Staring back at him was a
petite young woman with short curly black hair poking
from beneath her red-and-purple stocking cap. One
gloved hand covered her mouth and her brown eyes
widened in surprise.

"Hey, I asked you a question," Ben said in his
courtroom voice.

She removed her hand from her mouth, then smiled

with an expression he could only characterize as anticipation. "Who are you? The owner?"

"No."

"Then what are you doing here?"

Darn it, this was all backward. He was supposed to be the one conducting the cross-examination. He stepped toward her. "The owners asked me to check their property, and I don't think they'll be pleased that a trespasser was peeping in the window."

She raised her hands in a gesture of innocence. "I'm not a trespasser exactly. Well, maybe I am, but one with honorable intentions." She pivoted and spread her arms wide, as if to embrace the house. "How could I resist? This is the grandest place. I can just imagine generations of people having parties and picnics and reunions here, and—"

Ben signalled for a time-out. "Whoa. Can you slow down long enough to tell me who you are and what you're doing here?"

"Sorry, I guess I did get a little carried away. My name is Laurel Eden."

"Okay, that's a start."

"And you are…?"

"Ben Nolan, a local attorney—" that little tidbit ought to get her attention "—and the owners are my clients. So out with it. What are you doing prowling around Summer Haven?"

"Unbelievable as this sounds, I was walking along the beach, and when I saw this house—Summer Haven, you called it?—I had the strongest sense that I knew it. But that's crazy, because I've never been to Belleporte before. You know how it is when you have

that déjà vu feeling? You simply have to investigate."
She smiled engagingly. "So I did. End of story."

Ben had had no experience with déjà vu feelings,
but something in her manner made a believer of him.
She started around the corner of the house, then
stopped to admire the chimney. He trailed after her.
"Okay, Laurel Eden, where do you come from?"

"I live in Columbus, Ohio. At least for now. But
I'm hoping to move to Belleporte. Do you live here?"

For the life of him he didn't know why he was
continuing the conversation, why he didn't simply tell
her to get off the property. "No, but I grew up here."

"Don't you love it?" The young woman turned to
him, beaming.

"It's my hometown. What can I say?" She hurried
around to the front of the house, and despite the fact
he was totally flummoxed by her, he retained enough
of his male instincts to admire her well-formed legs,
encased in snug jeans, and the shapely curve of her
buttocks.

When he caught up with her, she stood before the
front door, studying the ornate wooden sign that identified the cottage as "Summer Haven."

"That's a beautiful entry. I'll bet the foyer is lovely,
too." She glanced over at him. "Is it? You've been
inside, of course."

He would not be snookered. For all he knew she
could be a cat burglar casing the place. Sidestepping
her question, he said, "Why might you be moving to
Belleporte?"

"If I find the right property, I intend to go into
business here."

"What kind of business?" he asked cautiously.

"A gift shop," she announced, climbing onto the front porch and running her hand over the wood of the door.

"This is a tough market."

She turned back to him, a quizzical look on her face. "Are you trying to discourage me?"

"Far be it from me." His ears were starting to sting in the cold wind, and Laurel Eden was showing no signs of leaving. He couldn't very well drive away on the outside chance she *was* an intruder with a convincing line. "Could I give you a lift back to—"

"Primrose House. You're sure you don't mind?" Then, as if having second thoughts, she held up her hands. "Wait. I can't climb into a car with a perfect stranger."

He stifled a grin. "I don't know about the 'perfect' part, but suit yourself." Unaccountably he found himself wanting to prolong their chance meeting. If she was, in fact, a cat burglar, she was a darned attractive one. He dug a business card out of his billfold and handed it to her. "In case our paths cross again…"

She studied the card, then studied him. "I think I passed your office on my walk today."

"It's next to the insurance agency."

"Right." She seemed to be reconsidering his offer. Finally she said, "It *is* cold and it's a long walk back. Maybe I'll take a chance on you."

Once she'd climbed into the car and buckled her seat belt, she rubbed her hands together. "The temperature must've dropped ten degrees."

"That'll happen. The wind off the lake can be brutal."

"But exhilarating, don't you think?" She turned toward him, her dark eyes capturing his, making it difficult to concentrate on the road.

"Are you always this enthusiastic?"

"Not always. Especially not recently." She fell silent, and in that moment seemed more wistful than exuberant. Then, as if collecting herself, she rushed on. "But that's about to change. What's not to be enthusiastic about Belleporte?"

He wouldn't be the one to disabuse her of her idealistic notions. "How long have you been in town?"

She checked her wristwatch. "Almost exactly eight hours. But long enough."

"Long enough for what?"

"To know this is the place."

"The place? That sounds downright ominous."

She laughed, a merry sound that caused a tightening in his throat. "For The Gift Horse," she said, as if he should have known.

He focused on negotiating the next curve in the road. "Um, your shop?"

She nodded. "Say, you would probably know if there are any commercial properties for sale."

"Not personally. But Ellen Manion, the local real estate agent, would."

"Good. I'll talk to her tomorrow. I only have two days before I have to report back to my job, so it's important that I move as quickly as possible and—"

"Don't you think you ought to do some market research, a demographic study or something?" He couldn't believe she would waltz into town and buy property on a whim. "After all, this is a big step for anyone."

"Do you always patronize people? Why would you presume I haven't done all of that?"

Hell, he'd dug himself in deep. "Guilty as charged. But you have to admit that to an outsider, the plan could sound precipitous."

"You don't have to worry. I've had lots of retail experience, and as for a market plan, I've done my homework. All I need now is the right property."

"Then I wish you good luck."

When he pulled up in front of Primrose House, Laurel didn't immediately get out. Instead, she turned toward him, eyeing him speculatively. "I appreciate your concern. Maybe you're right. Sometimes my enthusiasms do run away with me." Her voice turned serious and her eyes darkened. "But I know I can make this work."

Ben found the depth of her conviction touching. Except for opening his practice here, he'd never been much of a risk-taker himself, but her confidence almost made a believer of him.

"If you're sure you want to look in Belleporte, come by my office in the morning and I'll take you across the street and introduce you to Ellen." Now why in hell had he offered to do that? She was perfectly capable of going to the real estate office on her own. Although he preferred not to dwell on his motives for the rash offer, in a remote part of his brain, he knew it was because he wanted to see Laurel Eden again.

"I'd appreciate that. Nine o'clock?"

"Works for me. I'll look for you."

She opened the door, then paused. "Thanks for the lift. I promise not to trespass ever again." When she smiled for the last time, he found himself incapable of replying. "See you in the morning."

And she was gone, just like that.

Finally he started toward his mother's, trying to ignore the vague sense his life had suddenly taken an unexpected turn.

THE WHITE TWO-STORY frame house could use a coat of paint, Ben thought, as he pulled in the driveway behind the battered station wagon his mother insisted on keeping, despite its 200,000 plus miles. Paint and new cars, though, weren't high on the list of priorities—not with Terry in grad school in Chicago, Megan and Mikey still at home and their mom struggling to make ends meet between their dad's military pension and tuitions from her small day-care operation.

Yet Maureen Nolan never complained. When her husband was captured by the North Vietnamese, she had apparently come to grips with the fact life would never be the same. By the time he was released in 1973, she had made up her mind to deal with her lot cheerfully and resourcefully. The younger kids didn't get it, but being the oldest, Ben had seen the toll his dad's situation had exacted from her. Not that Matthew Nolan hadn't been a good father. He had. In fact, fatherhood had been one of the few pleasures that could pierce the gloom of his depression.

Whether it was his concentration, his ambition or his overall spirit that had been broken by those grueling months in the Hanoi Hilton, Matthew returned a far different man from the cocky, smiling pilot in the pre-Vietnam picture Ben's mother kept on her bureau. He'd never flown again, never spoken of goals. Instead, he'd perfunctorily and faithfully served as the greenskeeper for the Belleporte Country Club.

Only once had Ben dared to ask his father about his months as a prisoner of war, and he'd never forgotten the answer, or the anguished look on his dad's face. "I survived. Most didn't. Remember what I'm about to tell you. A man has to do what he has to do, but never let it be at the expense of your honor." It was a lesson Ben had vowed to take to heart.

Passing the children's fenced-in play area, Ben rapped on the screen door, then entered the kitchen. His mother looked up from the sink. "Thanks for coming, son. Have you eaten?"

"I'll grab a bite later."

"Nonsense." Maureen Nolan's naturally ruddy complexion and wavy chin-length red hair, now streaked with gray, increasingly reminded Ben of old photographs of his Irish grandmother. His mother reached into the cupboard and pulled out a bowl and a water glass. "I'll heat you up a few leftovers. I swear, you bachelors need to eat more regular meals."

Putting an arm around her thickened waist, Ben planted a kiss on her cheek. "And you need to quit worrying about me."

"Can't help it. I worry about all my kids."

He tilted her chin. "Especially Mikey, right?"

She sagged against him, momentarily resting her head on his shoulder. "Oh, Ben. He'll be the death of me yet."

"What now?"

"The school called." He couldn't miss the resignation in her voice. "He was caught smoking in the rest room."

Ben groaned. This was more serious than Mikey's previous capers. You could chalk up mouthing off to teachers and occasional tardiness to raging adolescence, but smoking was a different matter. "Smoking what?"

As if startled by his unspoken accusation, his mother looked up at him. "Don't jump to conclusions. I'm told it was just a cigarette."

"'Just a cigarette'? He knows better than that." Ben made a mental note of his mother's reaction. If she could dismiss smoking, she must be worried about something more threatening.

"Apparently not," Maureen noted dryly. "He's basically a good boy, Ben. I think he just misses his father."

"It's gotta be tough on him." Ben understood that grief and anger did funny things to people, but he had his hands full without Mikey pulling these half-assed shenanigans.

His mother turned back to the sink, plunging her hands into the sudsy water. "I don't know what to do with him anymore. He seems to resent me."

Ben's stomach lurched at the quaver in her voice. After all his mother had been through and the sacrifices she'd made, it seemed unfair his father had been taken away, leaving her to deal with the problems alone. She still went through the motions of being the strong one, but Ben could see her heart was no longer in it. If she could only share her feelings about Dad…but that wasn't her way.

"I'll talk to him. Where is he?"

"In the basement. Studying, he claims."

"I'll see if I can get through to him."

"And by the time you finish, I'll have the stew warmed up."

He patted his stomach. "I won't turn my back on a home-cooked meal." Besides, he knew it would make his mother feel useful to feed him. He opened the basement door. "Here goes nothing."

The fluorescent lights, whitewashed walls and tan carpet remnant brightened the basement rec room, which was furnished with a battle-scarred Ping-Pong table, several dilapidated recliners, a sagging couch and an old console-type TV. Sprawled on the couch, Mikey held the TV remote in one hand and a textbook in the other, but his eyes never left the mindless sit-com.

Ben settled into one of the recliners. "Think you could turn that off?"

"In a minute. This is the good part."

Ben bit back the retort forming on his lips. High-handed big-brother talk hadn't worked with Mikey before. He could wait.

The canned laughter reached a fever pitch, and the credits rolled. With painstaking deliberateness, Mikey made a show of turning off the television. His unruly auburn curls brushed the back of his collar and his freckles stood out in sharp relief. "I figured you'd be over. Old Man Moberly called Mom." He swung his feet to the floor and crossed his arms, his blue eyes blazing. "I'm listenin', man. Let's get it over with."

"Get what over with?"

"The lecture. How I've disappointed everybody."

Ben leaned forward. "What's going on with you, Mikey?"

"For one thing, quit callin' me Mikey. I'm not a little kid, you know."

He had to concede his brother's point. "Duly noted. Since when do you smoke, *Mike?*"

"What's it to you?"

"I'd like to have my brother around awhile."

"Ooh, the big 'C.' Is that it?"

Ben mentally counted to ten. "You've heard it in science class. You've read it on the labels. Smoking is bad for your health." He tried to find some chink in Mike's ice-hard expression. "But there's another issue. You knew it was against the rules to smoke on school grounds."

"Lotsa kids do it."

"So that makes it okay?"

The boy merely shrugged.

"You gotta help me here, Mike," Ben said, running a hand through his hair. "Mom and Dad raised you right. You're basically a good kid. Why're you pulling all this crap?"

Mike stood and went to the Ping-Pong paddle rack. He pulled out a paddle and a ball and began bouncing the ball on the table with an irritating rat-a-tat. Walking over, Ben scooped up the ball. "Damn it, I'm talking to you."

His skin mottled, Mike turned on him. "So what? You're not my father, you know."

"No, I'm not. But I'm the man of the family now." He got right in the boy's face. "Your behavior is unacceptable. It's hurting Mom, it's hurting me, and worst of all, it's hurting you. I'm sorry you lost your father. I did, too, you know. You're not the only one in pain here. But why you're determined to add to everyone's burden is beyond me. From now on, you'll present receipts for everything you spend your allowance on—''

"You can't do that!"

"—and that won't include cigarettes or beer." He stepped back, his chest working. "And if you think you're going to drive a car when you turn sixteen, think again. Unless—" he paused for emphasis "—you clean up your act. Understood?"

Mike made a mocking salaam. "Yes, oh great wise one."

"And cut out the smart mouth while you're at it," Ben said as he left the room.

When he reached the top of the stairs, his mother was ladling up a bowl of stew for him. Comfort food. Boy, did he need a generous helping of that about now. She raised her eyes. "Well?"

He recounted the conversation, including the restrictions on Mike's spending money. "He made a request I think we ought to consider."

"What's that?"

"He doesn't want to be called Mikey. Says he's not a kid anymore."

His mother set the bowl on the table, then handed him a napkin and spoon. Finally she sank into the chair across from him, trying, unsuccessfully, to smile. "So many things are changing. Mikey, too, I suppose." Blinking away a stray tear, she continued, "Maybe he's right. But it's so hard for a mother—for me—to give up my baby. To let him grow up."

Ben struggled to lighten the mood. "He'll look kinda funny as a forty-year-old in baggy jeans and untied Nikes." He laid his hand on hers. "I'm here, Mom. It's all going to be fine."

In her eyes was a hopefulness he found painful to observe.

WHEN LAUREL APPROACHED the law office the next morning, her nerves were tight as mountain fiddle strings, and not just at the prospect of meeting the real estate agent. She'd also be seeing Ben again, with his curly sand-brown hair, unforgettable blue eyes and broad shoulders. Yesterday in true attorney fashion, he'd been genuinely concerned she didn't know what she was doing, but it would have been inappropriate on such short acquaintance to tell him how carefully she'd prepared for the right opportunity. Well, she'd just have to show him.

In fairness, she had to admit she might have come on a bit strong yesterday, carried away by her enthusiasm for Summer Haven and Belleporte. But it had been far too long since joy had bubbled to the surface like that. Maybe, just maybe, she was finding her old self, the pre-Curt Laurel.

When she entered Ben's office, he was chatting with his receptionist. After introducing the two women, Ben grinned at Laurel. "Broken into any houses overnight?"

Laurel nodded at Janet. "What kind of impression will that make on this nice lady?"

Janet pursed her lips. "Where Ben is concerned, I'm not easily shocked."

Sheepishly Laurel explained about being caught trespassing.

"Give the woman a break, counselor," Janet said.

"Any female worth her salt would want to explore Summer Haven."

Ben eyed Laurel appreciatively. "Laurel qualifies, then."

Fighting a blush, Laurel acknowledged she'd enjoyed the implied compliment, perhaps more than she should have.

Ben caught her eye. "Ready?"

Her heart thudded. "As ready as I'll ever be."

As he escorted Laurel toward the door, a smiling Janet winked at her, as if they'd already formed a secret sisterhood.

Laurel could have sworn Ben deliberately lingered at the real estate office after introducing her to Ellen Manion, a young woman about Laurel's age with fly-away ginger hair, a radiant smile and sea-deep green eyes. Finally, he murmured something about a pressing appointment and beat a retreat. Although Laurel was eager to get on with business, she felt let down when he left. That puzzled her. It had been a very long time since any man had interested her.

Ushering Laurel into her office, Ellen immediately put her at ease. She listened intently to the plans for The Gift Horse, and when Laurel finished, Ellen propped her elbows on the desk and cupped her chin in her hands. "How much are you prepared to spend?"

Laurel named a figure, then added, "Of course, anything I do is contingent upon nailing down a loan. However, I do have a tentative financing commitment for that amount."

"Good. I have listings on two or three properties

that might work, but there's one in particular I think—''

"Could we look at it this morning? I have only one more day of vacation left, and if I find the right one—"

"You'd be prepared to move that quickly?"

"Yes." When she uttered the word, Laurel knew as if it had been preordained that today she would find the perfect location for her store.

Rising to her feet, Ellen said, "Come on then. It's vacant, I have the key, and the owners are eager to sell. To be safe, though, you really should look at the other properties, too."

While they quickly toured and dispensed with the first two possible sites, Laurel learned that Ellen was a lifelong resident of Belleporte, that she and Ben had been friends practically forever, and that, like her, Ellen was single.

When they approached the center of town, Ellen slowed the car. There it was. A former summer home, now zoned for commercial development, with English country cottage timber-and-stucco construction, peaked gables, multi-paned windows, a wonderful bay window overlooking a side garden and even a chimney. But it was the red door, just like the one Laurel had envisioned for The Gift Horse, that did it. "Oh, Ellen," she whispered, "I know I'm supposed to act aloof and businesslike, but—"

"It's perfect, isn't it?"

"I think so. I can't wait to see the inside."

It was going to happen, Laurel thought, hugging her purse to her wildly beating heart. Her dream was coming true.

CHAPTER TWO

JUST BEFORE NOON, Ellen finished preparing the sale offer. "You're sure I'm not rushing you into anything?"

Laurel picked up the pen and signed with a flourish. "Not at all. I've done a great deal of looking, and I know this is it." Then, setting down the pen, she studied her trembling fingers. "You *do* think the owners will accept, don't you?"

Ellen scanned the paperwork. "I can't promise, but you've come close to their asking price and the property's been on the market awhile." She smiled reassuringly. "I'll call them right away, and if I reach them, we should know something by noon tomorrow."

Laurel's mind teemed with plans for The Gift Horse. She'd sell decorative outdoor accessories in the garden area, kitchenware in the charming dining room, and if she knocked out the wall between—

"Are you planning to live above the shop?"

Laurel bolted upright in her chair. "Ellen, you're a genius. I'd just naturally assumed that would be a storage area, but if I used the basement and detached garage for that purpose, then I—"

"Yes, you could fix up a charming apartment and save yourself rental expense."

Immediately Laurel visualized her own cozy space filled with the oak furniture her father had made, hand-sewn quilts, the blue-and-white willowware dishes she collected… Then reality intruded. "It sounds wonderful, but I'd have to make arrangements now to have the space renovated while I'm finishing up my current job and preparing for the move."

"If the owners go along with your offer, I'll put you in touch with Arlo Bramwell, our local handyman. Since it's the off-season, he might welcome a project like this."

Laurel grinned. "Ellen, you just may be my new best friend. Thanks for the suggestion." Then, realizing Ellen needed privacy to contact the owners, Laurel stood. "I appreciate your help."

"My pleasure. I'll let you know when I hear something."

After she left the office, Laurel paused on the sidewalk studying the nearly deserted street. In her mind she fast forwarded to summer, picturing the broad canopy of leaves above, youngsters on bikes, the streets crowded with tourists. So much to accomplish in so little time. Despite the challenges, she couldn't hold back a satisfied smile. Nothing she'd ever done had felt so right.

IT WAS LATE AFTERNOON when Ben got back to his office. He'd made it to the courthouse in Lake City in time to file his brief in the Pendleton case. He didn't like doing tort work, but he couldn't be choosy. Not if he wanted his practice to thrive. Thrive? Survive was more like it.

He spread the phone memos on his desk. Two calls

from clients and one from Ellen Manion. Nothing urgent. He would return the calls in the morning.

It was nearly six before he finished reviewing the trust document Janet had prepared in his absence. Since she had already left, he was surprised when he heard someone in the reception area call his name.

He went to investigate. Ellen waited tentatively by Janet's desk. "Ellen? Hey, I'm sorry. I got your message. I planned to call you tomorrow."

"It's no big deal. I just wanted to thank you."

"For what?"

She smiled broadly. "Referring Laurel Eden."

Hell, the mere mention of the woman's name got his blood racing, and he didn't want to admit how often today he'd lost his concentration because of her.

"Ben?"

"Huh?"

"Laurel Eden." She snapped her fingers. "You remember."

He struggled to regain his poise. "What about her?"

"She made an offer on a property today."

"She *what?*" He had no idea why the idea both stunned and exhilarated him.

"The cottage on Shore Lane." Ellen was scrutinizing him. "The old Mansfield place."

"Oh."

"Is that all you have to say?"

He found himself stammering. "Well, er, congratulations."

"Congratulations are a bit premature. I haven't heard from the owners yet." She fingered the buttons of her coat. "But I hope it works out. Laurel is quite excited about her plans for the place."

"The gift shop?" He had a sudden urge to warn Laurel off. What she was undertaking was financially risky.

"I think her ideas have real promise."

"For her sake, I hope so." He had the feeling Ellen hadn't said all she came to say.

"If this sale goes through, I have you to thank. As a token of my appreciation for the referral, I was wondering if maybe I could take you to dinner tonight." She smiled crookedly.

Ben had known Ellen all his life. She'd played "Farmer in the Dell" with him in kindergarten, tutored him in Spanish in junior high and been his prom date their senior year. A guy couldn't have a better friend. Buddies, that's what they were. But in this pregnant silence, he had the uncomfortable notion she might have more in mind than a mere professional thank-you.

"I appreciate the offer, but tonight's out." He waved a hand in the direction of his office. "I have work that has to be wrapped up before morning."

Ever so faintly, her face flushed. "It was just a thought."

"Maybe another time," he suggested to fill the awkward pause.

"Sure." She opened the door, then looked back over her shoulder. "When you see your mother, tell her hello for me."

"I will."

After she left, he stood in the middle of the room wondering why he couldn't be attracted to her. Someday he'd have time to consider marriage, though not before things evened out with his family and the practice. As a prospective partner, Ellen made all kinds of sense. She was a lovely, talented, generous woman. They had lots in common. His siblings liked her. His mother liked her. Hell, he liked her.

But, improbably, it was Laurel Eden, about whom he knew almost nothing, who occupied his thoughts—and his fantasies.

LAUREL PULLED ON flannel pajama bottoms and a soft, worn T-shirt and climbed under the flowered comforter. Propping pillows behind her, she balanced the hardcover book that served as a writing desk on her knees and began a letter to her parents. If they had a computer, she could e-mail them on her laptop, but her folks had no intention of breaking down and entering the 21st century. Doing so would compromise the simple lifestyle they cherished—one that had made her growing up so magical.

She pictured her mother bent over the loom that occupied an entire corner of the living room, strands of colorful wool brightening the simple log interior of their home. In memory she smelled the pungent aroma of wood chips, sawdust and resin—byproducts of her father's woodcarving and furniture-making. At college, Laurel was the only one she knew who had grown up without television and been homeschooled until high school. Although at times she'd felt deprived, more often she'd appreciated learning in her own backyard—exploring the spring woods in search of animal spoor, uncovering West Virginia history from country cemetery markers, keeping weather records using her own barometer, thermometer and rain gauge. And there had been so much more—singing, dancing, playing the dulcimer, candle-making, quilting.

With a sigh, Laurel set aside her pen. Had she really been so naively happy? She shuddered, remembering how her life had changed after she had met and married Curt. A brilliant fellow graduate student, Curt was handsome, charming and…controlling. Laurel had only belatedly realized that he regarded her as a kind of Eliza Doolittle "project," ornamental, amusing, but not to be taken seriously. With an effort of will she banished her ex-husband from her mind—and that diminished self she was desperately trying to reconstruct. And she would, damn it!

She relaxed against the pillows. That was part of what had attracted her to Belleporte. Here she could rediscover the pure joy she'd felt for life before her disastrous marriage. Maybe she'd learn to trust again—even men. Her bitter experience had taught her one thing for sure. *Carpe diem* was more than an abstract philosophy; it was a way to leave the past behind and embrace life fully every single day. And that was exactly what she intended to do. Like acting on impulse and exploring Summer Haven. Like making an offer on the Mansfield property. And…like flirting with Ben Nolan.

She smiled in hopeful anticipation before turning back to her letter. Surely Ellen would have good news tomorrow.

Laurel studied what she'd written so far—an account of her travels and the dead ends she'd faced. She wanted to tell her parents about Belleporte—the way it felt like home, the beauty of the beaches, the charm of the resort town itself—but raised on mountain superstitions, she wasn't about to jinx the sale. Best not to mention anything until The Gift Horse was a done deal. Besides, regardless of their encouragement, she knew her parents would be disappointed she'd chosen Michigan over West Virginia.

Chewing the tip of the pen, she pondered her ending for a moment, then began to write.

I'm not giving up my dream, though. As you always told me, when you get discouraged, look for another bend in the trail, and that's exactly what I'm doing. Maybe I'll have some news by the time I visit West Virginia in a couple of weeks. Till then, give the dogs hugs—and cross your fingers for me. Knock on wood, too, if you'd like.

I love you,
Laurel

AT TEN O'CLOCK the next morning Laurel stood in the foyer of Primrose House, gripping the phone, listening intently. Then, unbelievably, Ellen confirmed the sale. It took a minute for the news to sink in. The charming cottage on Shore Lane, right here in Belleporte, Michigan, was hers.

She concentrated as Ellen recounted her conversation with the owners, who fortunately had given permission for Laurel to begin remodeling the upstairs apartment before the closing. When Ellen read her the handyman's number, Laurel fumbled for paper and a

pen and quickly jotted it down. "Yes, I've got it. I'll
call Mr. Bramwell right away. Could we get in the
house this afternoon if he's available?…Great. I'll get
back to you after I speak with him to set up a time.
And Ellen? You've made my day."

Still in shock at the end of the conversation, Laurel
slowly laid the phone in its cradle, unable to stop smiling. But after a few moments, reality set in. There was
no time to waste. She began making a mental list of
people to call. She'd have to notify her landlords in
Columbus and give notice at work.

By noon, Laurel had made an appointment with Mr.
Bramwell, called Ellen back, opened a local bank account and arranged for the florist to deliver flowers to
Ellen's office as a thank-you. She'd tried calling her
parents, but there was no answer. On second thought,
she decided to tell them in person, so she could soften
the blow about her choice of location.

Then there was Ben Nolan. She needed to thank him
for introducing her to Ellen. Maybe seek his advice.
He was an attorney, after all. Perhaps there were details she was overlooking. *Right. Is it really advice you
want? Or another look at his phenomenal blue eyes?*

She would hush that contrary inner voice later, Laurel decided, *after* she acted on her latest impulse. She
would go to Ben's office and invite the man to dinner.

BEN GLANCED AROUND the dark-paneled dining room
of the Dunes Inn, wondering what he was doing here.
He should have refused Laurel's invitation. He'd had
no trouble turning down Ellen yesterday. But when he
seated Laurel at their lakeside table and a whiff of
something lightly floral teased his nose, he remem-

bered why he was here. When Laurel had popped in his office this afternoon, catching him totally off guard, his reaction to her had been spontaneously physical. Without pausing for rational thought, he'd accepted her invitation—with the provision that he pick her up.

He toyed with the menu, unchanged in the many years he'd been coming here, and pretended to study it, all the time admiring Laurel. She looked stunning in a forest-green corduroy dress with a scoop neck that drew his eye to her softly rounded breasts.

"How's the walleye?" She chewed her lip as if the fate of the world depended on her meal selection.

"Fine. The prime rib's excellent, too."

He watched as she deliberated. He had absolutely no business entertaining thoughts about her provocative scent, her tantalizing figure, or her infectious enthusiasm. What with Mike, his mom, the practice and his personal financial situation, there were more than enough complications in his life.

She eyed him over the top of her menu. "What are you having?"

"My usual. Kansas City Strip. Medium rare."

"Just like a man."

"How's that?"

Cocking her head, she smiled. "It must be a gender thing." She gave an imitation of a caveman beating his chest. "Man need meat. Red meat."

It had been so long since he'd had a date, he couldn't tell for sure if she was flirting or being critical. He felt dangerously out of practice. Fortunately the appearance of their waiter spared him a reply.

After they ordered, she leaned forward. "Are you ready?"

He felt himself flush, wondering if she knew how provocative the question sounded. "For what?"

She spread her arms like a sideshow shill. "For the story of the birth of The Gift Horse."

He chuckled. "Do I have a choice?"

She quirked her mouth. "Absolutely not. Besides, I may need some legal advice."

"I'm your man." He was losing his grip. Surely he hadn't said that.

Fondling her wineglass between her fingers, she launched in. He tried to listen. Really. But the whole time he was acutely aware of her expressive hands, her breasts rising and falling with her breathing, her moist lips forming words he was having difficulty processing. He threw back a slug of his ale.

"…so what do you think?" She folded her arms on the table and waited for him to speak.

He hedged. "It sounds like an ambitious project."

"But won't the cottage be perfect? It's charming, conveniently located—"

"It's all of that."

"But…?" She leaned forward. "I can hear it coming, counselor. But what?"

How could he tell her people didn't come into an unfamiliar community, buy a significant piece of property within hours of arriving and then plan to open a retail business without so much as a feasibility study? "You'd like me to be enthusiastic, right?"

"That would help." A shadow fell across her face. "I've had enough discouragement in my life for the last few years."

He was tempted to pick up that last thread, but something in her posture let him know the topic was off-limits for now. "I'm not unenthusiastic. Just cautious, I guess. Have you done sales projections? Considered the off-season decline in business?"

She shook her head in disbelief, then smiled. "As I said before, 'just like a man.' Lucky I'm a brunette. Otherwise, you'd probably use me as the butt of one of those dumb blonde jokes."

He shifted in his seat. "I'm not saying that, it's just that the whole project seems…risky."

"You know, if I didn't like you so much, I could be downright offended." She raised her wineglass, studied the contents, then looked up. "Let me allay your concerns. Would it help if I told you I have an MBA in marketing and considerable business expertise?"

Abashed, he held up his hands in self-defense. "I apologize. Obviously you've figured in the risk factors. At least I hope so, because I'm interested in your success."

She brushed the goblet against her lips. "Why?"

He couldn't take his eyes off her—or her burgundy-red mouth. "I hope to enjoy observing the rehabilitation of a bona fide trespasser."

"Wow, I've gone from dumb blonde to felon in mere seconds."

He chuckled. "Believe me, you're much more than that."

She raised an eyebrow. "Go ahead. Lay it on."

His attorney's glibness failed him. He simply blurted out the truth. "You're an attractive woman I'd like to know better. I'm glad you're settling in Belleporte.'' He held up his ale. "Laurel, I wish you success and happiness.''

Her eyes found his, and in that instant he knew she was aware he had spoken from his heart.

As if delaying her response, she took a long time setting down her wine. "Thank you, Ben.''

Their dinner arrived, and for a few moments neither of them spoke. Then Laurel commented on the quality of the walleye and he made some inane remark about the steak living up to expectations. A high school classmate of his who ran an auto parts store stopped by the table, clearly ogling Laurel and angling for an introduction.

Ben stifled the urge to bust his chops. What was going on? He had no right to feel proprietary about Laurel, but he did. Involvement was a luxury he couldn't afford. Not now. Not with all his obligations.

Laurel squeezed a second lemon wedge over her fish. "Ben, I want to ask you something, and I want an honest answer.''

"Shoot.''

"I'd really like to know what exactly is worrying you about my plans.''

During the rest of the meal, he did his best to couch his reservations in nonjudgmental terms. Mainly he wanted her to be realistic about the seasonal nature of the business and the relatively small market area surrounding Belleporte and Lake City. When he finished, he added, "I hope you know I'm pulling for you. It's not my intent to cast gloom on the project.''

She laid a hand on his arm. "You didn't, and I appreciate your candor. Sometimes I have a tendency to take off like a soaring balloon, and every now and then I need somebody to yank my string. Thanks.'' She withdrew her hand and smiled at him. "Could you suggest a good CPA? I'm not so confident to think I can do without an accountant.''

"My brother Brian practices in Lake City.''

"If he's as straightforward as you, he ought to do fine. I'll call him when I get back in January.'' She took a last bite of the braised vegetables, then set down her fork. "Do you have other brothers and sisters?''

"There are six of us kids. Plus Mom. My father's dead.''

"Tell me about them.''

He ticked them off on his fingers. "I'm the oldest, then Brian, who's the quintessential young bachelor-about-town. My sister Bess is married and lives in Grand Rapids with her husband and two boys. Terry is a grad student at Northwestern. That leaves Megan, who's a high school senior, and Mike, a sophomore, still at home.''

"Wow, I'm envious.''

"Why's that?''

She smiled wistfully. "You're looking at an only child who always wished for a brother or sister.''

"Being part of a big family has its moments,'' he said with a grin, "not all of them wonderful.'' He sobered, thinking of Mike. "But I wouldn't trade mine for anything.''

"I hope to meet some of them when I get back in January.''

He chuckled. "You can't be in Belleporte long without bumping into one or another of us Nolans.'' He buttered the last half of his roll. "When are you leaving?''

"Tomorrow."

Despite reminding himself he didn't need the complication of Laurel Eden in his life, the news of her immediate departure hit him like a punch to the stomach. "Where will you live when you get back?"

By the time they were finished with dessert, she'd told him about her meeting with Arlo Bramwell and her plans for remodeling the cottage. Ben wished he could let her enthusiasm override his concerns. But he couldn't. The upstairs apartment was an additional investment she was making in the property. He didn't want to see her fail, yet he was fearful that was exactly what was going to happen. This was one time he didn't want to be right.

Ben drew up short, aware his thoughts were again following a dangerous path. Why should he be concerned about Laurel Eden and her success or failure? He couldn't allow himself the luxury of caring about her or any woman. No matter how tempting.

LAUREL HUNCHED HER SHOULDERS as Ben helped her into her coat. It had been a perfect day—The Gift Horse purchase, the meeting with Arlo Bramwell and this wonderful dinner with a man whose blue eyes made Paul Newman superfluous. Ben had insisted on paying. Another "man thing," he'd said.

She'd enjoyed herself—and enjoyed Ben and his genuineness. Maybe more than she should have. Slipping her arm through his as they walked toward the parking lot, she found herself wanting to prolong the evening. "Are you game for a little adventure, counselor?"

"That sounds remarkably like a dare," he said with a chuckle. "What do you have in mind?"

She nodded toward the lake. "There's a wonderful expanse of sand. I love the sound of the waves. And, look." She pointed at the horizon. "Nearly a full moon."

He eyed her footwear. "You sure?"

Grabbing his hand, she led him toward the beach. "Of course. Besides, what's a little sand in our shoes?"

"I'm game," he said, catching up to her and tucking her hand under his arm. "Why do I have the feeling this is just one in a series of adventures for you?"

"Because it is. Don't you see?" She looked up at him with teasing eyes. "That's what life's all about. Adventure. Excitement. All the good things."

"Tell me. How does one lead such a charmed life?"

"I know how simplistic it sounds. But for the most part, I *have* led a charmed life." Then she told him all about growing up in the mountains of West Virginia, the child of two former hippies for whom "peace, love, happiness" and "doing their thing" were priorities. She described her homeschooling, the success she'd enjoyed at the University of West Virginia, and how she fell into the job as the traveling rep for an Appalachian crafts cooperative.

"No failures, no disappointments, no broken romances?" he asked.

She slowed her pace. "You know, for a long time I didn't have what I would term genuinely bad experiences—at least not personal ones." They walked on a ways, listening to the splish-splash of the waves. The moon etched a silver vee across the surface of the lake, and dune grass swayed in the breeze. "Not until I…grew up, that is." She winced at the bitterness of her tone.

He stopped and turned to her. "Does this have anything to do with what you mentioned earlier? About having had enough discouragement?"

Ben was too sensitive a listener. She hadn't meant to get into this. She started down the beach again, wondering how to answer him.

He didn't press her, but fell in beside her, this time putting his arm around her and drawing her close. Finally, in the gentlest of tones, he merely said, "Laurel?"

"You know," she began slowly, "I can't imagine now how I could have been so naive, so trusting. The world was always a beautiful place for me and I took people at face value."

"That doesn't sound so awful."

"It's not, but it's idealistic. When I went off to college, I experienced a rude awakening. I was ill-prepared for the materialism and cynicism of many of my peers. Lord, I look back and wonder if I was in total la-la land."

"What happened?"

"I met the knight-in-shining-armor." She fixed her eyes on a point far up the beach. "Tarnished armor."

"Laurel, if you'd rather not talk about it—"

"No," she said in a firm voice. "I need to talk about it." She acknowledged her reaction was out of character; she rarely discussed her former husband. "Curt was a graduate assistant in the business department, well on his way to a brilliant career. He had it all—a great intellect, looks, connections, charisma.

You can guess the rest. I fell for him like a ton of bricks.''

"And?"

"Married him, of course. At the beginning, I couldn't believe my luck. But it didn't take long to see what he was really after."

"Which was?"

"A country bumpkin he could groom into the perfect companion and hostess. The ultimate self-effacing corporate wife.'' Laurel felt Ben's grip on her waist tighten. "He didn't want a woman with a mind of her own. He wanted a looking glass. 'Mirror, mirror, on the wall, who's the most successful man of all?''' She stumbled, grateful for Ben's support. "Let me tell you, that kind of life plays havoc with your self-esteem. I lasted four years."

"In the marriage?"

"Yes. For part of our time together, I assumed something was wrong with me. Then one day I woke up and thought 'Wait a minute. It's okay to like who you are, to do things to fulfill yourself.'''

"More than all right," Ben said.

"You asked me the other day if I'm always so enthusiastic. I used to be, and I'm trying hard to be again. That's what The Gift Horse is all about. This may sound corny, but it's not only my dream, it's my ticket back to me. The me I like. Even the me who's foolishly idealistic.''

Turning her toward him, he cupped her face with one cold hand. "I like this you, Laurel."

He looked so serious, so concerned. She laid her gloved hand on top of his. "I didn't mean to burden you."

He curled his fingers around hers. "You didn't."

Caught in the warmth of his gaze, she found herself immobilized. Afterward, she couldn't have said whether it was the magic of the moonlight, the shush of water on sand, or the naked longing in his eyes. All she knew was that, lost in the moment and without stopping to think, she gently drew his head close. At the same time he found her lips, and then he was lifting her off her feet and kissing her in a way that blotted out the lake, the moon, everything but the sensation of his mouth moving on hers.

Slowly, ever so slowly, he drew back, sliding her body down his until her toes once again made contact with the sand. All the while, he never stopped gazing at her. "Ben, I—"

He placed a finger on her lips. "Shh." This time he cupped her chin and kissed her gently, delicately, exploringly.

When at last he withdrew, he studied her with such intensity that she knew the kiss had taken on a deeper meaning than either of them could have foreseen.

THE AZURE-BLUE SKY RANG with the cry of a hawk, the fragrance of wood smoke floated on the morning-fresh air, and in the distance, the timbered mountains of West Virginia rose crest on crest as far as the eye could see. But Pat Eden heard nothing, smelled nothing, saw nothing—except for the return address on the envelope she held in her trembling hand. An envelope postmarked Belleporte, Michigan.

She sucked in her breath and stood by the mailbox with eyes closed, caught up in memories so piercing, so immediate she was convinced her heart would crack. She wrapped her arms around her chest, as if to shield herself from images too raw, too painful. But it was more than the sudden onslaught of memory that racked her. It was fear. Powerlessness.

Laurel in Belleporte? Unthinkable. Pat had closed that door long ago. Or, rather, had heard it slammed irrevocably behind her. And for thirty years she'd steeled herself to forget the family that had cast her out and ignored her attempts, early on, to renew contact. Finally, for her own peace of mind, it had been easier simply to cut them from her life as if they were dead. To mourn them and move on. And to protect her beloved daughter Laurel from ever knowing what had caused such a schism, or that there had even been one.

She opened her eyes, oblivious to the two German shepherds vying for her attention, and made her way slowly up the rutted dirt lane toward the log home that Noel had so lovingly built for the three of them. She should open the letter. Read it. Reassure herself that this was all some crazy, harmless coincidence. But despite her rationalizations, it didn't feel harmless.

"Pat?" Her husband stood on the front porch, his whip-lean body tight with concern. "Are you all right? You look like you've seen a ghost."

She held out the envelope to him. "Oh, God, Noel. I'm afraid I have. Look."

Stroking his beard, he studied the envelope. When he looked up, his eyes were warm with concern. "It's only a letter, Pat. Nothing has happened."

"Not yet. But—"

He handed back the letter. "Open it, darlin'. Maybe it's nothing."

She drew out the folded sheet of paper, focusing with difficulty on the elaborate graphics, the fancy script. "Primrose House, Your Belleporte Sanctuary." Quickly she scanned the page. "Laurel's spending a couple of days there before she goes back to work." She sagged against him with a sense of impending doom. "Read this last part. Oh, Noel, what if she chooses Belleporte for her shop?"

"That isn't apt to happen." He wrapped his arms around her and held her for a moment. Silently. But she could sense him gathering himself. Then the words came. "Would it be so bad if she found out?"

She pulled away, a flush of anger coloring her cheeks. "We agreed to leave all that behind." She looked up, momentarily resenting her husband for the reproof she read in his eyes.

"She's an adult. She has a right to know."

"To know what? That her mother has lied to her since birth? That the family who should have welcomed her and loved her cast us out without so much as a backward glance? We made a decision years ago. Don't fight me about this now, Noel."

He stood motionless, studying her as if he could see into the depths of her soul. "Does it still hurt that much?"

She knew she couldn't lie to this man she had loved enough to risk everything. "Yes," she whispered. Then, gathering her voice, she completed the thought. "But it doesn't have to hurt Laurel."

CHAPTER THREE

DUSK WAS FAST APPROACHING and storm clouds were massing when Laurel crossed the state line into West Virginia two weeks later. She kneaded the knots of tension in her neck. She was both eager and apprehensive to share her news with her parents. Undoubtedly they'd be disappointed she wasn't settling closer to home, but they'd always stood behind her, encouraging her to test her wings.

The Gift Horse purchase had gone through smoothly and quickly, and since leaving Belleporte, she'd managed to pack up her Columbus apartment, store most of her belongings and give her notice to the co-op. In addition to training her replacement there, she would spend most of December calling on artisans to arrange a line of supply for her store before coming back here for the holidays. Then, in January, she'd be back in Belleporte. She whispered the name under her breath. Musical. Magical.

In all honesty, it wasn't only Belleporte that was magical. Her memories of Ben—delightful and unsettling—had caused her more than a few restless nights. After Curt, she'd temporarily sworn off men. Ben was the first to cause her to rethink that decision. Besides the obvious sexual attraction, she admired the way he'd leveled with her about The Gift Horse. She'd even begun to think of him as a man she could trust.

At Clarksburg, she left the turnpike and meandered toward Elkins. As night fell, the first drops of rain splattered her windshield, and the road became slick as oil met water. She craned forward, watching for familiar road signs and landmarks. Only a few more miles now.

Turning onto the private gravel road, she downshifted, then jolted over the mile and a half to its end. She parked beside the detached garage housing her father's workshop. The downpour soaked her as she ran toward the cabin, burdened by her purse, laptop computer and overnight bag.

Flanked by Dylan and Fonda, the family dogs, her parents waited in the doorway. Laurel set down her luggage and found herself engulfed in a group hug, the scents of wet dog hair, wood smoke and cedar welcoming her home.

She drew back to study her parents—her father's ruddy complexion, keen gray eyes and trimmed beard; her mother's curly black hair drawn back in a braid, her makeup-free skin still flawless and her brown eyes luminous, magnified behind granny glasses. Although laugh lines and a few gray hairs hinted at aging, they both looked vital. "It's so good to be home."

"We waited dinner for you," her mother said.

Her father picked up her bags and carried them inside, putting them down by the staircase. "All of your favorite foods, posie."

Laurel smiled at the familiar endearment. She'd been named for the mountain laurel, and he'd been calling her "posie" ever since. "Does that mean vegetable soup, biscuits and blueberry pie?'' She knelt to greet the dogs, who nearly knocked her over in their enthusiasm.

''All of the above,'' her father said, as her mother turned away to the kitchen, wedged in one corner of the great room. He helped Laurel to her feet, then led her to the woodburning stove. ''Here. Take some of the chill off.''

She leaned toward the heat, rubbing her hands together. Then she turned around and spread her arms. ''I've been so excited to get here.'' Her mother continued busying herself with the meal preparation. ''Can I help, Mom?''

''It's under control. Relax and visit with your father.''

Laurel settled in the bentwood rocker. Fonda immediately put her head in Laurel's lap, demanding attention, while Dylan sprawled at her feet. Noel made small talk about the weather and his latest furniture project, but Laurel's thoughts wandered. When should she tell them? Now? After they ate?

Over dinner, her mother kept up a monologue about the weaving prize she'd won at the fair, about Noel's job teaching woodworking at the college in Elkins, about— It finally registered with Laurel. Her mother wasn't behaving normally. She was usually the one full of questions. The one who listened thoughtfully before finally commenting, her graceful hands punctuating her remarks. She was never the ''entertainer.'' But tonight she seemed on edge about something. It was odd, too, that neither had asked about her progress locating a site for The Gift Horse.

At one point Laurel ventured, "I have some interesting news for you about my store."

Instead of looking up, eyes dancing with curiosity, her mother bowed her head and drew a hand across her brow. "Can it wait, honey? I want to hear all about it, but I'm developing a blinding headache. Maybe tomorrow?"

Laurel noticed her father's surreptitious glance in her mother's direction. "Are you sure you're all right?" she said.

"Don't worry. I'll be fine in the morning."

"We'll clean up the dishes, Pat," Noel offered. Then, turning to Laurel, he added, "But we most certainly want to hear your news."

Laurel observed a tiny frown etch itself into her mother's forehead. "Go on to bed, Mom. I want you fresh for my big announcement, anyway."

After her mother left the room, Noel handed Laurel a dish towel. "You're sure you're not disappointed about waiting?"

"It's okay, Dad. My surprise can keep."

But later that night, snuggled into bed in her old room in the loft, listening to the rain pelt against the tin roof, she admitted she had been disappointed. She understood the delay, but it had taken the edge off her excitement. It was almost as if her mother hadn't wanted to listen. But why? Because she knew Laurel hadn't chosen a West Virginia site? Surely her mother was prepared for that. Was there something else going on? The thought nagged at her until she finally muttered to Fonda, snoring on the rag rug beside her bed, "What's the matter with me, Fonda? I need to quit imagining things."

Yet just before she closed her eyes, she had the sure sense that whatever her parents' reactions to her announcement tomorrow, they would seem anticlimactic.

PAT SPOONED PANCAKE BATTER into the sizzling skillet, then fixed her eyes on the cloud-shrouded mountains out the kitchen window. They'd always been a source of strength. Comfort. Today they mocked her.

Noel stamped his feet at the kitchen door, then entered with a blast of cold air. He hung his lumberjack-plaid coat on a peg and came into the kitchen, where he sidled up behind her and put his arms around her. She leaned into him, feeling the wiry strength of his body, his beard tickling her cheek. "Nothing's happened, Pat. Nothing at all."

"But if—"

He turned her in his arms and smothered the rest of her sentence against his shoulder. "No *ifs*. Even if we learn she has settled on Belleporte, to her it's just another town."

"I know, but—"

"We need to be excited for her." He cupped her face in his work-roughened hands. "All we've ever wanted is for Laurel to be self-sufficient, decent, happy. And she is. This is *her* dream, darlin'. We need to do everything we can to encourage her in it. If that means Belleporte, so be it."

Pat took one of his hands and drew it to her lips. "Of course I want the best for her. I'm overreacting, aren't I? Maybe it isn't Belleporte."

He chuckled in that warm way of his that had curled her toes from the first day she had met him at the university. "You said it, not I." He took the spatula from her hand. "You heat up the syrup. I'll finish the pancakes."

A few minutes later Laurel came down the stairs, wearing jeans and a red sweatshirt, her dark curls damp from the shower, her scrubbed face glowing. "Is there anything better in the morning than the smell of fresh coffee and pancakes? I don't know how I could be hungry after that great dinner, but I am."

Noel handed her a mug of steaming coffee, then took his place at the table. "Rest well?"

"Like a log. Once I got to sleep."

Placing the platter of pancakes before Noel, Pat sat down. "Problems?"

Laurel took her customary chair between them. "No, just excitement. I can't hold it in any longer."

"We're all ears," Noel said, giving Pat an encouraging nod.

"Okay, here goes. Trumpet blare! I am the sole proprietor of The Gift Horse, a charming cottage in beautiful Belleporte, Michigan."

Her daughter's exultation was almost too much for Pat to bear. Her worst fear was realized. "B-Belleporte?" she managed to stammer.

As if to deflect Laurel's scrutiny from her, Noel clapped his hands. "That's wonderful!"

"Oh, Daddy, I so hoped you'd be happy for me." She looked then at Pat. "And you, too, Mom."

Knowing she had to say something, Pat calmed her breathing. "If you feel good about this, that's what's important."

"Start at the beginning," Noel said. "Tell us everything."

Laurel did, but Pat could barely concentrate on her

daughter's words. Of all the places Laurel could have chosen. Her path to Belleporte sounded so innocent, even fortuitous. And she was clearly in love with the rustic house on Shore Lane and the village ambience. Pat couldn't look at Noel. She knew the Mansfield cottage, just as she knew the shops, the gazebo, the beach. With her fork she moved the soggy pancake around on her plate, but she couldn't swallow a bite.

Finally Laurel ended with "...and I'm moving there the first of January to get everything set up." She grinned engagingly. "Before then, though, I want to place orders with my two favorite suppliers. Mom, I'd love to sell your table runners and place mats, and, Dad, everyone will expect a shop called The Gift Horse to sell Eden-made rocking horses. What do you say?"

Pat covered her mouth with her napkin. When she drew it away, she tried to smile for Laurel's sake. "We'd be honored."

Laurel sat back and looked from one to the other. "It's the best thing I've ever done."

Tears threatening, Pat shoved away from the table and let the dogs out. Fog had settled on the mountains, obscuring her view. What irony! She felt lost. As if her whole adult life had been built on the shifting mist swirling in front of her, beneath her, around her.

IT WAS ANYTHING BUT a white Christmas, Ben observed from his mother's front porch. Blue skies, temperatures in the low 50s, with only a soft breeze off the lake. He shifted his armload of packages and knocked, wondering if he'd be heard over the din of family conversation. His sister Bess, her husband Dar-

ren and their two boys had driven in from Grand
Rapids, Brian was bringing a girlfriend, Terry had two
college buddies in tow, and that didn't count Megan,
Mike and Ben himself.

His mother, dressed in emerald-green, answered the
door and greeted him with a kiss. "Merry Christmas,
Ben. We'd about given up on you."

With his free arm, he hugged her. "It took me
longer than I thought to wrap these." He gazed at the
gifts he was holding. "And even then, they look none
too professional."

"It's the thought—"

"—that counts." He joined her in the familiar refrain, but sensed his mother's gaiety was forced. Understandable. The family had made a point of rallying
this year, knowing their first Christmas without their
father would be rough, especially on Mom.

"How are you doing today, *really?* It's got to be
tough without Dad."

Biting her lip, she shrugged helplessly.

He embraced her again. "I know," he murmured.
"I miss him, too."

"Hi, Ben!" Megan, her red curls caught up in a
ponytail, hurried toward him, eyeing the packages.
"Did you bring me something?"

He yanked on her hair. "You're shameless. Here,
help me with these."

Together the three entered the living room. Bess's
boys sprawled on the worn carpet, playing with their
Santa gifts. The contents of their emptied Christmas
stockings were strewn all over the floor. Ben added
his presents to those under the tree, then made the
rounds greeting everyone. Brian's guest was a busty

blonde wearing too much makeup. Terry's friends turned out to be exchange students from South Africa. Terry thrust an eggnog into his hand. ''Cheers, big brother.''

Ben raised his cup, then settled back to observe the festivities. Even Mike seemed caught up in the holiday spirit. When he opened Ben's present, a gift certificate from a Lake City music store, he cracked a wide grin. Amid the usual array of books, ties and socks, Ben was touched by his mother's gift to all of her children—a framed reproduction of the photograph of their dad in his Air Force blues.

The Christmas dinner went well, with only one spilled water glass. Predictably his mother teared up when she asked him to take his father's customary place at the head of the table. But Bess's youngest saved the moment by blurting, ''How can you be the grampa now, Uncle Ben? You don't got gray hairs.''

Just when Ben decided that Christmas was, indeed, about ''peace on earth, good will to men,'' all hell broke loose. First he stumbled on Brian and his date in a clinch in the pantry and overheard her whispering petulantly, ''Please, haven't we put in enough time here? All this family stuff is starting to bug me.'' *Brian, Brian,* Ben thought to himself with a grin, *this is not a bring-her-home-to-mother kind of girl.*

Then Terry cornered him, making sure their mother couldn't overhear them. ''Ben, can you help me out? I need three hundred bucks for the plane fare to my lab partner's wedding over spring break. No way can I ask Mom for any more.''

''What about your job? Aren't they paying you?''

"Yeah, they pay me, but, man, I'm barely making it. I wouldn't go except I'm a groomsman."

Ben sighed. "Stop by the office. I'll write you a check."

By the time he got back to the kitchen, his mother was elbow-deep in soapsuds while Megan and Bess were loading the dishwasher and drying the china and crystal. Ben untied his mother's apron and escorted her to the rec room door. "I'm taking over. Get down there and enjoy your grandchildren."

She ruffled his hair. "You're a good man, Ben Nolan. And I'm taking the credit."

Ben took his post beside his sisters, wondering whether the holiday meal was worth the mounds of dishes, pans, platters and glassware. He worked quietly, listening to Bess and Megan chat about Megan's work on her high school yearbook. When Mike hollered up the stairs that Megan was wanted on the phone, Ben couldn't help noticing his sister's blush as she scurried to the portable phone, lifted it, then disappeared in the direction of her bedroom.

Bess shook her head. "Love. Ain't it grand?"

Her tone, more sardonic than humorous, alerted him. He concentrated on scrubbing out the grease-encrusted turkey roaster. "You don't sound convinced. Is everything all right?"

When she didn't immediately answer, he turned to study her. She stood, hands braced on the countertop, head down, her auburn hair falling across her face and obscuring her features.

He dried his hands, then took hold of her shoulders and gently made her face him. "Sis?"

She collapsed against him, her back rigid, fingers

clenched against his chest. Finally she drew back. "It's Darren."

"What about him?"

"I haven't said anything to anyone. Please don't tell Mom. The last thing she needs today is something else to worry about." Bess's face was ravaged. "I'm afraid my husband has developed a serious drinking problem."

If she'd told him Lake Michigan had suddenly dried up, he couldn't have been more surprised. Sure, the guy tossed back a few beers and occasionally had been known to tie one on, but...

In a small voice she said, "I'm finding bottles hidden around the house."

"Have you talked to him?"

"Of course, till I'm blue in the face. He claims he's not drinking on the job. That he's got everything under control. But how can I be sure? Would you talk to him, Ben? He's always admired you."

Merry Christmas. "I don't know if it'll do any good, but I'll give it a try." Someone was coming up from the rec room. He leaned close and said, "Bess, you know I'm here for you. Any time."

She looked up, her eyes misty. "Thanks, Ben. I don't know what I'd do without you. What any of us would do. You're our rock."

When one of the exchange students walked into the kitchen, Ben renewed his attack on the roaster, regretting that family problems could not be so easily cleaned up. *A rock.* So that's what they thought. He hadn't had a clue what was in store for him when his dying father asked him to assume the role of head of the family.

It was a heavy responsibility. One Ben didn't begrudge. But there were truths to be faced. Take Laurel Eden, for instance.

His obligations didn't leave much time for personal relationships, and that reality saddened him, because Laurel deserved so much more than he could give right now.

TRYING IN VAIN to curb her excitement, Laurel drove straight to the cottage when she returned to Belleporte. Arlo Bramwell, bent to his work, barely acknowledged her, but when she breathed an ecstatic, "Wow!" he laid down his screwdriver and turned to observe her reaction. He'd transformed the second-story attic into one large combination living room-kitchen-bedroom with a bathroom tucked into one corner and a built-in desk in another. Shelves, still smelling of stain, lined one wall, and the refinished hardwood floors looked like new. He'd even built window-seat storage units.

"It's wonderful, Mr. Bramwell. I couldn't be more pleased."

He shrugged. "Don't rightly know if this is how you wanted these cabinets, but, missy, this is the only way they'll go." He stood back for Laurel to inspect his work on the apartment kitchen.

"I trust your judgment."

He harrumphed, but Laurel noticed a nearly imperceptible gleam in his eye.

"How soon can I move in?"

"Depends."

"On what?"

"Whether you want hot water. Plumber's comin' tomorrow."

"I'd like to talk with you about the work I need done downstairs. When would be a good time?"

"Now's as good as any."

While he went on working, she outlined her ideas for the first floor, explaining that she wanted to open by April fifteenth.

When she finished, all he said was, "Reckon I can handle it."

She spent the rest of the afternoon selecting mini-blinds, getting set up for trash pickup and ordering phone service. Until her apartment was ready, she planned to stay at Primrose House.

Later, at the drugstore, she ran into Janet Kerns, who greeted her by saying, "Welcome home."

Laurel beamed. "How did you know? That's exactly what it feels like."

"I could boast it's woman's intuition, but, sweetie, the bounce in your step is a dead giveaway. Best of all, you're back just in time for Twelfth Night."

"Twelfth Night?"

"Tomorrow is January 5, the eve of the Feast of the Epiphany. Those of us who stick it out here for the winter get together for our annual Christmas-tree-burning party. It's how we celebrate the official end of the holiday season. It will be a marvelous way for you to meet some of the year-round residents."

"I'd love to come."

Janet gave her the details, then, with a cheery wave of farewell, said, "Hope to see you then."

Laurel paid for her merchandise and strolled back to Primrose House. Would Ben be at the Twelfth Night festivities? They hadn't seen each other since their dinner at the Dunes Inn. Maybe she'd romanticized their kisses. Laurel shook her head. No way had she imagined the electric charge between them.

BEN CLOSED THE BLINDS, donned his parka and left his office. The cold, clear night air fairly crackled. Christmas lights on homes and storefronts twinkled merrily, and in the distance he made out a glow in the city park. Then he remembered. Twelfth Night. Hell, he'd been so buried in work, he'd totally lost track of time. He checked his watch. He was supposed to meet his mother fifteen minutes ago.

Setting off at a jog through the light dusting of snow, Ben headed toward the park. He didn't want to miss this long-standing Belleporte tradition, especially the refreshments afterward at the community center.

Clustered around the bonfire were children bundled in snowsuits, adults in boots and parkas, and old-timers with hats pulled low over their ears. Mike, bare-headed, stood with some of his buddies, and Ben spotted Megan huddling closer than necessary to a tall blond kid in a Lake City letter jacket. The burning Christmas trees, now fiery skeletons, sent smoke spiraling into the sky. He sidled up to his mother, who was chatting with Mrs. Arlo, as everyone called Bramwell's pudgy, dough-faced wife. "Did I miss much?"

"The traditional torching and singing of 'We Three Kings.' We could've used your baritone. Working late?"

There were never enough hours in the day. Not if he wanted to keep his practice afloat. "Yeah."

"You young people," Mrs. Arlo said with a shake of her head. "You work too hard. Never enjoy the simple things."

"Ellen's here," his mother remarked, her nonchalance unconvincing. "Why don't you go say hello?"

"You trying to get rid of me, Mom?"

"Never. But you need to have some fun."

Fun? The last time he could remember fun involved Laurel Eden. Maybe he would go talk with Ellen, after all. She might have news about Laurel's return.

In her bright blue coat and purple ski band, Ellen stood out in the crowd. Her eyes lit up when he walked toward her. "Hi, Ben. I was hoping you weren't going to miss the festivities."

"No way." He stood beside her, his hands thrust deep in his pockets, his ears burning in the cold. When a couple of teenagers threw the last of the trees onto the blaze, a man with a strong voice began singing "The Twelve Days of Christmas," and soon the crowd joined in.

Without looking at him, Ellen slipped her arm through his, her warm, rich alto blending with the others. It was uplifting to see the community come together on occasions like this, their petty squabbles left behind. But as Ben knew, things were seldom what they seemed.

Take Bess and Darren, for instance. To the casual observer they were a happy, upwardly mobile family. Yet Darren's defensiveness when Ben had tried to talk to him about his drinking had raised all kinds of red flags. He didn't want to think about the man driving with his kids if he was under the influence. Ben had encouraged Bess to try Al-Anon. Darren, on the other hand, hadn't even wanted to discuss AA.

The last chorus died away and firemen began dousing the smoldering ashes. "Heading for the community center?" Ellen asked.

"Have you ever known me to turn down food?"

They followed the crowd toward the lighted building at the end of the park. Out of the corner of his eye, he noticed his mother's approving smile. He could swear she'd been born part matchmaker.

Breaking the silence, he said, "Have you heard from Laurel Eden?"

He detected a momentary hesitation before Ellen answered. "Yes. She got back yesterday. Any particular reason for asking?"

"Just curious."

"She's up to her ears in the remodeling project, but I imagine she's here tonight. She wouldn't want to miss her first Twelfth Night."

They had reached the door of the hall. She still clung to his arm. "Can I get you a piece of cake, Ben?"

He scanned the crowd, admitting to himself he was looking for a head of curly black hair. "That's okay." He nodded toward Megan. "My sister needs to introduce me to that teenage heartthrob she's hanging all over. See you later."

It wasn't the most gracious exit line, but he didn't want to give Ellen any false hopes. Besides, he really should meet Megan's latest boyfriend.

Most of all, though, he wanted to find Laurel.

LAUREL HUNG at the back of the crowd gathered around the bonfire, delighted she'd arrived in time for the ceremony. Already she'd greeted the Bramwells, the florist and Janet, who had introduced her to her family. She was eager to meet some of the others, especially the Nolans.

Was Ben here? She craned her neck, but couldn't see over the people standing in front of her. Finally, when the crowd dispersed, she spotted him. Arm in arm with... Her jaw dropped. Ellen. They stood close together, and there was no mistaking the adoring look on the woman's face. Laurel felt sick.

She watched as the two sauntered toward the community center, still arm in arm, Ben's head bent close to catch whatever Ellen was saying.

Laurel liked Ellen—valued their new friendship. Why hadn't Ben said something that night on the beach? *Carpe diem,* indeed. She'd seized the day all right—or, more accurately, the night. She'd kissed a man who appeared to be already taken.

She was tempted to flee to Primrose House. But why deprive herself of the pleasure of the celebration? After all, she hadn't come to Belleporte because of Ben Nolan. He'd merely been an added attraction.

Arlo Bramwell's wife grabbed Laurel's arm when she entered the community center and ushered her around, introducing her to everyone she encountered. Finally she directed Laurel to the refreshment table, where they each picked up a slice of cake and a mug of hot chocolate. "Now—" Mrs. Arlo looked around "—where shall we sit?" Then she waved across the room and nodded her head. "There. By Maureen."

They shouldered through the crowd and settled at a long table by the window. "Laurel, this is my friend Maureen—she runs the village day-care."

A friendly-looking woman with russet hair and sad green eyes smiled. "I'm delighted to meet you."

Mrs. Arlo practically bounced in her chair. "You must know about Laurel. She bought the old Mansfield place. For a gift shop."

"Of course. I've heard about you from my son Ben."

Laurel nearly dropped her fork. "Yes, he introduced me to Ellen, who handled the sale for me."

"Ellen's a great real estate agent and a wonderful person," Maureen Nolan continued. "She and Ben have known each other ever since grade school."

Approval echoed in every syllable. Laurel's heart sank, but she did her best to recover, asking the two women about the history of the Twelfth Night observance.

"Part of the fun is the Epiphany cake," Mrs. Arlo said. "Whoever finds a pea in their cake will be crowned king or queen."

"Of what?" Laurel asked.

"Misrule," Maureen responded. "It all goes back to an old Epiphany tradition. We do it here mainly for fun."

"In just a minute there will be the announcement," Mrs. Arlo said.

Sure enough, the mayor hushed the crowd, then held up a pasteboard crown. "Okay, folks, who has the pea?"

A jaunty silver-haired gentleman with a military mustache stood and made his way to the front. "Quincy Axtell, I declare," the mayor said, "this is about the fifth time you've been king."

"Wouldn't you know it would be Quincy," Mrs. Arlo whispered to Ben's mother, but Laurel noticed both women gazed on the man with affection.

After the coronation, Laurel politely excused herself and headed for the door. She had taken only a few steps when she stopped dead.

From the other side of the room, walking directly toward her in a yellow sweater and gray flannel slacks, was the man who'd filled her thoughts for weeks now. Someone jostled against her, but she didn't move.

Ben wasn't looking at the mayor nor at the new king.

Nor was Laurel looking at anyone else.

Despite the press of the crowd and the hearty conversations raging around them, they may as well have been alone—the only man and woman on a moonlit, windswept beach.

BEN STRODE toward Laurel, ignoring those in his path. It would've been so much easier if his memory had idealized her or if, at this moment, he felt ambivalent about seeing her. But when her dark eyes met his and her lips parted in welcome, relief washed over him. He hadn't imagined her, or the physical attraction that even in a crowd of people threatened to make itself visible.

As others turned away to finish their refreshments or head for home, Ben said quietly, "I'm glad you're back." Talk about understatement.

"Me, too. I wish you could see the wonders Arlo's worked on my apartment. Monday he starts on the shop itself."

He smiled. "Still think you haven't undertaken too much?"

"For your information, Mr. Pessimist, I'm more convinced than ever that I made the right choice. Just wait till you see some of the merchandise I've lined up. Really, it's all coming together nicely."

What was the matter with him? He had no right to discourage her. But that didn't stop him from worrying. "I'd like to drop by so you can show me."

"Anytime. I'm almost always there."

He couldn't read her comment. She hadn't set an exact time. Maybe the kiss on the beach had meant little to her. Maybe she hadn't spent these intervening weeks reliving it, the way he had. Before he could respond, he felt his mother's hand on his shoulder.

"There you are," she said. Then she turned to Laurel. "I didn't have a chance earlier to tell you how pleased we are you decided on Belleporte for your shop."

"Thank you. I can't think of a better place."

"If the good will of the community means anything, you should be quite successful." Maureen smiled warmly. "I enjoyed visiting with you earlier."

"Likewise."

"If you'll excuse us—" Maureen took Ben by the arm "—I promised Ellen you'd walk her home."

His mother's timing was flawless. Laurel's ever-so-slightly raised eyebrows signaled more question than accusation. For Pete's sake. Ellen was *not* the woman he wanted to walk home, but what could he say without seeming rude?

Laurel's smile looked forced. "Remember, you're welcome anytime to inspect the cottage."

"I'll come by soon. Good night, Laurel."

Steering him through the crowd, his mother whispered in his ear. "Before you leave, could you locate Mikey—I mean, Mike? He was hanging around that

Ingram boy tonight. I'm afraid they're outside smoking.''

Ellen stood by the door watching their approach expectantly. He felt a twisting in his gut. Ellen was a nice person, but she stirred no romantic impulses. Period.

''And, honey, could you stop by the house tomorrow or the next day? I've received some paperwork from the Veterans Administration. That government legalese is incomprehensible to the ordinary person.''

He sighed inwardly. Whatever adrenaline rush he'd experienced when he'd seen Laurel had effectively been squelched. His mother hadn't done it on purpose, of course, but she'd served up a timely reminder that with his many responsibilities his life was not his own right now. If he could manage it, and he wasn't sure he could, he needed to keep his distance from Laurel. Anything else would be unfair to her.

CHAPTER FOUR

Winnetka, Illinois
Late February

KATHERINE SULLIVAN DIDN'T know when she'd felt
so good. Liberated, actually. She surveyed the half-
empty walk-in closet with satisfaction. After so many
years, she was tired of having clothes, jewels, furs—
things—define her. Tired of endless golf games and
charity benefits. Tired of having to live up to the expectations of others. Especially Frank.

Oh, she'd loved him. But he'd been a difficult man
to live with. She had quietly prided herself on making
the necessary accommodations to keep him happy.
But, then, that's what wives in her generation did.
Kept themselves attractive, sublimated their own needs
and talents, and smoothly ran a household around their
husbands' schedules and social obligations.

She slipped two fur-trimmed jackets off hangers and
added them to the pile on the king-size bed. Ball
gowns, cocktail dresses and beaded jackets lay in a
heap beside rows of designer shoes and bags.

Frank had been dead for almost a year, and though
at first she had felt helplessly adrift, in the last few
weeks it was as if sunshine had displaced the gray of
her soul. And in that light, the seed of an idea had

sprouted, gradually taking root and growing stronger day by day.

She had a life. Not Frank's definition of her life. Or her daughter's. Hers. Finally. And she was going to claim it.

Flinging open the pale-green brocade curtains, Katherine looked out over the immaculately landscaped yard sloping toward Lake Michigan. Whitecaps surged in the wind. Wild. Free. Just like she felt.

She could predict what her friends would say. "Katherine's bizarre behavior is a reaction to her grief" or, "Poor Katherine, do you suppose Frank's estate was that small?" She smiled to herself, triumphantly aware she didn't care what others thought. She planned to advance way beyond "When I'm an old lady, I shall wear purple."

The only place she had ever truly been able to be herself was at Summer Haven—years ago. Even before Frank. It made perfect sense to begin her new life there. The giddy high of possibility dizzied her, and she turned away from the window and sank into the dressing table chair, studying her reflection in the mirror. The years—and expensive beauticians—had preserved her better than most. Her naturally white hair smoothly waved back from her high forehead, and her complexion remained soft, the wrinkles evidence of character. Her eyes, brown with hints of green and amber, were the same as those of the little girl who had built sand castles on the beach below her father's happiest monument to success—Summer Haven. She tilted her head in wonderment. Where had the time gone? She didn't feel old, despite the evidence in the mirror. How could she possibly be nearing seventy-five? It didn't make any sense.

But what did make sense, now that her life was no longer dictated by her often demanding, though charismatic husband, was doing what she wanted in whatever time remained to her.

In the distance, she heard the front door chime. Greta, her housekeeper, would answer it. Undoubtedly it would be her daughter Nan, who checked on her nearly every day, as if she were senile. Not that she didn't appreciate Nan's solicitude, but she still had a will of her own, thank you very much.

"Mother!" Nan burst into the bedroom. "Have you lost your mind?"

"Quite the contrary. In fact, I'm simply beginning to exercise it again. Why?"

"John just called. A friend of his who's on the board told him you've resigned from the country club." Nan pulled a chair close to Katherine and sat down, leaning forward in concern. "Surely it's a mistake."

Katherine pivoted to face her daughter. "Not at all. What do I need the club for now?"

"But your friends…your bridge foursome…"

Katherine tried to hide her amusement. How could Nan know she despised the vacuity of the fashion-obsessed women in the bridge group? "I won't be needing the amenities of a club membership."

Belatedly, Nan looked at her mother's bed. She jumped to her feet and rifled through the satins, silks and velvets. "What's all this?"

"Discards for the hospital auxiliary thrift shop."

"*Discards?*" Katherine recognized the symptoms.

Nan was working herself into high dudgeon. She held up a silver-gray chiffon gown with a sequined jacket. "Why, this is your Versace."

"Yes," Katherine replied. She knew she shouldn't be taking such delight in her daughter's distress.

Nan fondled a mink cloche. "Daddy gave you this one Christmas." She flung her arms wide in bewilderment. "You can't do this."

"Watch me," Katherine said, unable to refrain from smiling.

Nan sank onto the bed. "Mother, are you sure you're all right?"

"Darling, I'm better than I've been in a great long while." She fingered her wedding band before continuing. "I loved your father. I hope I made him happy. I didn't always agree with him, as you know all too well, but he was a very forceful individual. Early on in our marriage, I had to make a decision. To bend to Frank's will or oppose him. I'd promised to love and obey. If I wanted our marriage to last, there was only one choice. I made it gladly. At least at the time. He's gone now. Maybe I let him protect me too much. Pampering can be easy to get used to. It can also be suffocating. Limiting."

"You're worrying me. What are you trying to say?"

"I've made some plans. I didn't want to tell you until I had everything arranged because I knew you'd try to dissuade me."

"What plans?"

"Unless you and John want to buy this house, I'm selling it and moving permanently to Summer Haven."

Judging from Nan's slack jaw and wide-eyed expression, Katherine couldn't have shocked her more if she'd said she was taking up residence in a bordello. "That's crazy," Nan finally managed to say. "You need to be here, close to family. You're…you're an old woman."

Katherine smiled acerbically. "Thank you for that timely reminder. It's precisely because I'm an old woman that I'm doing exactly what I want to do for a change. Living *my* life, for as long as God permits me that privilege."

"But Summer Haven?"

"Why not Summer Haven? My happiest, most productive days have been spent there. And you don't have to worry about a thing. Greta is moving with me, and your son Jay's nice young friend Ben Nolan is helping me with the financial arrangements for transferring my bank accounts and that sort of thing." She rose from her chair and joined Nan on the bed. "Please." She picked up both her daughter's hands and clasped them firmly. "I'm not crazy. I'm more alive than I've been in a long time." She sought her daughter's eyes. "I need this time in Belleporte. And I need you to understand." Katherine saw the flicker of pain in Nan's eyes and knew that she, too, was remembering. "The house here goes on the market next week."

"There's no talking you out of this?"

"No possibility at all."

Nan studied her mother, as if hoping to find a crack in her determination. Finally she slumped and merely said, "I'll miss you so much."

Katherine embraced her firstborn. "I'll miss you,

too, but I'm hoping you, John and Jay will be frequent visitors.''

''Just like always,'' Nan whispered against her mother's ear.

In her heart, though, Katherine knew nothing was going to be just like always. That was the exciting part. How many women her age seized the opportunity for a new beginning?

AFTER WEEKS OF FOG, bone-chilling temperatures and occasional snow, March blew in like an obsessed hausfrau—sweeping the brilliant sky clear of clouds and scrubbing the trees clean of dead leaves. Invigorating, Laurel thought as she walked briskly along the windswept beach. She inhaled deeply, then spread her arms and ran for a hundred yards or so. She'd been cooped up far too long, even though progress on The Gift Horse kept her energized. Arlo was nearly finished with the modifications to the downstairs, and the painters should wind up their work within the week. Then the fun would begin—stocking the shelves.

In the last few days, shipments of merchandise had started to arrive. Opening the boxes, she'd felt like a pampered child at Christmas. So many beautiful things. She hoped her customers would think so, too.

Ads had been placed in the Michigan tourism guidebook, as well as in the regional newspapers. She had established her account with major credit card providers and, with Brian Nolan's help, secured a tax identification number and set up her bookkeeping system.

Brian didn't fit the stereotype of an accountant. On first acquaintance, he seemed more fun-loving than serious. But as soon as he started to work for her, he became all business. He was already worth his retainer in what he'd saved her in time and expense.

Ben had been by several times after the Twelfth Night party to check on the progress Arlo was making, but he'd never once come by himself. Nor had she experienced anything like the response he'd given her that night on the beach when they had kissed, or the kind of look he'd telegraphed her on Twelfth Night. Had she imagined the whole attraction thing?

She had to face facts. Ellen was the most likely explanation for his keeping a polite distance.

Laurel slowed, then stood panting on the beach, letting the fine, cold mist off the breaking waves bedew her face. She'd been naive not to expect a handsome man like Ben to be spoken for. It made sense. But why had he kissed her? That part didn't make sense. She should know better than to get her hopes up where a man was concerned. Had her experience with Curt taught her nothing?

She couldn't really fault Ellen, who had been particularly welcoming, inviting Laurel to supper once and another time to the movies in Lake City. She was generous and fun, the kind of friend Laurel could have confided in. Except whenever Ellen mentioned Ben, Laurel heard the skipped beat in her voice.

Laurel pulled down her stocking cap over her ears and began jogging back toward town. A couple of times Ben had brought his sister Megan to the store. Laurel was immediately drawn to her infectious personality and appreciated the girl's genuine curiosity about the merchandise. On her second visit, Megan had tentatively asked if Laurel needed any part-time summer help. "I can do better than that," Laurel had responded. On the spot she'd offered Megan a job—part-time until school was out and then full-time over the summer.

Ben had drawn her aside. "Are you sure? She's just a kid."

Recalling the look on his face, Laurel chuckled to herself as she dodged the runoff from a breaking wave. It was as if Ben had said, *Another of your harebrained impulses?* Yet she already knew hiring the teenager was one of her soundest decisions. Megan had started coming in voluntarily after school to help sort stock, even though she wouldn't officially be on the payroll until the first of April.

At Megan's suggestion, Laurel had even engaged Mike Nolan to move boxes on Saturdays. Later in the spring, he'd tend to the lawn and plantings.

But had it been a good idea to surround herself with Nolans? Or had she subconsciously been insuring that she'd see Ben? Because no matter how much she tried to talk herself out of it, she had by no means lost interest in him.

The pounding surf dinned in her ears, reminding her that you couldn't force nature. Either there was something between her and Ben or there wasn't.

And despite evidence to the contrary, she was convinced there was.

BEN FOUND the dark interior of the Rathskeller oddly soothing, despite the volume of conversation from nearby tables. While he waited for Jay Kelley, in town briefly from Chicago, he nursed his dark beer and absently studied the collection of steins aligned on a shelf behind the bar. The pub was a Lake City landmark, the first place red-blooded males frequented when they were old enough to buy a drink, carving their initials and dates into the worn tables to mark the occasion. He and Jay had been no exception. Jeez, that seemed like a long time ago.

Ben sighed. Now they were adults, weighed down by responsibilities to their families. It was a different world from their carefree adolescent days, and his recent trip to Grand Rapids to visit Bess had demonstrated that all too clearly. She was getting nowhere with Darren, who refused to admit his drinking problem, much less do anything about it. Frazzled and weepy, his sister had fallen apart when she'd confided in him.

There was one big difference between him and Jay, though. His friend didn't have money worries.

Crap. He was feeling sorry for himself, and on top of everything else, he was having a heck of a time keeping away from Laurel Eden. Every time he saw her, he wanted to take her in his arms, taste those soft lips again, stare into her dusky eyes. Willpower was killing him. He didn't know how much longer he could hold out. Hell, he didn't even want to hold out.

"Hey, Ben, why the long face?" Jay slipped in across the booth from him. "We're celebrating, remember?"

Ben worked up a smile and shook Jay's hand. "I was waiting for you before beginning the party. Happy birthday, pal."

"Thanks. Seems appropriate to be spending it here. Nobody in Chicago goes as far back with me as you do."

Ben chuckled. "Are you sure you want me to remind you of the past? Like the time we spied on your cousin making out on the beach with that Evans creep? Or the night we got drunk on that bottle you swiped out of your grandfather's liquor cabinet?''

"Hmm. Maybe some things are better left to the mists of time." Jay signaled the waitress, pointed to Ben's beer and held up two fingers. Then he leaned forward, elbows on the table. "So tell me, are you getting my Granny Sullivan settled?"

"Your grandmother is a rare lady. I expected her to be more or less clueless about relocating to a different state, but she's sharp as a tack. She's squared around with insurance, driver's license, bank accounts—all that kind of stuff. Naturally we've made amendments to her trust based on her Michigan residence and the sale of the Winnetka property."

Seamlessly, the waitress removed Ben's empty and set two more beers on the table. "It's the strangest thing," Jay said. "She's been like a kid looking forward to this move." He shook his head in bewilderment. "Go figure. I mean, who would have thought she'd give up that suburban lifestyle she enjoyed. Especially at her age."

"I'm not sure how much she enjoyed it, particularly after your grandfather died."

"It's true. She's always loved Summer Haven. Maybe she put up with the Chicago scene all those years for Granddad's sake. To see her now, she could be the Gray Power poster girl." With a twinkle in his eye, Jay held up a fist and affected an oratorical tone. "Seniors of the world, unite. Live your own life!"

"That's what Katherine is doing, and I think it's great." Ben had to admit her decision had been timely—throwing him business when he desperately needed some billable hours.

"Mom might have tried to stop her, but Granny was too quick for her. She and Dad'll probably be over here a lot more now, checking on Granny."

Ben raised his glass. "You, too, I'll bet."

Jay grinned. "You know me pretty well. I'll do anything to keep my grandmother happy." He took a long swig of beer. "What's happening about the improvements she wants to make on the cottage?"

"Arlo's slated to begin on Summer Haven as soon as he finishes with The Gift Horse."

"The *what?*"

"The new gift shop opening in the village."

"Who's doing a crazy thing like that?"

Ben muffled a groan by taking a mouthful of beer. So he wasn't the only one skeptical of the project. "Laurel Eden."

"Who's she?" Before Ben could answer, Jay snapped his fingers and said, "I remember now. Myron Fiedler at the Lake City Bank mentioned her. Small, good-looking woman with some big merchandising ideas."

That about says it. Except for one thing. She's sexy as hell. "That's the one."

"You know this Laurel?"

For some idiotic reason, he found himself clutching his knees and praying his voice wouldn't crack. "In case you've forgotten, buddy, Belleporte isn't that big a place."

Ben felt his friend scrutinizing him. *Son of a bitch.*

Then, as if making an important discovery, Jay shook his head and leaned back in the booth, laughing.

"I never thought I'd see it. You're holding out on me, Nolan."

It took great effort for Ben to control his expression. "What in hell are you talking about?"

"You, buddy. It's plain as day. Lord, you always were the world's worst poker player." He clinked his mug against Ben's. "Congratulations, hotshot."

"What for?" Ben growled.

"Finding the one."

"Now, wait a minute—"

"Give it up. You're busted. So what're you doing about this Laurel Eden?"

"You're way off base, Kelley, but even if you weren't, I'm in no position to pursue her or any woman."

"Maybe that'll change soon."

"Whaddya mean?"

"This is confidential for now, but Dad's getting ready to merge the Sullivan Company with Allied Tech. He wants you involved in the legal work on the tax implications. Could be a healthy retainer, my friend."

"You must have counsel in Chicago—"

"Sure we do. But nobody we trust as much as we trust you. So quit trying to talk yourself out of work."

Ben studied his beer. This was a big deal. A very big deal. He didn't want to disappoint the Kelleys, but neither did he want to feel indebted to them for his success.

"We believe in you, Ben. And we need you."

Jay's eyes held his, and Ben knew he couldn't let down his oldest and best friend. "Okay."

"And while you're at it, give yourself a break. Ask The Gift Horse lady out."

He wanted to. He really did. But it wasn't that simple.

PAT STOOD at the kitchen window and watched Noel finish loading the rocking horses and children's cane-seated rocking chairs into the truck. He paused then and, as he always did in moments of repose, gazed around, taking in the mountain view before him. Even after all these years, her heart filled with love. Noel was a fine man, and they'd lived a good life. One very different from what might have been. Of course, she'd never know if that other life would have been better, but she doubted it.

Now she waited, knowing Noel would come into the house and force on her the question she'd been expecting from him ever since the phone call from Laurel last week, asking if they could deliver Noel's pieces and her weavings to Belleporte. Laurel wanted them to see The Gift Horse.

Noel was leaving in the morning, and would stop overnight in Ohio to pick up an order of jewelry made by a supplier of Laurel's.

She heard his boots on the porch, then the door opened. He entered the house, followed by Dylan and Fonda.

"All set?" she asked.

He hung up his jacket, then approached her. Slowly he removed her glasses and set them on the counter. "Not quite."

His eyes sought hers, but she couldn't bear the re-

crimination she read there and twisted away. She knew
what he was going to say. She didn't want to hear it.

He held her loosely in his arms. "Please come with
me tomorrow. Laurel wants you to come. I want you
to come."

A moan built inside her, but instead she rasped the
words, "I can't. You know that."

"Oh, Pat, darlin', I know no such thing. Let it go."

She bit her lower lip. "Please, Noel. Don't ask me.
It's too much. It's not time." Then more softly she
added, "It may never be time."

He rubbed his hands up and down her arms, then,
with a resigned sigh, stepped away. "I'll tell Laurel
you send your love."

"Yes, do that," Pat said, feeling ice penetrate every
bone in her body. The same ice that had formed on
that awful afternoon so many years ago.

WRAPPED IN A CASHMERE THROW, Katherine Sullivan
sat on the sunporch in her favorite easy chair, survey-
ing the lake, choppy on this blustery March Saturday.
In her hands, warming her fingers, she cupped a mug
of hot mulled cider. It felt so good to be here. Home.
At last.

On the horizon a steamer made its way across the
lake, like a tiny target in a midway shooting gallery.
The endless motion of the water, the sunlight glinting
on the frothy whitecaps, the wind whipping the flag
flying outside were balm to her soul. Maybe this moment represented the silver lining of Frank's death.
Before, she couldn't have considered living full-time
at Summer Haven.

She and her family owed a great deal to Frank. Who

knows? Except for him, there might have been no Summer Haven to come home to. Her father had been a gregarious man with a deep laugh and an endless supply of stories, and Katherine had adored him. But in retrospect, she recognized that besides being a born raconteur, he was also the ultimate wheeler-dealer. Making it big, losing it even bigger, then somehow miraculously landing on his feet. Until that last time.

Katherine pulled the throw tighter around her shoulders. She'd never forget the day he gathered the family to tell them he was putting Summer Haven on the market. Up to that point, no one, not even her mother, had known the extent of his losses. Despite his attempt to maintain a confident front, Katherine had recognized and been frightened by the fear in his eyes. If the cottage didn't sell immediately, he told them, they would have one last season in Belleporte.

So began the bittersweet summer of 1947. Katherine was twenty. World War II had put a damper on Belleporte socializing, but now several young, single men, dressed in whites, frequented the clubhouse. Gradually the younger set resumed their beach parties, tennis tournaments and treks to Lake City dance halls. For most, it was a giddy time of relief that the war was over, but for Katherine, it was an anxious succession of days and nights passing too swiftly, racing toward the end of Summer Haven.

Setting down her cider, she turned and gazed at the inked caricature of Frank hanging on the wall. The artist had captured his strong chin, high forehead and bushy brows—and the acquisitive gleam in his eyes. Katherine had first seen him at the 1947 Belleporte community Fourth of July celebration. He'd been leaning against a tree, a beer in his hand, talking earnestly with her father. After the two had shaken hands, her father had led Frank over to her and made the introduction. She'd immediately responded to the proprietary way Frank suggested a stroll on the beach, then took her by the arm and, in a manner that brooked no argument, led her away from the crowd.

Katherine sighed. Had it been love at first sight or something else? She was captivated by his take-charge attitude, a relief in the sea of uncertainty generated by her father's business failures. Until Frank, she'd never realized a girl could literally be swept off her feet. Handsome and witty, he exuded power, and she needed the security he represented. They were engaged by Labor Day, married by Christmas.

Only in the last few years had she permitted herself to consider the ramifications of that summer. Frank had bought her father's failing company in November of 1947, Summer Haven had miraculously been saved, and everyone had lived happily ever after. With one painful exception. But she couldn't—wouldn't—think about that.

In the distance, she spotted two figures on the beach, walking toward Summer Haven. As they approached, she spun her tale to its conclusion. Had Frank genuinely loved her, or had she merely been part of a transaction?

She stood and folded the throw, then approached the window, idly observing the couple on the beach. No matter, she scolded herself. Frank had taken care of her, and she'd always acceded to his wishes like the dutiful wife she'd been brought up to be. Even when it had cost her so dearly. Yet surely he'd loved her, hadn't he?

She noticed now that one of the figures below was a petite, dark-haired woman. The other, a lanky teenage boy. The teenager held a colorful kite with a dragon design, while the woman walked backward away from him, unspooling the kite string. Then, with a wave, the woman signaled the boy, who let the wind catch the kite. Off they went, running down the beach, the kite lofting high above the dunes. The sound of their laughter failed to penetrate the pane of glass, but Katherine could read it in their carefree expressions.

She ached to join them, to throw off her memories and exult in simply being on a windswept beach on an early spring day with nothing more pressing to do than fly a kite.

BEN SAT on the cedar bench Laurel had installed outside the main entrance of The Gift Horse and waited for his brother. He was fuming. The place was locked up tight. No Laurel. No Mike. Was the kid pulling another fast one? He was supposed to be working. Ben checked his watch. Four-thirty. He jerked to his feet and paced up and down the sidewalk.

Where the hell were they? Mike had been grounded again, this time for coming in past his curfew after a friend's sixteenth birthday party, and Ben was keeping close tabs on him.

Reversing his steps, he returned to the shop and peered inside. Boxes were stacked all over the floor and a few items were clustered on the counter, although some display areas were beginning to take shape. He frowned. Laurel was planning to open for business on April 15, but it looked to him as if she still had a long way to go.

Which brought him full circle. Why wasn't she here working? And where was Mike?

As he pivoted away from the window, he saw them. Mike, his face raw with windburn, strode up the boardwalk from the beach, grinning and holding, of all things, a kite. To keep pace, Laurel literally skipped along beside him, both of them absorbed in an animated conversation.

What did they think they were doing? This didn't look like work to him. He didn't want to react to Laurel, but, damn it, his heart had kicked into overdrive. She looked so alive, so carefree.

When they spotted him, they both stopped in their tracks. "Ben? Hey, am I late or something?" Mike at least had the wits to look nonplussed.

"Half an hour," Ben mumbled.

"But it's such a glorious afternoon!" As if oblivious to the tension between the brothers, Laurel went on. "Spring is in the air and it was a perfect day to fly a kite, wasn't it, Mike?"

Ben couldn't enter into their shared glee. "What about work?"

"Work is always there," Laurel responded airily. "But kite-flying weather isn't. Besides, Mike's been working hard. He deserved a break."

"But what about your opening? Will you be ready?"

"Of course, but you know my motto. *Carpe diem.*"

Oh, yeah. It figured. *Seize the day.* Apparently that was her answer to everything.

She took the kite from Mike and eyed Ben over the top of it. "You ought to try it sometime."

Like that was practical. Between his workload and family obligations, he could hardly squeeze in an occasional game of racquet ball or a night at the Rathskeller with his buddies. "Maybe I'll just do that."

As he uttered those words, he could hear Jay's taunting voice, *Ask The Gift Horse lady out.*

Steeling himself against the temptation, he was reminded that right here was an example of their differing values. It would be a cold day in hell before he walked away from his responsibilities to fly a kite.

Laurel propped the kite against the door and finger-combed her unruly curls. "Thanks, Mike. I really enjoyed that. See you next Saturday?"

"Sure." He eyed Ben sheepishly. "Let's go."

The idiotic thing was, Ben didn't want to go. He wanted to touch Laurel's rosy cheeks, run his hands through her hair, take her inside the shop and spend the evening with her.

She pulled out her door key, but paused, looking back at Ben. "Come by soon and see how the shop's shaping up now that some merchandise is in."

"I will." He gulped, then found words tripping off his tongue with an ease that surprised him. "How about tonight? I'll pick up some pizza and be back in an hour."

The smile she gave him chased any second thoughts right into left field. "Super. I love showing off our progress."

"Later then."

When Ben started for the car, Mike didn't move. Instead he gaped at his brother. "No way," he said, shaking his head in disbelief. "No friggin' way."

CHAPTER FIVE

LAUREL DIDN'T KNOW what to make of Mike's skeptical reaction to Ben's suggestion, which surely was nothing more than friendly interest in her shop. Until today, Ben had kept a polite distance almost as if that night on the beach had never happened. His standoffishness would be amusing if it wasn't such an obstacle to their friendship. In fairness, she acknowledged he had his own problems, his own prior relationships.

Perhaps that was just as well. She needed to focus on business, not on a man, even Ben. Just in case, though, she decided to freshen up, change her clothes and put on a little makeup.

After her shower, she ran a brush through her damp hair, pondering the fact that Ellen hadn't mentioned Ben lately. Nor had Laurel seen the two of them together, although that didn't necessarily mean anything. Laurel made a face at herself in the mirror. *Hypocrite.* She *did* care.

She was waiting in the shop, rearranging items on the counter, when Ben came to the door, looking way too handsome for indifference in khakis and a slate-blue pullover that accentuated the deep cobalt flecks in his eyes. She took his suede bomber jacket and draped it over a chair.

He set down the pizza box, then, with hands shoved

idly in his pockets, studied the interior of the shop—
from the antique general-store counter she'd rescued
from an old barn in Pennsylvania to the pie cabinets
stacked with pottery, candles and dried flower arrangements, and then to the children's nook, filled with an
assortment of rag dolls and wooden toys and puzzles.

"Nice," he said, stepping around a packing crate to
examine a selection of intricately woven baskets.

"It's coming along." His monosyllabic reaction
wasn't exactly a vote of confidence. Couldn't he see
the possibilities? "Let me show you the kitchenware
section." She led him to the rear, where she stood
aside for him to view the bakers' racks, pot hangers
and freshly installed cutting-board counters. Drawing
her hand across a pile of cookbooks, she said, "This
area's where I'll display the cookware, and over
there—" she gestured to the large kitchen window
"—I'll hang stained glass suncatchers. And here—"
she nearly tripped over a ceramic flower pot "—I'll
stock gourmet food items not available locally."

He hadn't moved. "Like what?"

"You know, herb vinegars, chutney, pickled baby
corn."

"People *eat* pickled corn?"

"All the time. You ought to try it."

His lips twitched. Perhaps he was actually going to
grin. "Maybe I will. Will you serve free samples to
lure the wary?"

She looked up at him in surprise. "That's not a bad
idea. I could offer samples the first week I'm open,
and then again for the grand opening—"

"Grand opening? Sounds fancy. When will
that be?"

"I'm waiting until school is out so the summer people will be here. Of course, I'll be in business before that, but I want the official opening to be a total community event."

"As in 'everyone who's anyone' will be here?"

"Exactly."

He gestured at the mounds of boxes. "You really think you'll be in business by April 15?"

"With Megan and Mike's help, and putting in lots of hours myself, I'll make it."

"Mike working out okay?"

She tilted her head. "You sound dubious."

"Well?"

"He's a good worker. You can quit worrying."

Laurel thought she heard him say under his breath, "I wish."

She wandered back toward the counter where the pizza sat. "Honest verdict—what do you think of The Gift Horse now?"

He hesitated, then laid a reassuring hand on her shoulder. "You've worked hard and deserve success." He smiled. "And as soon as you offer those pickled corn samples, it'll be in the bag."

As they started upstairs to her apartment, he added, "Hey, have you thought about stocking those little fruit stick-candy things with the chocolate covering? They'd be a real draw for Belleporte hostesses."

"Reception sticks," she mumbled automatically, wondering if he was serious or putting her on. She hoped the latter. A sense of humor was an enormous asset in a man. Especially one in whom she had a particular interest. Like Ben.

Damn. Why couldn't life be simple?

AFTER A THIRD SLICE of pizza, Ben sat nursing a brew and listening to the soft dulcimer music playing on the stereo. He didn't know what he'd expected, but Laurel had made an inviting home out of what, last time he'd seen it, had been an empty barnlike space. Now it was filled with comfortable, if worn, upholstered furniture, an oak rocker, braided rugs. Quilts and weavings decorated the walls, and wooden and ceramic bowls were strategically placed to hold magazines, pencils and fresh fruit. Homey without being too feminine or artsy. A man could get comfortable here. Heck, he already had.

With swift, efficient movements, Laurel was rinsing the dinner plates. When she leaned over to put them in the dishwasher, he stifled a groan. For such a small woman, she had a deliciously rounded backside. *Jay, old buddy, what were you thinking, putting these notions in my head?* Right, like he hadn't coveted Laurel Eden long before Jay knew anything about her. He needed to come back to earth, and there was one guaranteed way.

"Laurel, about Mike…"

She wrung out the sponge with which she'd been wiping the counters, set it down and turned toward him. "Yes?"

"He's having some problems you need to be aware of."

"Do I?" she said, settling at the other end of the sofa from him. "He's been a perfect gentleman. Why prejudice me?"

"That's not what I'm trying to do." He fumbled to explain himself. "It's just—"

"You thought it was frivolous of me to take him to

the beach today for something as unproductive as kite-flying.''

Her neutral tone put him on guard. ''Well, yeah. I mean, he was supposed to be working. He's irresponsible enough without encouragement. For Pete's sake, the reason I had to pick him up today is that he's grounded.''

''So you've been elected to keep his nose to the grindstone?''

She made it sound like a bad thing to be a caring older brother. ''I think there are some things you don't understand.''

''And I think there are some things *you* don't understand.''

''Like?''

She drew her knees up and wrapped her arms around her legs, studying him. ''Oh, Ben, I don't mean to be confrontational. It's just that Mike is a good kid who seems kind of, well, lost. He works hard, and this afternoon we'd accomplished a lot. I had an urge to see him smile, which he doesn't do very often, and it was a perfect day for kites.'' As if seeking his agreement, she raised her eyebrows and quirked her mouth in a tiny smile. ''Don't you agree?''

''That's not the point.''

''What is?''

He raked a hand through his hair. Damned if he knew what the point was. How could a man concentrate when she was looking at him with those depthless eyes of hers? He drew a deep breath. ''When our dad died last spring, it really threw Mike. It was hard on the rest of us, of course, Mom in particular, but Mike's turned into a different kid. Rebellious, defiant. He's started hanging out with some guys that aren't exactly stellar performers. Mom can't handle him all by herself, so I do my damnedest to keep him on the straight and narrow, but—''

"He's angry. You're the punching bag. He resents you."

Boy, she'd gotten that right. "Big time."

"And it hurts."

God, now her eyes were swimming with concern. "That goes with the territory."

"It must be tough being the one others depend on."

Tell me about it. "I'm the oldest. It's my responsibility."

"And you take it very seriously."

"Sure."

"He's a teenager, Ben. He's going to make mistakes. But here at work? We get along great. He's polite, follows directions. Maybe the job is just what he needs." She paused. "But if there's anything I can do to help…"

"Thanks. I appreciate that." And he did. He hadn't realized quite how alone—or helpless—he had felt. Except for Jay, he couldn't have talked about this stuff with anyone else.

She pulled her legs under her and laid an arm across the back of the sofa. "We've both been through some rough times and talking about them helps. At least, talking with you about Curt helped me. It's funny, but without that relationship, miserable as it was, I wouldn't be where I am tonight."

She seemed both vulnerable and determined. "Where's that?" he asked.

"Starting a new life. Confident, for the first time,

in my own instincts and abilities. Making new friends." She paused, then looked up at him. "Ben, I don't want to do anything to jeopardize those friendships."

"What are you talking about?"

"You and Ellen. I mean, should you really be here this evening?"

His first instinct was to laugh, then he realized what she was saying. She'd assumed he and Ellen were... "Excuse me?"

She drew her hand back into her lap and fidgeted with the crease of her slacks. "Aren't you...a couple?"

"A couple of friends, that's all." Like most men, he wasn't a great student of feminine nonverbals, but he could swear she was relieved.

"So..." She smiled. "Being here tonight, you're not compromising yourself?"

He moved beside her and put his arm around her, cuddling her close enough to catch a heady whiff of her perfume. "No," he murmured huskily, "not yet."

She raised her chin, her moist lips barely a breath from his. He realized he was in real danger here. More than anything he wanted to kiss her. Holding back, remembering his resolve, was pure hell. "You know that night on the beach?" she asked.

Know it? He'd only relived it a record-setting number of times. "Yeah?"

"Did it mean anything or were you merely being nice?"

"Why?"

"I just wondered."

What was he supposed to say to that? He wasn't in

a position to encourage her, but she deserved the truth. "I'm never 'merely nice.'"

"Good," she said with a contented sigh.

Then, unbelievably, she didn't say anything more about it. Instead, she suggested they play a board game, which turned out to be a lot of fun. It wasn't until he was standing at the door, ready to leave, that he became aware of a longing in her eyes that matched the thud of his own heart. He couldn't focus on anything except the way her lips were poised, ripe for kissing. All he had to do was make the first move, but he found himself paralyzed.

Apparently sensing his hesitation, Laurel stepped back, offered him her hand and said softly, "Thanks for the pizza."

He was darn near blindsided by the letdown, except for the fact that she'd saved him from making the mistake he'd worried about all the way over here tonight—letting this relationship get out of control.

But, damn, he'd wanted to kiss her.

SO CLOSE, Laurel thought the next morning as she unpacked a shipping box full of Appalachian jams, jellies and fruit butters. She'd been so sure from the hunger in Ben's eyes that he was going to kiss her. She'd wanted him to, but since that time on the beach, she'd known it had to be his initiative, not hers. Then he'd stiffened, loosened his grip on her hand, and the moment passed.

Glancing at the clock, Laurel realized she still needed to make room for the horses, rockers and other items her parents were bringing. She set aside the rest of the jam order, quickly cleared a spot near the front door and had just time to grab a quick lunch before she heard a horn toot in the driveway.

Noel was halfway up the walk when she flung herself into his arms. "Daddy, I'm so glad you're here!" Until she saw him, she hadn't realized how eager she was for her folks to visit The Gift Horse. Over his shoulder she noticed the empty truck cab. Pulling back, she studied her father, his kindly gray eyes full of love and approval. "Where's Mother? Didn't she come?"

When he answered, his voice was calm, but his smile faded. "It's a long trip. She didn't want to leave the chores, the dogs. Maybe another time, posie."

Laurel choked back her disappointment. She had naturally assumed her mother would come. "Daddy?" Laurel paused before opening the door. "Is Mom all right? She's not sick or anything?"

"She's fine. She sent her love, and I have strict orders to return with a detailed report." He gestured toward the red door. "So are you going to show me or not?"

Just as she'd hoped, her father was blown away by the cottage, the different thematic areas and the obvious quality of her merchandise. "Certain you can sell all this stuff?" he asked with a twinkle in his eye.

"Pretty sure. I've checked out the competition around here, but I haven't seen many handcrafted items as skillfully done as what you, Mother and the others in the co-op do."

After the complete tour, including her apartment, they spent the better part of an hour unloading. They were nearly finished when Laurel noticed right behind the cab a large item covered with a tarp. "What's that?"

Her father looked at her fondly. "A surprise. I hope you'll like it." He lifted the object to the ground. "Are you ready for the grand unveiling?"

"I'm ready."

"Close your eyes."

She dutifully obeyed, enjoying his playfulness.

"Now you're official. Open your eyes."

Laurel stared dumbfounded at the one thing, unbelievably, she hadn't thought of.

"It's to go outside your door during business hours," Noel said.

"Oh, Daddy, it's perfect." She laid her hand on the head of the giant oak rocking horse he'd made, complete with mane and tail of thick strands of rope. Woodburned on the flank was the name of the shop. In his mouth the horse held an oak bucket.

"I thought you could put seasonal items in the bucket—kind of an advertisement."

She could already see it—the bucket overflowing with bunny hand puppets or Fourth of July napkins and flags or gaily wrapped Christmas gift boxes...

"Hey, posie. You with me?"

She chuckled. "Oh, I'm with you." She left the horse and put her arms around her father. "Thank you. I'll think of you every day when I put him outside." As she kissed his cheek, another thought came to her. She stepped back, thunking her forehead with her hand. "A logo. I can use him for my business cards and ads, maybe have a stamp made to put on my gift bags, and—"

"That's my girl. If enthusiasm and creativity count for anything, you should do well."

Late that afternoon she gave him a walking tour of Belleporte, introducing him to several of her acquaintances, before ending up at the Hungry Gull, a small sandwich shop. "You've accomplished quite a bit in a short time," Noel said over dessert. "Your mother and I are very proud of you."

She studied the piece of carrot cake impaled on her fork. *If she's so proud of me, why isn't she here?* "Thank you," she said quietly.

Her father studied her intently. She'd never been able to hide anything from him. "Posie, about your mother—"

"It's okay, Daddy. She was busy. I understand."

But she didn't. Not really.

There was something her father wasn't telling her. But what? They'd never been a family that kept secrets. Or maybe she was merely paranoid. After all, the world didn't revolve around her. She'd have to accept his explanation. Her mother was busy.

KATHERINE STUDIED HERSELF in the full-length mirror. She couldn't hold back a smug grin. If her bridge partners could see her now! Her well-broken-in athletic shoes, two-piece lavender jogging suit and jaunty pink sun visor were a far cry from the standard matron "uniform" of designer pumps, elegant silk blouse, linen skirt and pearls.

The lake air and independence had been true tonics. She felt better than she had in years. Each day she'd added a few more yards to her morning walk, and today she was going clear into town to the post office.

Then, after Greta completed the grocery shopping, she would pick her up at Ben Nolan's office.

For the first time, they'd been able to open the windows to the gentle April breeze, bearing with it the scent of growing things. Springtime. Katherine knew they'd get one or two more cold snaps, but she was going to revel in today's promise. She strapped on a fanny pack and set off down the sandy road.

When had she ever walked in Winnetka? Or been surrounded by nature, glorying in the cry of a gull and the kiss of wind on her cheeks? Never. Exercise was done with personal trainers or in posh athletic clubs. The way her heart now pounded and her breath came in deep, jagged pants suggested her body was coming alive like an awakened Rip Van Winkle. Winded by the time she reached the village, she paused at the gazebo and sat for a few minutes to allow her pulse rate to return to normal. Looking at three recently built fabulous lakeside homes, she sighed. Not everything new signaled progress. The houses were on the site of the original community center, razed several years ago. She had loved the building, with its rustic stone and timber construction and its wide veranda overlooking the lake. So many fun times back then— dances, sing-alongs, amateur drama productions. Lordy, was she getting to be one of those snively old ladies lost in "the way it used to be"?

Then, catching her off guard, came another memory. Nan's rehearsal dinner all those years ago. The community center had been decorated with fresh lilacs and swags of white netting. She and Frank had brought in caterers and a string quartet from Chicago for the occasion. It was to have been a happy, festive family celebration. Even now, like an icicle driven into her chest, the pain came, piercing and all too real. Everything had changed that late May afternoon. Numbed by Frank's shocking announcement, she'd somehow managed to stumble through the evening and the wedding the next day. Nan had been devastated by what had happened. But she, too, had carried on. Neither of them had ever understood, though. Not really, despite Frank's assurances that he'd done what he had to do.

Katherine eased to her feet and started down the street toward the post office. Some pain never went away. Some memories never dimmed, no matter how many years passed.

Ever since that day, a huge part of her had been missing.

Fiddle-faddle, she admonished herself. She couldn't let the grim, gray cloak of depression ruin this God-given day. She held her head higher and quickened her pace. The innkeeper from Primrose House waved at her, and Mrs. Arlo beeped her horn as she tootled past in her Volkswagen bug. Rounding the corner onto Shore Lane, Katherine stopped short. What was going on with the Mansfield cottage? Then she recalled reading in the weekly county paper about someone opening a gift store in Belleporte. The Gift House, or something. Curious, she crossed the street and approached the shop. As she came closer, she saw the large rocking horse and the sign. Oh, yes. That was it. The Gift Horse.

What a delight to see someone paying attention to the Mansfield house. Why, the yard had been cleaned up, the multi-paned windows shone in the morning sun, and the welcoming feel of the shop beckoned the passerby. The front door opened and a petite young woman who looked strangely familiar emerged, carrying two pots of flowers, which she arranged on either side of the gate.

Katherine hurried toward her. "Good morning. Are you open for business yet?"

Smiling warmly, the curly-headed lady wiped her hands on her jeans. "We open this weekend."

"Oh." Katherine was disappointed. "I'll have to arrange to come again then."

The proprietor cocked her head. "I'm getting ready to pour a cup of tea. Why don't you join me? That way you can have a sneak preview."

Katherine's first impulse was to say no. She didn't want to intrude. But the invitation had sounded genuine. Besides, she was curious where she'd seen this woman before. "I'd like that."

"Good." As the young woman preceded Katherine up the walk, she said, "I'm Laurel Eden. Ordinarily I'd shake hands, but I'm covered in potting soil."

"Delighted to meet you, Laurel. I'm Katherine Sullivan."

Laurel spun in her tracks, her face alight with pleasure. "Please tell me you're the Katherine Sullivan who lives in Summer Haven."

"The very same. Have we met?"

"Oh, no. It's just that I have a love affair with your house. It's…it's…special."

Katherine studied the young woman. "Yes, it is."

Laurel seemed to come out of a trance. "Forgive me. I've forgotten my manners. Please come in." She stood aside and let Katherine pass. "Well, here it is. The Gift Horse."

Katherine couldn't believe the profusion of color and texture, the faint fragrance of flowers, the rustic, yet sophisticated display pieces. Everywhere she looked was something she wanted to examine more closely. She turned to the young woman. "Laurel, I can't believe it. We've never had anything like this in Belleporte. It's amazing. Show me everything."

As Laurel explained the various sections of the store and pointed out the one-of-a-kind merchandise, Katherine grew even more entranced. "I'll be here the day you open. Complete with my credit card."

"Next Friday." Laurel rinsed off her hands, then pulled down two cups and filled them. As she handed one to Katherine, she said in a low voice, "I'm a little scared." Then before Katherine could reassure her, she went on. "I don't know why I'm telling you this. Up to now, I've been excited, confident. I mean, I think this place is wonderful, but will anyone else?"

"I do," Katherine said.

"Thanks. That means a lot. Especially from you. You've been coming to Belleporte for years. You must have a good sense about the people here."

"They will love The Gift Horse, dear. I'm sure of it." Katherine permitted herself to inhale the soothing almond fragrance of the tea before taking a small sip. When she set down her cup, she smiled. "Now tell me why you like Summer Haven."

Laurel's eyes lit up. "You know how there are places that capture you? Where you can imagine what goes on inside, what kind of people live there? The first time I saw it from the beach, I had that reaction." She sat back in her chair. "This is going to sound silly."

"Please. Go on."

"It was as if I could hear children laughing and playing and adults chatting over cocktails on the deck. The house itself was like a living being, surrounding its inhabitants with loving arms. It seemed like—" Laurel ducked her head as if in embarrassment "—well, such a happy, family place."

"It was. *Is*." A companionable silence followed, and Katherine knew that she and Laurel were destined to be friends. In the distance a clock chimed eleven. "Oh, dear, I'm late." Katherine stood and carried her cup to the small sink. "Thank you so much for the tea, but I have an appointment with Ben Nolan." She turned. "Do you know him?"

"Yes, I do."

If her eyes weren't failing her, Katherine detected the first hint of a blush, and there was no mistaking the glow in Laurel's eyes. "He's a fine young man. My grandson's best friend, in fact." Nothing like putting in an endorsement. Ben was too darned serious. He needed a lively young woman like Laurel. No harm in playing matchmaker, was there? "I'm going to tell Ben to bring you out to Summer Haven soon. You haven't been inside the house, have you?"

"No, I haven't. I'd love that, Mrs. Sullivan."

Katherine held up her hand. "Please. I want us to be friends. Just 'Katherine.'"

"You've made me feel so much better. I hope you know you're welcome anytime."

As they strolled toward the door, Katherine noticed a beautiful kite with a rainbow design on the wall above the counter. Then it struck her where she'd seen

Laurel before. "You're the kite-flyer," she said delightedly. "That's why you looked familiar."

"You saw us that day?" Laurel hugged herself. "It was so much fun. The wind was just right, and it was exhilarating running down the beach, feeling the tug on the string."

Katherine had a sudden memory of herself racing down the beach behind her father, thinking if only she could run a bit faster, she could fly. "You make me feel young again, simply hearing about it."

"You are young. Age is a matter of the heart. You are *not* old."

"Thank you, my dear. For everything." She opened the door, then paused in the entry. "And if I have anything to say about it, our Mr. Nolan will be calling you soon. I can't wait to show you Summer Haven."

If a septuagenarian could be said to skip, that's exactly what Katherine did as she headed down the street toward Ben's office. What an extraordinary young woman. Exactly who Ben needed to put a spark in his life.

CHAPTER SIX

PAT SNUGGLED under the quilt, waiting for Noel to come to bed. He'd driven back from Michigan in one day and seemed unusually reticent. Or tired. He'd wrapped her in his customary hug when he'd come home, but his answers to her questions about Laurel and her store had been perfunctory. Yes, their daughter was fine. Yes, she'd done a great job with remodeling the premises and displaying the merchandise. Of course she'd liked his gift of the outdoor display horse.

And, no, Belleporte didn't seem much different from her descriptions of it.

Although Noel claimed to understand her reasons for staying home, she knew he didn't approve. The light in the bathroom went out and her husband entered the darkened room, opened the window to the moist spring air, then slipped in beside her. He lay on his back with his hands locked behind his head, saying nothing.

Usually he turned on his side, pulling her to him in a comforting spoon position. She waited, slowing her breathing to match his. The emotional distance vastly exceeded the few inches separating them. After a few moments, she slid closer, nestling her head in the crook of his shoulder. Almost reluctantly, he disengaged one arm and slowly draped it around her.

"Are you angry with me?" she whispered.

"No."

"Disappointed?"

"Laurel missed you. She's concerned. She asked me if you were ill."

Didn't he grasp how much she would have liked to go with him? Anywhere but Belleporte. "I'm sorry."

"I know."

She gathered her courage. "Did you, you know, see…anyone?"

"No." He traced a finger up and down her shoulder. "I think you're overly concerned with the past."

"Don't, Noel. I'll never ever forget. And I can't forgive."

"'Never' is a long time."

She lay still, listening to the steady beat of his heart, remembering her intense youthful idealism. "It all seemed so right at the time. Young men were dying in a senseless war. It was crazy. Somebody had to stop the madness." As clearly as if it was yesterday, she could picture a stern-jawed Noel on the steps of the university administration building, megaphone to his lips, his anti-war rhetoric persuasive and inflaming. He had moved her out of sophomoric complacency into passionate conviction and action.

She felt his body tense, but he didn't comment. "Noel, were we too radical?"

"If you believe in a cause, you have to have the courage of your convictions. Hindsight is a resource we didn't have, but even so, I'd still do what I did. I believed then, and I believe now, that there are just and unjust wars. Vietnam was unjust."

"Our principles cost us a great deal, didn't they?"

"You, in particular."

In the distance an owl hooted. A gust ruffled the muslin curtains. "But they also gave us this wonderful home. This safe place to raise Laurel."

Noel grunted. "We live in a world now where there are no safe places."

"That's why it's so important to preserve what we have as long as we can."

He didn't answer, and from his breathing, she concluded he was asleep. But then, just before rolling away from her, he said, "Or to risk setting right the things we can still control."

Shivering, she pulled up the covers and stared at the ceiling, willing away her tears. She couldn't go where he wanted her to.

MEGAN FINISHED gift-wrapping a package for the last customer. The minute the door closed behind the woman, she let out a delighted whoop. "We did it!"

Laurel nodded with satisfaction. "It feels good, doesn't it? I didn't have time to sit all day."

Ellen, who'd been straightening the display of place mats, sauntered toward them. "Who *did?*" She grinned. "But that's the price of success, huh?"

The steady flow of customers, many from Lake City and beyond, had surprised Laurel, who'd figured The Gift Horse would get off to a slow start. If Ellen hadn't volunteered to help out on the opening day, they'd have been caught shorthanded. "This calls for a celebration. Megan, are you old enough for bubbly?"

The teenager grinned. "I could lie and say yes, but I won't. Thanks, though." She shrugged into her cheerleader letter jacket. "I can't stay anyway."

Ellen eased onto one of the stools behind the counter. "Big date tonight?"

Megan blushed. "The first bonfire beach party of the season."

"Could be mighty cold," Laurel suggested.

Ellen jabbed her in the ribs. "I doubt Miss Megan will freeze with that handsome boyfriend to keep her warm."

Megan's blush intensified. "Jeez, I can't have any secrets around here."

Laurel suddenly felt old. "Just be careful."

"Oh, brother. Not you, too." Megan shook her head. "You sound like my mother. And Ben. Trust me, I know the score. And I *will* be careful."

Ellen chuckled. "Now look what we've done. Don't let us envious spinsters spoil your fun."

With a flourish, Megan wrapped a scarf around her neck. "No way," she said as she opened the door. Then she turned back. "Congratulations, Laurel. It was an awesome day. Good night."

"She's right, you know," Ellen said after Megan left. "It *was* an awesome day."

"I may need you to bring me back to earth. The customers really seemed to like what they saw. And bought."

"Why wouldn't they?" Ellen gazed steadily at Laurel. "You've accomplished miracles here. In fact, I'll be frank. When you came to my office that first day, I thought maybe you were overly optimistic. But you were unstoppable." She rose to her feet and ushered Laurel to the stairs. "Now get your jacket. Dinner at The Rusty Bucket is my treat."

"Only if you'll let me spring for the champagne."

"Deal. I'll call for reservations while you get ready. It's celebration time, girlfriend."

The Rusty Bucket looked like a roadhouse from the outside, but the interior, with its white linen table-cloths, muted lighting and live piano bar, was strictly first-class. Laurel sipped her champagne, reveling in the satisfaction of a successful opening and Ellen's welcome company.

Guiltily, she acknowledged Ellen had been a far better friend to her than she had been in return. She shouldn't have let Ben's relationship with Ellen keep her from suggesting more get-togethers. "I'm glad you didn't have any property to show today."

"Business is slow right now. It'll pick up in May when people start looking for vacation rentals. It was fun helping out. Where did all those beautiful things come from?"

Laurel told her the backgrounds of some of the artisans and how she'd discovered them.

"Those woven place mats were stunning. I may have to buy a set myself."

"My mother made them," Laurel said quietly.

"No kidding? And your dad made the rocking horses? Quite a talented family. Will they be coming for your grand opening in June? I'd love to meet them."

"I'm not sure." When she said the words aloud, she recognized their truth. For one of the few times in her life, she couldn't be certain of her mother's support.

"Why's that?" Ellen asked.

"I can't put my finger on it. My father seems excited about The Gift Horse, but I don't know about my mother.'' In a desperate attempt to change the subject, she added, ''Next to Ben Nolan, she's my biggest skeptic.''

''Ben? Pooh. What does he know? He's a man.'' With a knowing look, Ellen raised her champagne flute.

Belatedly, Laurel regretted mentioning Ben. ''A fiscally responsible man who thinks The Gift Horse is risky business.''

''That figures. Has he tried to protect you from yourself?''

Laurel managed a wan grin. ''Yes. Obviously I paid no attention.''

''Ben can't help himself. He simply has to take care of people.''

''Like Mike, you mean?''

Ellen studied the amber fluid in her flute. ''Like everyone. Mike, Megan, his mother, his brother Terry and God knows who else. It's in his nature.''

''That should be admirable.''

''Oh, it is. But sometimes the family takes advantage of him. Poor guy, here he is trying to establish a law practice, which can't be easy in a place like this. Then his father died, and everything just fell to pieces.''

''And Ben's the one doing the picking up.''

''Exactly. Sometimes I think their dependence on him is a way to avoid taking responsibility for their own lives. It doesn't leave him much time for anything else.''

Laurel had a sick feeling where this was headed. ''His personal life, you mean?''

Ellen shoved her empty goblet aside. "I used to think maybe Ben and I—"

"You've known him forever. It's only natural you'd get together."

"I don't think so. I've recently come to some conclusions about Ben. He's my friend, that's all. If he had any other ideas, he's had more than enough time to act on them."

Laurel eyed her friend with concern. "Are you okay with that?"

"Surprisingly, I'm better than okay. Maybe it was loneliness, a fear of remaining single or something, but those aren't good enough reasons for pursuing a relationship. My big *aha* came when I realized I'm comfortable with Ben, but I'm not in love with him." She sat back in her chair. "I can't tell you what a relief that discovery was."

I'm relieved, too. But for an entirely different reason, Laurel thought.

"Are you ready to order, ladies?" The waiter stood attentively beside their table, ending their conversation.

Later, over coffee, Laurel couldn't help returning to the subject. "Tell me, Ellen. What was Ben like in high school?"

"He was loads of fun, but he was always the responsible type—the designated driver, captain of the football team, the spokesman for the students when the school administration was on our case. Now, with all the family obligations, it's as if he can't let down. I'm hoping this summer when his friend Jay Kelley is here on the weekends that Ben will lighten up."

"Jay Kelley?"

"Katherine Sullivan's grandson. He and Ben have been pals since boyhood."

"Ben could use a friend about now," Laurel said quietly.

"I'm one." Ellen paused. "You can be one, too."

THE NEXT DAY, a Saturday, was even busier in the store. Mike worked on the flower beds and hauling trash, and Megan was a dynamo at the cash register. One woman from South Bend bought three children's rockers, a dried floral arrangement and a case of apple butter. Another ordered an eight-piece place setting of pottery made by a ceramicist Laurel had discovered near Morgantown, West Virginia. Realistically, she knew every day wouldn't be like these two, but it gave her a rush of satisfaction to see how her inventory delighted customers.

Ellen had been in to help this morning but had to leave for a two o'clock showing. Relieved that Ben was no longer a potential obstacle between them, Laurel looked forward to an even deeper friendship with Ellen, whose warmth, common sense and clear-eyed view of Belleporte Laurel was coming to appreciate more and more.

Half an hour before closing time, the sleigh bells on the front door tinkled, announcing another customer. "Mom," Laurel heard Megan saying, "what are you doing here?"

As Laurel wove her way between displays to the front, she heard Maureen Nolan reply, "I wanted to see where you and Mike are working." She turned toward Laurel. "And what Laurel has done with the Mansfield cottage. I couldn't come yesterday," she added apologetically. "I didn't think you'd appreciate my day-care toddlers parading through the place."

Laurel smiled. "That might have been an interesting challenge." She held out her hand. "I'm glad you could come today. Let me show you around."

Ben's mother paused to inhale the scented candles and examine the workmanship of a rag doll. She ran her hands over the surface of a wooden cutting board. "These are beautiful, Laurel. You've done well." Maureen laid a hand on Laurel's shoulder, checking to be sure they were out of earshot. "I'm grateful to you for hiring Mike and Megan. It's a big help to me. Not just financially, but because they feel useful."

"They *are* useful. In fact, I don't know what I'd do without them."

"That's nice of you. Mike, in particular, can be quite a handful."

In the distance, Laurel heard Megan finishing up with the only other customer in the store. "Not around here. He's a good worker."

"That's a relief." Maureen picked up a bottle of maple syrup. "This looks like the real stuff."

"It is."

"I'll take one."

Laurel had a sense Maureen felt obligated to buy something, yet it would be insensitive to insist that wasn't necessary. Laurel picked up the syrup, and the two returned to the front of the store. "Megan, how about showing off for your mother and handling the sale?"

Megan grinned impishly. "Watch, Mom. Megan, the all-star entrepreneur." With dramatic flair, she took her mother's money and opened the cash drawer.

While Megan was wrapping the maple syrup, Mike wandered in, his jeans muddy at the knees. "Anything else, Laurel?" Noticing his mother, he paused, his cheerful smile replaced by a mask of indifference. "Mom, what're you doing in here?"

"I'm picking you up."

"Megan could've taken me home."

Maureen's words were carefully neutral. "Yes, but I wanted to see the store."

"Whatever." Laurel noticed the nearly imperceptible shrug and heard him mutter as he walked out of the store, "Like I wouldn't figure out you're checking on me."

The pleasant mood had turned chilly. Laurel didn't know what to say. Fortunately, Megan came to the rescue. She gestured toward the sack. "I can't wait to try this syrup. You gonna make your famous pancakes tomorrow morning, Mom?"

Maureen's features softened. "I just might." She addressed Laurel. "All my kids will be home tomorrow. We're having a big family brunch. Pancakes and syrup might be just the ticket to go with the ham."

"I've got an idea." Megan's cheeks flushed. "Since so many people are coming, I mean, it wouldn't be any trouble to add somebody else, would it?"

Maureen eyed her daughter challengingly. "I'm sure your boyfriend has his own plans."

"Not him, Mom. *Laurel.*" Before Laurel could offer an excuse, Megan rattled on. "Laurel's here all by herself. Sundays have to be lonely. Besides, I want her to meet Terry and Bess." She finished triumphantly. "Then she'll know all us Nolans."

Maureen chuckled. "Are you sure Laurel's up to taking on our entire brood?"

"I'm sure." Megan bounced up and down on her toes. "Say yes, Laurel. Please."

It was on the tip of Laurel's tongue to ask, "But what will Ben say to the idea?" But she couldn't do that. "I'd love to come. Thank you for asking."

Maureen slipped her change back into her billfold. "Eleven in the morning?"

"I'll be there."

"Well, that's settled." Maureen turned to her daughter. "I'll see you at home." She exhaled a theatrical sigh. "Now on to the Mike challenge."

After her mother left, Megan helped Laurel straighten the merchandise before she, too, departed.

Laurel dimmed the lights, then stood a moment at the kitchen window, from which a small wedge of lake was visible. As the shadows grew longer outside, she indulged in a moment of pure satisfaction. Two days did not a season make, but The Gift Horse might be filling a niche in Belleporte.

The same niche she wanted for herself. She felt at home here. People had been unbelievably supportive.

Except for Ben.

Ironic. The one person in Belleporte from whom she most craved approval was the one who continued to withhold it.

She had mixed feelings about Maureen and Megan's brunch invitation. She liked the Nolans she'd met and was eager to meet the rest of the family, but she suspected Ben wouldn't be overjoyed to see her there.

Yet it could be interesting to observe him interact-

ing with his family, she thought, turning away from
the window. Maybe she could get a clue what she was
up against.

Because the truth was—she couldn't banish the man
from her thoughts.

LAUREL TOOK a deep breath, then rang the bell on the
Nolans' front porch. From inside she could hear children shouting "I'll get it" and the thundering of several someones bounding down the stairs. The door
flew open and she was greeted by two red-haired,
freckle-faced boys, practically identical except one
was three inches taller than the other. "Who're you?"
the shorter one demanded, eyeing her up and down.

"Are you selling something?" the taller boy asked.

Laurel smiled. Admittance past these gatekeepers
was going to be hard-won. "No. I was invited to
brunch."

"I got it," the shorter one said, a grin of comprehension lighting his face. "You're one of Uncle
Brian's bimbo girlfriends."

"Paulie, you know Mom said never to say that
word."

"Bimbo? Why not? What's it mean?"

Just when Laurel began to imagine herself barging
on in, right past the adorable—and candid—munch-
kins, Mike clambered down the stairs in flannel box-
ers. "Jeez, you two. Don't you have any manners?"

From somewhere upstairs came Megan's raised
voice. "Mike, is she here yet?"

Like an echo, another voice, deep and male, joined
in from the front room. "Quiet, people! How do you
expect a guy to study around here?"

A pale-faced young woman with a bright copper pageboy approached the boys. "Paulie, Patrick. Why are you standing there with the door open?"

"There's a lady here," Paulie said.

"That's no lady," Mike corrected. "It's Laurel, you dummy."

The woman shot Mike a disgusted look. "She is very much a lady, Mike. And for God's sake, go get some clothes on." The woman shoved the boys in the direction of the living room, blew her bangs off her face and ushered Laurel in. "I'm so sorry. My sons are completely uncivilized and their uncles aren't much better." Smiling, she offered her hand. "You must be Laurel. I've heard so many nice things about you. I'm Bess, the big sister."

"I'm delighted to meet you."

"C'mon with me. I'll save you from the Nolan men. Mom's elbow-deep in pancake batter and wants to see you."

On the way to the kitchen, Laurel noticed a series of low-hanging pegs on the wall. Above them were strips of masking tape labeled with names. Plastic bins filled with books and toys lined the hallway. "Don't mind that stuff. Mom's day-care equipment is all over the place."

The refrigerator was plastered with children's colorful art work, and on a bookshelf beneath the kitchen window were a fish bowl and terraria, one inhabited by a huge tarantula. Maureen stood at the island counter stirring batter in an industrial-sized mixing bowl. "Laurel, welcome. I hope you're hungry."

"Ravenous." The brisk walk over had restored the

appetite her nerves had threatened to eliminate. "What can I do to help?"

"Not a thing right now. We're waiting on Brian and Ben."

Well, that answers one question. "Bess, you live in Grand Rapids, right?" Laurel asked.

The woman hesitated before answering in a soft voice. "Yes." Then, as if distracted, she went on. "Ben and Brian have both settled in the area, but who knows what Terry will do."

"Did you meet Terry?" Maureen asked.

"Not yet." Laurel grinned. "He must be the one trying to study."

"That's his claim anyway," Bess said.

Maureen ducked her head toward the living room. "I don't think he's doing much of that now. Sounds like Patrick and Paulie have that darned Nintendo going."

Bess started toward the door. "I'll say something."

"Oh, honey, don't bother. We're about ready to eat, and a few minutes playing with his nephews will hardly affect Terry's GPA."

In addition to the noise from the living room, the ceiling above Laurel's head vibrated with a steady bass thrump. "Is it always this lively around here?"

Bess rolled her eyes. "Just wait. Brian and Ben haven't even arrived." She seemed to catch herself. "By the way, have you met my other two brothers?"

Laurel hoped she wouldn't blush and give herself away. "Brian's doing the accounting work for my business and Ben introduced me to Ellen Manion, who negotiated the purchase of my shop."

"Mom, speaking of Ellen, anything going on with Ben and her yet?"

Laurel drew in a breath, waiting for Maureen's answer.

"That boy." Maureen accelerated her spoon-action. "I don't know what he's waiting for."

"Maybe Ellen isn't the right woman," Bess suggested.

"Maybe," her mother agreed.

A lanky young man with unruly black curls appeared in the door. "Mom, any chance of a guy getting fed around here?"

"Not until you meet our guest."

Laurel waved her fingers in the air. "Hi, I'm Laurel Eden."

"I'm Terry. Glad to meetcha. You with Brian?"

Laurel couldn't wait till the family playboy arrived. She would look at her CPA with totally different eyes. "Actually, Megan and your mother invited me."

"Laurel owns the shop where the kids work," Maureen explained.

"Where is that lazy sister of mine, anyway? Did she have a hot date last night?"

He was nudged aside by Megan, wearing baggy jeans and an oversized man's shirt. "Not that it's any of your business, but, yes, I *did* have a hot date."

"How hot, sis?"

"Children!" Maureen glared at both of them. "Cut it out. We've got company."

Paulie barreled between Terry's legs and smiled up appealingly at Laurel. "Hey, lady, wanna play Nintendo?"

Overhead, something like a dead weight went *ker-*

thunk, and everyone in the kitchen heard Mike's muffled, "Damn!"

Paulie clapped a hand over his mouth. "Uncle Mikey said a bad word."

All her life Laurel had heard about large, close-knit rollicking families, and now she was witnessing the real thing.

A gust of cool air from the back porch caused the group to turn toward the door. "I told you the White Sox pitchers were no good. But would you believe me? Hell, no." Brian came into the kitchen, followed by Ben. "Look here, bro. A regular welcoming committee."

Paulie whooped, ran across the floor and flung himself at Brian, who braced for the onslaught. Catching his nephew up in his arms, he grinned at Laurel over the youngster's head. "Hey, Laurel. You're a surprise!"

Ben looked at Laurel, then at his mother. In a noncommittal tone he said, "Mom, I didn't know we were having company."

"Laurel's not company. She's practically one of the family," Megan said, draping an arm around Laurel. "If she can put up with Mike, she oughta be able to put up with you two."

Engaging as the Nolan family's camaraderie was, Laurel felt almost overwhelmed. She'd always thought having siblings would be interesting, but she'd relished being the center of her parents' world and savored her privacy. She couldn't imagine where a Nolan would find a quiet corner in this household.

Mike stumbled into the scene. "I'm starving. When are we gonna eat?"

"As soon as I get some help." Maureen pulled a huge clove-encrusted ham out of the oven. "Ben, would you carve? Bess, you and Megan can finish setting the table." She handed a spatula to Brian. "Here, you do the pancakes while Laurel and I pour the juice." She eyed Terry and Mike. "As for you two, keep my wild grandchildren out of harm's way until we're ready to serve."

As if the movements had been choreographed and practiced for years, the family members swung into action. Laurel was grateful for the task she'd been assigned. It gave her an excuse not to talk to Ben. But when she passed by him carrying the juice glasses to the table, he caught her eye. "Welcome to the Nolans," he said in a wry tone, but the inexplicable sadness in his eyes belied the smile on his lips.

"Thank you," Laurel murmured, wondering again whether she should have accepted the brunch invitation.

Had she only made things worse?

DAMN IT. WHAT WAS Laurel doing here? Ben impaled the ham with his fork and began sawing again. She'd already invaded his thoughts; now she'd invaded his family. This brunch couldn't be over soon enough to suit him.

By the time the meal was underway, something else became clear. She'd won them over. She and Bess acted like twins separated at birth, Paulie demanded that he sit next to her, and Brian was ogling her in a way totally inappropriate for an accountant and his client. That didn't even count Megan and Mike, who acted as if they had brought home a prize. Then there was the way his mother kept looking from him to Laurel and back again. He could almost read her thoughts. At least there was a bright side, he told himself. Maybe she'd get off his case about Ellen.

Meanwhile, Laurel resembled a bewildered spectator at a tennis match, as family jokes flew around the table. She also looked like a million bucks in that form-fitting lavender sweater. But, hey, who was noticing?

Surely she could see why he couldn't get involved. All she had to do was look around the table, for cripe's sake. Bess had called earlier in the week. She needed to talk with him, she'd said. Things were getting worse with Darren. Over his second stack of pancakes, Terry had made noises about wanting a new suit for the summer internship interviews he had lined up. Guess who would get to pay for dapper Dan?

The conversation flowed around him, as if he were a boulder rooted in a rushing stream. He heard snatches from Laurel about her store, from his mother about some new state day-care regulation, from Mike about his geometry teacher, the sadist.

Then Patrick's whiny voice intruded on his thoughts. "Why not, Mommy? You promised. You said we could call Daddy."

Paulie took up the chorus. "Yeah, I wanna talk to Daddy. I wanted him to come with us here." He glared at Bess. "You're mean, Mommy."

"Yeah," Patrick said. "Why couldn't he come?"

Ben looked at his sister. Her freckles stood out against her mottled skin. "Boys, go upstairs."

"But—"

"Now!"

Reacting to Bess's discomfort, Megan shoved back her chair. "I'll take them. C'mon, guys, wanna hear my new CD?"

"Where is Darren anyway?" Mike blurted, his mouth full of pancake.

Maureen studied her plate. "Mike, hush."

"Sis, is something wrong?" Ben asked, experiencing a sudden sinking sensation.

Terry, who was sitting by Bess, picked up her hand. "Are you okay?"

Bess tried to speak, but couldn't manage to get the words out. Fat tears oozed down her cheek and she jumped to her feet, looking wildly around the table. "Sorry," she mumbled, her hands covering her mouth before she ran from the room.

No one said anything. Laurel's eyes found Ben's. In them he saw compassion tinged with concern. "Mom, what's going on?"

Maureen carefully set her napkin beside her plate, then stood. "Bess hasn't told the boys yet, but she's come home to stay."

Brian bolted up. "What do you mean?"

"She's leaving Darren." Maureen touched her son's shoulder. "She'll tell you more later. When she's ready. Right now I'm going to her."

"Darren is such a shithead," Mike mumbled.

"That's all Mom needs," Terry said in a hushed voice.

No one said anything more until Laurel slowly rose. "I know this is a sad time for all of you. Thank you for the meal, but I think I should leave now."

With the females all upstairs, Ben forced himself to his feet. "I'll walk you outside," he said.

Neither of them spoke as they made their way to the porch. There, Laurel faced him and laid a hand on his arm. "I'm so sorry, Ben. This must be very difficult for Bess and your family."

She had no idea how difficult. "I'm the one who should apologize."

"Nonsense. These things happen. Please give Bess my best." She withdrew her hand and turned to go.

"Laurel?"

She stopped, then faced him, her eyes wide with concern. "What?"

How could he tell her he needed her? That he didn't know how much of this load he could carry by himself? He bit the inside of his cheek. "Nothing."

"Ben..." She hesitated as if deciding something. "You might want to talk. If you do, well, I'll—"

He shrugged. "Thanks."

"I care, you know," she said, before setting off down the walk.

Yes, he knew. With those four words, she'd undone him. He knew, too, that despite how hard he was fighting it, he was falling in love with her.

CHAPTER SEVEN

BEN HAD PUT IT OFF as long as he could, but Katherine Sullivan had called to remind him in no uncertain terms that nearly three weeks had elapsed since he'd promised to bring Laurel to visit Summer Haven. Much as he knew he ought to avoid Laurel, the fact of the matter was he missed her. Now, thanks to his most important client, he had a reason to see her again.

It was not only fear of his own need that had kept him away from Laurel. Between the demands of his practice and counseling Bess about the legal implications of separation, he'd had little free time. His sister had given Darren an ultimatum. Either he go to Alcoholics Anonymous and show he could stay sober or the marriage was over. Meanwhile Bess was barely holding herself together. On top of that, Mike had been none too pleased to move into Terry's old room to accommodate Patrick and Paulie, and every day their mother looked more exhausted.

When he arrived at The Gift Horse, Laurel suggested walking along the beach to Summer Haven. Typical Laurel. It was such a "heavenly day," she said. "Too nice to waste in a stuffy car." So here he was, trudging along, fully aware he wasn't the most affable companion. He listened to her prattle on about the flowers she'd planted in her garden, the B and B owner who'd placed a large order for candlesticks, and plans she had for a Web site. Grunts and uh-huh's constituted his response.

Concentrating on the beach in front of him prevented him from looking at her and being taunted by her wind-tossed curls and tempting figure. Apparently she hadn't picked up on his mood or had chosen to ignore it, because she was her same effervescent self. He balled his fists and shoved them into his pockets, thankful she hadn't asked him about his family, because that might have prompted him to tell her they were sucking him dry. God, he loved them all, but he didn't see any end to their reliance on him. Megan was applying to colleges now, and if she didn't get a scholarship, he had no idea how his mother would pay for her education.

After a few more paces, he became aware Laurel had stopped. He turned around. There she stood, staring up at Summer Haven with a delighted grin. "See? Isn't it the best house on the beach?" Then she ran past him, grabbing his hand on the fly and heading for the stairs.

Somehow jogging those last few yards in the fresh air lightened his mood. She was right. It was a wonderful house, home of more good times than he could count.

Katherine had apparently been watching for them, because she came out on the deck, looking particularly youthful in a fitted lime-green pant suit. "There you are! It's about time, Ben Nolan." She turned to Laurel. "Do you know how long I've been asking him to bring you here?"

Laurel raised her eyebrows questioningly. "No. Has he been dragging his feet?"

"You know how men are. The more a woman asks them to do something, the longer it takes them to get around to it. It must have to do with standing their ground, proving their manhood."

Ben's foul mood threatened to return. Why the hell were they talking about him as if he were invisible? He figured the best defense was a good offense. "Man is the provider. It's serious business."

Katherine's eyes sparkled. "But that doesn't mean he's in charge."

Ben laughed. "Boy, you've got that right. Otherwise, Laurel and I would've driven over here."

Laurel punched him on the arm. "You have to admit the walk was invigorating."

Invigorating and awkward as hell. "I bow to the superior wisdom of your suggestion."

Katherine took each of them by the arm. "Come in, children. Greta has our tea ready, along with her fabulous ginger cookies."

Entering Summer Haven, Ben was immediately swept into the past by the comforting smells of wood smoke and cinnamon he'd always associated with the cottage. Katherine ushered them to commodious chairs by the full-length window overlooking the lake.

"Oh, Katherine, this room—" Laurel twirled around before sitting down. "It's fabulous. That's an unbelievable view."

"We've spent many happy times here over the years."

"I can sense it. This room has a homey, lived-in feel."

Ben settled back, letting the women carry the conversation. Watching Laurel as he munched on Greta's moist, chewy cookies, he stifled a smile. She was such a lover of life. And so was Katherine. The two of them chatted on as if they'd known each other for years. Katherine was particularly fascinated by Laurel's homeschooling.

"Did you ever wish you'd gone to public school?" she asked.

"Sometimes. But usually when I'd begin whining about it, Mom and Dad would whisk me off on some educational adventure, as they called it. It's pretty hard to argue with firsthand learning at places like Williamsburg, Philadelphia and the Outer Banks." Laurel picked up her cup, but didn't drink right away. "I guess I was pretty pampered, now that I think about it."

"But from what I can tell, not spoiled," Katherine said.

Laurel chuckled. "I hope not. But as an only child, I ran the risk."

Ben roused himself. "Speaking of risks, Katherine, how's yours working out? You know, moving here?"

Katherine slapped the arm of her chair with the flat of her hand. "Best thing I ever did. Life is full of silver linings, and this is one. If Frank were alive, I'd still be in Chicago rattling around that huge house. But Summer Haven is home now."

"Is Nan getting used to the idea?"

Turning to Laurel, Katherine explained, "Nan is my daughter." A mischievous grin enlivened the older woman's features. "She still thinks I'm certifiable, but she'll change her tune when she comes this summer and spends time with me. Surely if I feel ten years younger, it'll show.''

"It does," Laurel hastened to agree. "When I grow up, I want to be just like you."

"You could do a whole lot worse," Ben offered.

"Hush, you two. I'll get a big head."

"Oh, I doubt that," Laurel said.

Katherine rose to her feet. "Well, enough of this. Ben, I have some papers I need you to glance over while I show Laurel the house." Teasingly, she said to Laurel, "You *do* want a tour, don't you?"

Laurel was so animated with wonder and delight, Ben could hardly bear to look at her.

"Katherine, ever since I first saw this house last November, I haven't been able to stop thinking about it. Show me everything, each nook and cranny."

"You keep Ben company while I get those papers, and then I'll give you the deluxe tour."

Brimming with excitement, Laurel sat on the edge of her chair. "Ben, thank you."

"For what?"

"Bringing me. It seems right somehow that you're here."

"Since I'm the one who caught you trespassing?"

"No." She paused. "Since you're part of this place, too."

How did she know his times at Summer Haven with Jay had been so important? That he'd been more himself here, more at home, than at his own house. There had been space and light and the solid male companionship of Jay and his father John, who in some ways had been a role model for Ben.

Katherine entered the room, flopping down a manila

envelope. "This is an annual report and proxy. After you look it over, I'd like some advice." She patted his shoulder. "Take your time. Laurel and I may be a while, but I'll be sure to bring your girl back to you safe and sound." She turned to Laurel. "Ready?"

After they left the room, Ben ignored the paperwork and stared out at the calm lake. *Your girl? Not very subtle, Katherine.*

God help him, he was surrounded by matchmakers. Within the last week his mother, Bess, Megan and Ellen had all cleverly worked Laurel into their conversations with him. Now Katherine. Resisting such a formidable lineup and his own substantial temptation was taking more energy than he had to give. With a heavy sigh, he picked up the report and started reading.

But it was damned difficult to concentrate. In the distance he could hear the lilt of Laurel's voice, followed by warm, shared laughter.

"YOU LOVED IT, didn't you?" Ben asked Laurel later as they left Summer Haven and started back down the beach.

Laurel wasn't sure she could put her feelings into words. "Yes."

He cast her a sidelong glance. "That's all you have to say?"

"No, but—" Would it sound fanciful to say Summer Haven had wrapped her in its arms?

"But?"

She stopped, then scooped up a flat, smooth stone. With a practiced side-arm delivery, she skipped the stone over the surface of the water before turning to him. "Whatever I say, I'm afraid it will somehow dilute the sensation." She brushed off her hands, then resumed strolling toward the village.

"It's okay. You don't have to say anything."

And she didn't for a quarter of a mile or so, appreciating his understanding. Part of her knew it was ludicrous to so instantly attach herself to a piece of property. But the other part knew she'd come home, crazy as that sounded. Even Katherine had picked up on her feelings. "I don't think anyone until now has understood what this place has meant to me for so many years," she'd said. Then she'd added, "Thank you, child."

"Ben?" Laurel slipped her hand into his, welcoming the warmth of his flesh against her cold fingers. "How do you explain déjà vu?"

"Still feel as if you've seen the house before?"

"Not the inside, although it was very like what I'd pictured in my imagination. But I have the strongest sense I was supposed to come here to Belleporte and discover Summer Haven." She glanced up to see if he thought she was nuts, but he looked at her with interest.

"So what do you make of it?"

"I don't know." She walked on several paces, then laughed self-deprecatingly. "At the very least I have Katherine for a friend. Isn't she amazing?"

"She's always been the stabilizer in that family."

"What was her husband like?"

"Frank?" He seemed to choose his words carefully. "A powerhouse. Big-time defense contractor. More or less self-made. I'd have to say he opted to run his family very much with the same firm hand he ran his company."

"Sounds formidable."

"He was, but he could also charm his most jaundiced competitor. You might not have liked him, though."

"Why's that?"

"He was typical of some men of his generation. A male chauvinist of the first magnitude."

"Hmm. That makes me admire Katherine all the more for striking out on her own at her age."

"Just goes to show you never know what's going on behind the scenes in families."

The edge in his voice took Laurel by surprise. Was he talking about his own? She decided to seize the opening. "How's Bess?"

He shrugged helplessly. "Miserable. I wish I knew how to help her. But the only person who can do that is Darren. I could knock his teeth out."

"What happened?"

"I don't know whether it was the stress of his job or what, but about a year ago he started drinking heavily. Bess says he's out of control now. She felt she had to remove the boys from the situation."

"Will he get help?"

"I hope so, not only for Bess's sake, but Mom's as well. After the shock of Dad's death, I don't know how much more stress she can take."

"What about you? How much more stress can you take?"

He didn't answer immediately, but moved steadily forward, his head bent.

"Ben, I don't mean to pry."

"I know you don't."

"It's because I care."

Dropping her hand, he stopped, then, placing his hands on her shoulders, anchored her. "Don't," he said, his expression raw with pain.

"It's too late," she said, her eyes never wavering from his.

"You can't begin to understand, Laurel. The family is my responsibility. That doesn't leave time for anything else." His voice trailed off. "Any*one* else."

Laurel hooked her hands over his elbows and drew his arms down, then meshed her fingers with his. "It's not about time," she said. "It's about feelings."

He bit his lower lip and stared out at the lake. "I can't," he said raggedly.

"Can't what?"

"Give you what you want. Not now."

She stepped closer. "It's too late."

He looked down at her. "What do you mean?"

"Ben, if I can get the shivers from an old house, I ought to be able to intuit the feelings of the man I care about and who, I'm pretty sure, cares about me."

Roughly he pulled her into his embrace, burying his chin in her hair. "Oh, God, Laurel. I've been fighting this so hard."

Laurel's whole being flooded with warmth. "You don't have to." She kissed the tender place in his neck, where his pulse throbbed beneath her lips. "I understand about your family and your obligations there. Let me help."

He stepped back, holding her at arm's length, searching her face. "Why?"

She felt the words bubbling up from somewhere

deep in her chest. "Are you sure you want the answer?"

Dumbly, he nodded.

"Because, if I'm not careful, I could be falling in love with you, Ben Nolan."

"Laurel, I—"

"Don't you dare say another word." She kissed him lightly on the mouth, then turned in his arms, wrapping his hands around her waist. "Look," she said, nodding her head to the west, where the setting sun gilded the surface of the vast lake. "This is today. The sun will come up again. And again. I'm not asking anything from you now. But one of those tomorrows, you'll have time." She sank back against him. "Till then, I'll wait. We'll take it one day at a time. Remember, I'm a bit commitment-shy, too."

They stood enveloped in silence for several minutes, then she shifted around to face him. "At the risk of contradicting myself, what are you doing this evening?"

He caught her to him and his voice thickened. "I'm loving you, Laurel Eden. I'm loving you silly."

She rubbed her fingers over his light beard, and with the remaining breath in her body, whispered, "What are we waiting for, then?"

KATHERINE STOOD at the window, binoculars pressed to her eyes. She fumbled with the focus and the image cleared just in time for her to catch sight of Laurel skipping a stone. There were distinct advantages to being an eccentric old woman—no one to tell her it wasn't polite to snoop, no one to admonish her to mind her own business.

The house seemed emptier, chillier somehow with the young people gone. She felt a renewed affection for Laurel just thinking about her delighted reaction to the house. Katherine could spot a phony, but there was no pretense in the young woman's appreciation. People could have a special affinity for places. She herself did. Summer Haven was the home of her soul. But it was interesting that Laurel, after only one visit, also seemed so attached.

Katherine had taken great delight in watching Ben follow Laurel with his eyes. Bless his heart, he was trying so hard to resist her, but his expression was a dead giveaway. The man was besotted!

Laurel was exactly what he needed. Katherine remembered him and Jay as little tykes—Jay, the mischievous troublemaker, and Ben, the steady, calming influence. He'd always been bright and mature beyond his years. That was one reason she'd entrusted so much of her legal business to him. Yet he could use a strong dose of Laurel's zest for life. Surely he wouldn't be a big enough fool to let her get away.

She squinted. Things were getting interesting on the beach. Darn this fading sunlight anyway. The two figures were mere specks now, but not too distant for Katherine to miss seeing that Ben had his arms around Laurel and neither seemed in any hurry to move.

"Perfect," she muttered with a satisfied sigh. "I couldn't have arranged it better myself."

As soon as the door of her apartment closed behind them, Laurel launched herself into Ben's arms, her body molding itself to his. On the walk back, Ben had tried to talk sense to himself. *What are you doing?*

Get a grip, Nolan. But now those thoughts were drowned out by the blood rushing through his body, humming over and over, *I want her.*

As if incapable of control, he slipped off her jacket, driving his hands down her back, cupping her buttocks as her mouth moved hungrily against his. Her fingers fluttered across his chest and, one by one, she undid his buttons, then pulled the shirt out of his jeans. When he slid his hands around her tiny waist, she strained against him, her breasts cushioned against his chest. Her scent—the outdoors mixed with the lemony tang of her shampoo—was driving him wild.

Somehow he managed to frame her face with his hands. "Laurel, I don't know how much of this I can take. If you want me to stop—"

She pressed a hand against his backside, drawing his erection against her body. "Stop now and jeopardize your chances of…ever going skinny-dipping with me," she said, nuzzling the line of his collarbone.

"Now, there's a genuine threat," he mumbled, distracted by the sensation of her fingers fumbling with his belt buckle.

"You're not going to chicken out, are you?" She looked up, her eyes revealing both playfulness and a raw need that matched his own.

Before he could answer, she began kissing him and they somehow edged their way to the bed, like crabs caught in a mating dance. Gently she pushed him down and let him watch, fascinated, as she removed her shoes, then slowly shed her jeans, all the time gazing at him with hungry, smoky eyes. When she stripped off her T-shirt and stood before him in her lacy bra and bikinis, his mouth went dry. "You're amazing," he said.

Catlike, she crawled onto the bed and curled up beside him. He wove his fingers through her curls and met her mouth with all the pent-up need he'd denied for so long. As if with a mind of its own, his hand found her breast, peaking the nipple beneath his fingers.

Her soft skin, abrading his, was like warm lotion. Somehow in the frenzied next few minutes, he managed to toss his clothes on the floor and retrieve the foil packet that had been in his billfold for months. He had only time to sheath himself and utter a frantic prayer that the damn thing would work before Laurel straddled him, the dark tips of her breasts beginning to bob in rhythm as she guided him inside her.

Then a force, powerful and driving, took over, and he was aware only of her hands braced on his shoulders, her hot, fragrant skin and her voice intoning his name again and again.

Naturally he'd had sex before, but nothing like this. He'd wanted to claim her and make her part of him. Life without her seemed unimaginable. And as he gripped her hips and rose to meet her in a cataclysmic release, he knew, as he had never known before, that Laurel Eden commanded not just his body but his heart.

She collapsed against him, her ragged breathing matching his. "Oh, Ben. Wow!" she whispered in his ear, the words echoing his thoughts.

"Yeah," he murmured, "wow!" But *wow* didn't begin to say it all. "It's too late for second thoughts now."

He felt the tip of her tongue tickle his ear. "Hmm...I've got some second thoughts."

Alarm bells rang. "You do?"

Rubbing the palm of her hand over the flat of his belly, she crooned, "I sure do. But they're more like second *actions*."

He tried to rise up on one elbow. "You mean—"

"Yessir." She pushed him down and her hand moved lower. "I liked the sample."

Then, before he could even assess his state of readiness, she was guaranteeing it.

CURLED IN THE CURVE of Ben's arm, here in Belleporte, Michigan, above her very own gift shop, Laurel knew a contentment she wasn't sure any human being deserved. He was a passionate, caring lover, stirring in her a fierce need to take care of him, to smooth over the troubles he took to heart.

"You okay?" he whispered.

She'd thought he was dozing. "I'm better than okay. How about you?"

He ran his forefinger down the hollow space in her neck, then over the swell of her breast, until it rested on her nipple. "Wonderful." He paused a beat, then chuckled. "And hungry. Can I take you out?"

She struggled to sit up. "What time is it?"

He checked his wristwatch. "Nine."

"How do you feel about bacon and eggs?"

"Food for the gods."

"Coming right up." She slipped from beneath the sheet, pulled on her panties and T-shirt and crossed to the kitchen. Lady Luck was with her. Using the green peppers, onion and cheese she found, she could whip up a Spanish omelet, topped off with Enrique's Salsa, which she just happened to carry in the store.

While the bacon cooked, she put on a bluegrass CD, then heated the oven to bake the refrigerated biscuits she'd found behind the eggs.

"Hey, the woman can cook, too!" Grinning like a satisfied tomcat, Ben wandered barefoot into the kitchen, his unbuttoned shirt hanging out over his jeans. In the bright light, she felt suddenly self-conscious, finding it hard to look anywhere but at his well-toned chest and taut stomach.

"We mountain girls have a multitude of talents."

He approached, put his arms around her and lightly ran his sandpapery beard across her cheek. "You can say that again."

"Keep up that sweet talk, mister, and you'll never get your supper."

"I need that supper. Gotta keep my strength up, you know." With that, he released her and straddled one of the kitchen chairs, watching her thoughtfully.

As Laurel prepared the food, she hummed along with the CD, almost afraid to trust her happiness. Ben looked like he belonged here. And, Lordy, could he make love. She whipped up the eggs and poured them over the chopped pepper and onion sautéing in the pan. But she couldn't get her hopes up. Not until he sorted out his family. Besides, she'd promised to wait. Damn, though. It wasn't going to be easy. Ben was like the last piece of her dream dropping into place. The most important one.

"I've been sitting here thinking whether I ought to apologize," he said.

"For what?"

"For taking advantage of you."

Laurel took a moment to set the wire whip on a spoon rest. "Why would you say something like that?"

"I don't know whether I made it clear that right now I'm not in a position—"

"Ben, stop." She turned down the burner and took the seat across from him. "I know you're tied up with your family. That's what I meant about waiting."

"But that doesn't seem fair to you."

"It works fine for me. After all—" she gave him a knowing grin "—I'm the *carpe diem* girl, remember?"

"I remember."

"You could do with a little of that philosophy, too."

"Mine's more like trying to make ends meet each day," he said, his bitter tone catching her off guard.

"What do you mean?" She wanted to see his expression when he answered, but she had to check on the eggs. She rose to her feet, dread building.

"I'm looking at a lot of expenses. Terry's in college, Megan will be going soon, followed by Mike, if he ever gets his act together. We're still sorting out what Mom'll have to work with financially. Then there's Bess and the boys."

Carefully she slid the omelets onto their plates. Equally carefully she asked, "Is all of that solely up to you?"

"I'm the oldest. Dad left me in charge."

"I understand your sense of obligation, and I admire you for it. But does that automatically let the others off the hook?"

"What are you getting at?" There was no mistaking the edge in his voice.

She set down their plates, then turned back to get the biscuits and bacon. "It's probably none of my business, but it seems to me Brian could pick up some of the slack. Terry could put himself through school and maybe Megan could work a year after high school, save some money and then go to college. Perhaps Bess could eventually get her own place."

"It's not that simple."

"I'm sure it's not." Laurel tasted the omelet. Sawdust. How had she so quickly managed to screw up a perfect evening?

"My family must seem wild to you. Lord, that day you came to brunch it was a madhouse. You probably can't imagine having brothers and sisters, and I can't imagine not having them. Until you know more about us, you can't possibly understand what I'm up against."

"You're right, but I'd like to learn, to try to get used to a big family." She swallowed hard. "If you'll let me."

He slathered a biscuit with butter, then looked up. "I knew I shouldn't have let this happen. It's not fair to need you and not be able to give you much in return."

Laurel slipped out of her chair and walked behind his. Leaning over, she cradled his head against her breast. "Darling Ben, you don't have to save the world, and you don't have to save me. I've already had one man try to protect me, thank you very much. For now, all you have to do is—"

He set down the biscuit and captured her hands.

"Live the day with you." Then he chuckled sugges-
tively. "Or the night."

She kissed the top of his head. "That's good enough
for me."

"And when it isn't?"

"I'll let you know."

He stood and pulled her close. "Deal," he said quietly. She laid her ear against his heart, listening to its
steady, reassuring beat, understanding in a way she
hadn't until this evening how his family drew strength
from him. It was easy to do.

CHAPTER EIGHT

BEN THREW a forearm over his eyes, shielding them from the shaft of sunlight slanting across his bed. With all his worries, insomnia often prevented the kind of deep sleep from which he'd just awakened. Then memory kicked in, accompanied by a slow-forming, satisfied grin.

Laurel. Lovemaking.

He groaned as his body responded to the images delighting his brain. Passion. Abandon. Tenderness. Release.

And Laurel's promise. Time to get his life on track.

He swung his feet over the edge of the bed and sat up. When was that likely to happen? No sooner did he put out one fire than another erupted. Mike was in danger of failing geometry, Bess was filing for a separation, the economy was hindering Terry's job search, and Mom?

Ben ran his palms up and down his thighs. She was carrying on, but lately she'd seemed brittle—as if the effort of keeping the family together was too much.

He lurched to his feet. So much for euphoria. Laurel's words from last night came back to him. *I understand your sense of obligation…. But does that automatically let the others off the hook?*

She didn't get it. How could she? Her family was

very different from his. That night on the beach she'd
referred to most of her life as "charmed." Must be
nice. Quickly he censored that thought. He wouldn't
trade his family—difficulties and all—for any other.

Moving to the open window, he breathed in the
smell of freshly mown grass, acknowledging that he
couldn't get her out of his mind.

She'd said she could wait. He hoped so, because
regardless of all his reasoned arguments about not getting involved, he could no longer stay away from her.

Didn't want to stay away.

He raked a hand through his hair, then headed for
the shower.

A cold one.

"KATHERINE, YOU'RE TOO GENEROUS. I couldn't ask
that of you. At least let me pay you." Laurel perched
on the wooden bench beside the older woman in the
garden of The Gift Horse, where she'd just finished
arranging statuary, pots and wind chimes.

"Nonsense, child. I don't need the money. Besides,
what else do I have to do? And think of all the people
I know. I'm a natural hostess."

Katherine was in the habit of stopping by the shop
in the course of her morning walks, and from her questions, Laurel knew she took a sincere interest in the
business. But this? "I would want our arrangement to
be flexible."

"Understood." The older woman put her arm
around Laurel's shoulder and gave her a quick hug
before getting to her feet. "Greta will provide the
cookies and I will pour for your weekend teas. It's a

delightful touch and should be a draw for your female customers.''

''It's only a week until the grand opening. You're sure about this?''

Katherine's gaze was steady. ''My dear, I'm as sure as I've been about anything. It will give me a sense of purpose and help you in the process.''

Laurel stood quietly, fingering a fern, as she watched Katherine stroll jauntily down the street toward the post office. One day Laurel had casually mentioned she planned to serve refreshments for the grand opening. Katherine had seized upon the idea, appropriating it as her own and expanding it to include a midafternoon tea each weekend during the tourist season. She insisted on presiding herself, claiming she needed worthwhile activity. It was a gift Laurel graciously accepted.

Katherine's was a friendship she valued. Despite the difference in their ages, they had much in common, including an optimistic outlook on life. In fact, Katherine was an inspiration. Laurel didn't know many women her age who would embrace such a radical change of lifestyle with such energy and enthusiasm. When Laurel had infrequent doubts about The Gift Horse and the financial obligation she'd undertaken, she had only to think about Katherine to receive an infusion of confidence.

She checked her watch. Time enough to hang the gourd birdhouses before opening for business. She dug in the packing box and pulled out the first—painted with a dogwood design—and hung it under the eaves. When she turned around, she noticed Mike slowly approaching the shop, head low, the bill of his ball cap shielding his face. When he entered the garden, his usual smile was missing, replaced by a sullen look.

"Good morning," Laurel said cheerfully.

"Right." He stood in front of her, avoiding her gaze.

"Ready for work?" She gestured toward the box of birdhouses.

"I guess."

She handed him two gourds, took two herself and nodded toward the nearby tree. "Let's hang these over there."

He followed her, but said nothing, and his movements as he adjusted the birdhouses betrayed irritation. This was a side of the boy Ben had hinted at but Laurel hadn't seen before. When they finished, she stood back admiring their work. "Birds ought to love these."

"Birds don't buy them," Mike said. "People do."

Laurel grinned. "A bit of humor. That's a good sign. For a while there, I was afraid you'd gotten up on the wrong side of the bed."

Mike stared at her, his lip curling. "I did." He hesitated. "But it's got nothin' to do with you."

"Want to talk about it?"

"No. You'd just take Ben's side anyway. 'Specially now you've got the hots for each other."

Ignoring that last comment, Laurel said, "Try me."

"He's ruined my whole sophomore year. I've been grounded again." The boy kicked the dirt. "I hate him!"

"I'm sure he's only trying to do what he thinks is best for you."

Mike glared at her. "See? I knew you'd stick up

for him. Screw it,'' he said as he stalked off toward the garage, where the lawn tools were stored.

Laurel's instinct was to go after him, but she had no right. It wasn't any of her business. Ben was trying so hard to hold everything together, but Mike wasn't making it easy for him. Maybe what the boy needed was to get into trouble and be forced to face the consequences. Ben couldn't indefinitely save Mike from himself by grounding him. Her life with Curt had proved experience could be a powerful teacher.

Sighing, Laurel turned and entered the shop. At the counter, Megan was breaking wrapped coins into the register drawer. "Your brother doesn't seem too happy this morning."

Megan looked up and rolled her eyes. "Tell me about it. Final exams are next week and he has to get a B on the test in geometry to pass. Except for work, Ben's grounded him so he can study. Mike is *not* happy. He's missing all the end-of-the-year parties."

"What happens if he doesn't pass?"

"He'll have to take geometry again in summer school."

"Would that be the end of the world?"

Megan shrugged. "I guess Ben thinks so."

At that moment a customer entered, and Laurel shifted her attention to locating just the right basket for the woman's kitchen. Later, though, she wondered if she should risk talking to Ben about Mike. Things were going so well between her and Ben. And not just in bed. She grinned in satisfaction. Well, that, too, but they'd also had the best conversations. She didn't want anything to upset this newfound harmony.

And interfering with his family would.

Still, they couldn't live in a cocoon, no matter how cozy. More and more, she had to admit, she wanted a future with Ben, even though that thought filled her with both exhilaration and wariness. But she'd made him a promise.

One that was becoming increasingly difficult to keep.

THE EVENING BEFORE the grand opening of The Gift Horse, Laurel was too nervous to sit still. She paced the garden, running over in her mind last-minute details. Balloons. New gift bags with the rocking horse logo. Entry forms for the door-prizes. Good weather was forecast and already most of the summer homes were occupied.

"Hey, Miss Proprietor, keyed up?" Ben leaned on the gate, studying her with a bemused grin.

Laurel spread her arms wide. "Oh, Ben, I want tomorrow to be perfect."

He moved toward her. "It will be."

"I wish I could be as sure as you are."

He tucked her hand under his arm. "You'll see. Meanwhile, lady, we're going for a stroll along the beach—get your mind off business."

It worked. As she walked hand-in-hand with Ben, the sounds of water lapping at the shore and the soft strains of jazz emanating from one of the beach houses calmed her. She inhaled deeply, breathing in the lake-freshened air.

"That sounds a lot like contentment," Ben said, tightening his grip on her hand.

"It is. Regardless of what tomorrow brings, this

place is where I belong.'' The unspoken words flashed like a marquee in her mind, *Like I belong with you.*

On the horizon, the last rays of the setting sun winked across the lake and the evening stars took on added luster. They walked in companionable silence. Up ahead, beyond a modern multi-decked house, which Laurel secretly thought was a monstrosity, she spotted Summer Haven, solid and welcoming, its twin chimneys silhouetted against the darkening sky.

Abruptly she stopped. Whether it was an angle of light or an instantaneous image in her brain, she didn't know, but...

Something was different.

She squinted, then shook her head dazedly. Whatever the ''something'' was, it was gone, leaving the square brown house planted firmly on the land's end, looking exactly as it always had.

''Laurel?'' Ben studied her closely. ''What is it?''

''Nothing.'' She started walking. He came alongside her and put his arm around her waist, drawing her close. Until then, she hadn't realized she was chilled. Keeping her eyes on Summer Haven, she willed the change to manifest itself again.

''It must be something,'' Ben said.

She tried a self-deprecating laugh. ''For a minute there, I thought Summer Haven looked...never mind.''

''Your imagination working overtime?''

''Something like that.''

''It figures—as many hours as you've been putting in.''

She wasn't accustomed to seeing things, so he was probably right.

"Let's sit." He motioned toward a set of steps leading up from the beach. He sat on the fourth one, cradling her between his knees, his fingers playing idly through her curls. The wind died and snippets of conversation wafted down from above, indistinguishable sounds reminding them they were not alone. Ben gently massaged the nape of her neck. When he finished, he leaned down and kissed the hollow under her ear, raising gooseflesh.

"You make me happy," he whispered.

"I'm glad."

"I almost forget about things when I'm with you."

She scooted back against a rail post so she could observe him. "By 'things,' do you mean your family?"

"Family. Business."

"You don't really want to forget them, do you?"

His grin came slowly. "No. Actually, the practice has had a boost. I'm going to Chicago next week on some business for the Kelleys."

"And Bess? Mike? Your mother?"

He leaned back, bracing his elbows against a higher step. "Bess is keeping up a brave front, but I know she wishes she could wave a magic wand and restore her marriage. Mom?" He shook his head. "She's bottling up everything."

"Mike?"

"Nothing works with that kid."

"Megan told me about the geometry."

"He's bright. He can do it if he wants to."

"Maybe he doesn't want to."

"Why the hell not? He's only punishing himself."

Laurel leaned closer and spoke quietly. "And you."

"Me?"

Laurel debated whether she should say something more and ruin the magical spell of the evening. "You," she said simply. "Think about it."

He stood abruptly. "Exactly what is it you think I should do about Mike?"

"Let failure be his choice...and his lesson."

He didn't say anything. Instead he moved a few feet toward the water's edge and gazed out over the lake. Laurel watched him, fearful she'd crossed a line. Minutes passed. She hugged her knees to her chest, feeling, as if by osmosis, his distress.

Finally he turned back, holding out his hand to her. "Let's walk."

And they did, each lost in thoughts too personal to share. When they reached The Gift Horse, he paused at the door and framed her face in his warm hands. "I'll think about it," he said simply.

Then he lowered his mouth and kissed her, his lips gentle, caressing. She cradled his head, welcoming the warmth—and relief—spreading throughout her body. She'd been concerned she'd offended him.

"Good luck tomorrow," he murmured, before turning to walk toward the street.

"Thanks." The word echoed in her mind. She stepped back and studied the painted sign over the door. Her own place. She ran a tentative finger over the lips Ben had just kissed.

One dream realized. One to go.

"MOTHER, you're doing *what?*"

Stifling a grin, Katherine faced Nan across the breakfast table. "I'm serving tea at The Gift Horse."

"That shop you told me about?"

"Laurel Eden's shop. Have I told you about Laurel? She's a fascinating young woman. You'll like her."

Taking a sip of coffee, Katherine decided to go ahead and drop the next bombshell. "In fact, I'm going to serve tea every weekend through the season."

Nan's eyes widened. "You can't do that. What about golf? Entertaining?"

Katherine wondered how long it would take Nan to get the picture—her mother had a new life. "There'll be time for that. When I'm ready. *If* I am. But right now, I'm going to do exactly what I want to do. And what I want to do is help Laurel."

Nan set down her fork and pushed back in her chair. "Mother, I don't know what to say. You seem quite attached to this young woman."

"Relax. It's not as if she's after the family jewels or anything. She's pleasant, hardworking and fun to be around. What do I need with a bunch of old biddies in golf carts, anyway? You and I'll walk down to the village this afternoon and I'll introduce you before I begin my shift as the tea server."

"Walk?"

"Oh, haven't I told you?" Katherine twirled her finger airily. "I'm up to three miles a day now."

She would have traded her best pearls for a photograph of the expression on her daughter's face. Yes, indeed, wearing purple was minor league.

BEN BENT OVER his desk Saturday morning, determined to finish the most pressing paperwork before his trip to Chicago. He still didn't quite understand why Jay and his father were involving him with the merger work, but he'd be a damn fool to turn his back on the opportunity. After he finished preparing a couple of filings, he turned to the thick folder Jay had provided him and began studying the financial figures for Allied Tech.

Lunch was crackers and cheese at his desk while he jotted down the questions he needed to ask Jay. Finally around three, he glanced at his watch and decided to call it a day. Besides, he wanted to drop by The Gift Horse to see how things were going for Laurel. And Katherine. He chuckled. Laurel had told him how insistent the older woman had been about serving tea. Frank Sullivan was probably rolling in his grave, but Katherine had clearly shed any of the social pretensions he'd ingrained in her about ''working'' outside the home. Besides, Katherine knew everybody in the village. Her presence could only help the turnout. Even he had to admit Laurel had done wonders with the shop, but he still worried about her long-term prospects.

Just as he was leaving, the phone rang. He was tempted not to answer. After all, it was a Saturday and he was not officially ''in.''

''Oh, what the heck,'' he said to himself as he picked up the receiver.

''Ben? Thank God I caught you.'' Bess's voice was on the edge of panic.

His gut tightened. ''What's wrong?''

''Darren just called. He's on his way here. I don't know what to expect. Can you please come home?''

''Now?'' Ben fought down an irritation he knew was irrational.

"He was on his cell phone. He's only a few miles away."

"Where's Mom?"

"She took the boys to the park. I—I don't know when they'll be back. I don't want them walking in on Darren if..."

"He's drunk?"

"Yes. Please, Ben. Help me."

Ben briefly closed his eyes. "Hang on, sis. I'll be right there."

As he left the office and drove toward home, he glanced regretfully down Shore Lane, thronged with pedestrians heading toward The Gift Horse.

LAUREL COULDN'T BELIEVE IT. A steady stream of customers, full of compliments, kept Megan and Ellen vying at the cash register to ring up sales. Katherine's tea was eliciting oohs and aahs. One mother had even outfitted her little girls in long dresses and gloves. They sat now in the garden contentedly munching wafer-thin cookies and sipping lemonade, which Katherine had decided at the last minute to add just for children. Laurel had lost count of the number of people to whom Katherine had introduced her. It was clear she was providing a social coup as well as practical help.

Late in the afternoon, Megan found Laurel straightening the display of place mats and had just time to whisper, "We've taken in over four thousand dollars," before a gentleman holding one of the children's rocking horses asked to have it rung up.

Laurel's feet ached and her voice was raspy from answering questions all day, but Katherine was the picture of grace. Hovering solicitously near the tea table was Nan Kelley, immaculately coiffed, her dark, thick hair pulled back in a chignon, her flawless complexion the careful result of understated makeup. But it was her eyes that arrested Laurel. Deep brown, they followed Katherine, revealing the depth of her caring.

"I'll be fine, Nan," Laurel overheard Katherine saying. "Go on home. Be there when John arrives. Greta is planning to pick me up at five." She fixed a sharp eye on her daughter. "I'm not made of porcelain, you know."

"I don't want you to get overly tired."

"Tired? I'm having fun, and fun is energizing."

Laurel watched the daughter lean over and kiss her mother on the cheek. "Very well. I *would* like to be home to greet John."

Observing the exchange, Laurel acknowledged the ache in her heart. She had so desperately wanted her parents to share in the celebration, but they had rented a booth at a crafts show in Pennsylvania this weekend. Laurel couldn't help wondering, though. Her mother had asked all the right questions about The Gift Horse, yet her enthusiasm had been tempered by…what? Surely Laurel was imagining things. But there had been no mistaking the caution, maybe even doubt, in her mother's voice.

By four-thirty only a few late-arriving customers remained. Katherine and Ellen were washing the tea service and cups while Laurel set the garden area to rights. That was her excuse anyway. What she was really doing was keeping an eye on Shore Lane, hoping that at any moment Ben would appear. She wanted to tell him everything—about the very first customer of the day, who had clapped her hands and said, "This is just what Belleporte has needed for years!" And then there was the woman from Grosse Pointe who had bought five hundred dollars' worth of merchandise, and the charming little girls dressed for high tea and…

"You look as if you could use a pick-me-up." Laurel turned to find Katherine standing beside her, offering her a cup of tea.

"That sounds divine. Thank you."

Katherine handed her the cup, then sat on the bench, indicating the place beside her. "Sit." She nodded toward the interior. "The girls have things well in hand. Besides, my dear, you deserve to gloat."

Laurel beamed. "It was even better than I dared hope. In large part, thanks to you."

"Nonsense. Nobody turned out today merely to chat with a resident septuagenarian. They came because you had a unique idea on which you expended creativity, time and money. Not to mention love. And the results speak for themselves. Laurel, dear, you're in business!"

In business. Magic words. Soothing words. "Thank you, Katherine. I can't explain it, but it feels… vivifying!"

Katherine eyed her with amusement. *"Vivifying?"*

"I've always wanted to work that word into a sentence, and now I have." She set her cup on a plant stand. "Vivifying." Her expansive gesture included the garden and the shop. "That's exactly how this feels." She picked up her tea and, taking a sip, let the spicy flavor play on her palate.

"Almost everyone in town came," Katherine said.

Almost everyone. But not Ben. Laurel wished his absence didn't matter so much, but it did.

As if reading her thoughts, Katherine said, "Where was that scalawag Ben Nolan?"

"I don't know."

Katherine rearranged the fabric of her skirt. "You're disappointed, aren't you?"

Laurel sighed, knowing she couldn't lie. "Are you a mind reader in addition to being a tea hostess?"

Chuckling softly, Katherine patted Laurel on the knee. "You know, of course, that you wear your heart on your sleeve."

"I thought he'd be here," Laurel murmured.

"And so he would have. Something came up. I just know it. Ben is conscientious. He wouldn't have deliberately let you down."

"I don't suppose so." Laurel desperately wanted to give him the benefit of the doubt.

"It's probably his family. They run him ragged sometimes. Always have."

"Do you know why?"

"When Matthew Nolan returned from Vietnam, nothing was ever the same." Katherine paused, staring beyond the garden, beyond the street. "I wish you could have seen him before. A rugged, jaunty, smiling, handsome man. He and Maureen were a beautiful couple, young and full of life. It was a joy to be around them."

Laurel closed her eyes, remembering the sadness etched in Ben's mother's face.

"When he was declared a prisoner-of-war, Maureen never gave up hope. Then he came home. Wounded. Not just in body, but in spirit." Katherine turned to

Laurel. "Matthew was someone else, someone we didn't know. He was a good father and did his best to provide by working at the golf course. But, oh, the wasted promise."

Faintly Laurel heard a customer leave and Megan close the door behind her.

"Ben was just a little boy. But he was the oldest. Somehow he knew the others depended upon him. As the babies came, it was always Ben who made the sacrifices. His father, especially, came to count on him. But now? He needs his own life."

"And they can't let him go."

Katherine seemed to be reflecting on Laurel's words. "Oh, they can. But will they?"

"That's partly up to Ben, isn't it?"

"Yes. But, Laurel, you'll always have to share him, you know."

It was comforting to have Katherine put into words exactly what Laurel had been feeling. She covered the older woman's hand with her own. "I know."

"Say, if you have time tomorrow, I'd like you to come to Summer Haven for dinner. I'm eager for my daughter Nan to get to know you."

"Thank you, I'll look forward to it." Warmth spread through Laurel as she pictured Summer Haven the way she'd seen it from the beach the evening before. Rooted beside the vast lake, permanent, welcoming. Then—like a flash—the image changed, giving her just enough time to capture the fragment before it was gone again. The same inexplicable sensation as last night.

The older woman rose to her feet. "Good. We'll see you around six."

Slowly Laurel stood, preoccupied with the strange question forming in her mind. "Katherine, was Summer Haven ever painted white?"

The older woman swayed slightly, as if caught by surprise. Then, recovering, she studied Laurel. "Why do you ask?"

Laurel realized instantly she'd been foolish. "It's nothing. Except…"

"Except what?"

"Ever since I first came to Belleporte, I've had the strangest feeling that I know Summer Haven. Yet I'd never been to Belleporte until November. The clang of the flagpole, the chimneys, the windows—it was all somehow…familiar."

"Go on."

"But last night, when Ben and I were walking on the beach, I don't know whether it was a trick of the moonlight or simply a figment of my imagination, but for an instant the house looked…white." Laurel dimly registered Katherine's hand on her arm. "And just now, in my mind, it was white again." She sought Katherine's eyes. "That's crazy, isn't it?"

Katherine paled. "No. It's not crazy. Summer Haven *was* white until after our…" She seemed to check herself. "Until my husband had it painted brown in the early '70s." She hesitated, then said as if to herself, "But however could you know that?"

CHAPTER NINE

WHEN BEN GOT TO the house, Bess sat in the living room, spine stiff, hands clenched in her lap, red hair framing her pale face. "What am I going to do, Ben?" The ache in her voice unnerved him. She raised her eyes. "Darren sounded so…determined. I think he's coming to try to talk me into going home."

"Could you tell if he's been drinking?"

"No, that's why I needed you here. Just in case."

Ben pulled a chair closer to his sister and sat down. "What do you hope to have happen?"

"I'm nearly beyond hope." She waved a hand in front of her face. "I want this all to go away. I want my life back the way it used to be."

"And how was that?"

"We were so in love. The kids were, well, just an added blessing. We've never had a lot of money. Maybe I complained some about that, but there was nothing so bad we couldn't have figured it out together. At least I didn't think so."

"Maybe Darren didn't see it that way."

Bitterness crept into her voice. "Apparently not."

He picked up her hands. "Bess, do you love him?"

Her lips trembled. "I'll always love him." She withdrew a hand and swiped at her tears. "But it's hard the way he is now."

A car pulled into the driveway and Bess shot Ben an anguished look. "He's here."

"Reserve your judgment. Give him a chance."

"If Mom and the kids come home—"

"I'll head them off."

"Okay, then." Bess took a deep breath and crossed to the front door.

Ben waited until Bess led her husband into the room. Darren's face was sallow, marred by a razor nick on his chin, but his eyes were clear, steady. He nodded and returned Ben's gaze. "Ben," he murmured by way of acknowledgment.

"Darren."

"If you'll excuse us, I need to talk with Bess."

Ben caught Bess's eye and she shrugged assent.

Picking up on the implied question, Darren cleared his throat. "I haven't been drinking, if that's what you're wondering."

"Good," Ben said, returning his chair to its accustomed position. "I'll be in the rec room."

Pausing in the kitchen to get a soda from the refrigerator, Ben couldn't help overhearing Darren's first comments to Bess.

"I want you and the boys back. But before you say anything, I need to tell you something. When I got passed over for that promotion, it hurt. Bad. More than you ever knew. All I could think of was how you deserved better. How Ben is always here for all of you and I could never measure up—be the kind of dependable guy he is. I let resentment and self-pity swallow me in a bottle."

Ben knew he should go downstairs. Instead he waited in the silence. Then came the words he knew his sister needed to hear. "Bess, I've started going to AA. I hope someday I'll be man enough for you—like your brother—and that you'll forgive me. That you'll turn to me the way you've always turned to him."

Now Ben did slip downstairs, leaving the door open so he could catch his mom and the kids before they intruded. He switched on a televised baseball game, hit the mute button and settled back in the worn recliner to ponder Darren's assessment of him. He hardly regarded himself as some model of dependability. Then came another thought. Maybe he was a crippler instead. Was he overly protective of his family as Laurel had suggested?

Idly he watched a fly ball soar toward the right-fielder, knowing in his gut that hidden in Darren's words was an accusation he needed to think about.

LAUREL TUCKED ONE FOOT up under her as she hunched on the counter stool, studying the day's receipts. The final total—$5,713.62. She glanced around the empty store, once again orderly and ready for business, thanks to the efforts of Ellen and Megan. The grand opening had been an unqualified success, although she knew to rein in her enthusiasm. Once the novelty wore off for her customer base, would they return again and again as she needed them to in order to be successful? Only time would tell.

Tonight, though, she wanted to celebrate, but her parents were in West Virginia and Ellen had a date. She tried not to think about Ben. He knew how much the opening meant to her, yet she hadn't seen or heard from him all day. She tried to rationalize that something had come up as it seemed to with great regularity, particularly where his family was concerned. This was an aspect of their relationship that worried her. She enjoyed the Nolans and the idea of family, but the reality was a different matter. What did she know about sibling relationships?

Yet despite her lack of experience, she couldn't help thinking Ben's responsibility to his family went too far, and in the process, he denied himself a life. If she wanted a permanent relationship with him, his family would be a major consideration. And there was nothing she could do to change the situation. That was up to Ben.

She made out the deposit slip, then scooped up the bills and coins and secured them in a bank bag. Okay. She'd take the money to the night deposit box, pick up a submarine sandwich and a six-pack and have her own party of one. No thoughts of Ben Nolan were going to spoil her celebration.

When she returned home, to her surprise, Ben was sitting on her doorstep. He leaped to his feet and ran a hand nervously through his hair. She walked slowly toward him, aware she ought to be miffed with him, but the abject apology she read in his eyes made that impossible. "I'm sorry, Laurel," were his first words. "I intended to come, but—"

"Something came up," she finished for him.

"Bess needed me."

The thought occurred to her that if it hadn't been Bess, it would've been Mike or Terry or his mother, but that was petty. Nor could she bring herself to say, "I needed you, too."

"Well, you're here now."

He stood awkwardly, hands in his pockets. "Megan said the opening was a great success."

"It was."

He eyed the deli sack in her right hand. "Dinner?"

She held up the six-pack. "And party."

"I want to take you out. Do the whole champagne and toasts thing."

Weariness and a sense of too-little-too-late swept over her. "Some other time, Ben. I'm beat."

"Next Saturday? A table for two at the Dunes Inn?"

He was trying. She could be gracious, she guessed. "I'd like that."

"Meanwhile—" he took the six-pack from her "—would you share a brew with me and fill me in about today?"

What was it about the man that was so irresistible? Besides, she needed—wanted—to replay the day in glorious living Technicolor for someone. And "someone" was here.

He made a slight bow and motioned to the door. "After you, ma'am."

LAUREL USHERED HIM to the kitchen table, handed him a beer, then gave him half of her sandwich. "There's plenty for both of us."

Ben remembered he'd skipped a real lunch, and after that the events with Bess and Darren had taken away his appetite. Suddenly, he was famished. "Looks good. Thanks."

Between bites, she began telling him about the grand opening. Finally, she put down her sandwich, the better to gesture enthusiastically as she described

Katherine and the success of the afternoon tea. For a grand finale, she stood up and spread her arms ringmaster-style to announce the day's take.

He applauded and she made a theatrical bow. "That's impressive," he said, wondering if he should caution her that one day did not a season make.

She grinned at him. "I know what you're thinking, counselor." She affected the deep voice of an accomplished orator. "Temper your optimism. Every day is not a grand opening."

He held up his hands. "You nailed me dead to rights."

"We optimists can also be realistic."

"And this realist doesn't mean to come across as a pessimist." He set down his beer and picked up her hand. "I just don't want you to get hurt."

Her expression sobered. "I'm a big girl, Ben. I'm fully capable of taking care of myself."

He struggled to read between the lines. Was she implying she didn't need anyone? Didn't need him? "What's that supposed to mean?"

"That you can stop worrying about me. You have enough on your plate without that."

He pulled his hand away and leaned back in his chair. "I guess we should talk about this afternoon. I wanted to be here."

"But?"

"Bess called. Darren was coming to see her. She wanted me there."

"For what?"

Laurel's neutral tone carried a hint of criticism. "In case Darren was drunk."

"Was he?"

"No."

"What did he want?"

"He's been to AA. He's asked Bess and the boys to come back. After he left, she wanted to know what I think."

"Isn't the bigger question what Bess thinks?"

Something important was being said. "What are you suggesting?"

Her fingers were tightly clenched around her beer can. "Ben, have you ever heard of enabling?"

Anger, hot and defensive, filled him. "Do you think that's what I want to do?" He had to move. He stood, rotated his chair, straddled it and sat back down. "I want them to be able to cope on their own, but right now they all turn to me."

She was studying the top of her can intently. "And because of that you avoid having a life of your own?"

"Avoid? Damn it, Laurel, spill it. Go ahead. I can see you're dying to enlighten me."

She sighed. "I've said too much."

He pounded the table. "Not by half. Go ahead, lay it on me."

"I can't talk when you're so angry."

Frustration seized him. "I'm not angry. I'm confused, damn it. You started this. Finish it."

Instead, she carefully folded the deli sack and napkins, rose to her feet and disposed of the trash. When she turned back to him, she said, "I need to touch you while I talk. Please." She nodded toward the sofa. "Sit with me."

His legs were wooden, but he did as she asked. Like a fragile Buddha, she sat cross-legged, facing him, holding his one hand between her two. She began tentatively, "I know I'm no expert on families, and I'm not minimizing the needs and problems that exist in yours. But in the long run, are you doing the people you love any service by being their savior?"

"*Savior?*" He laughed bitterly. "Not me."

Laurel rubbed a thumb up and down the back of his hand before continuing. "Why did Bess call you this afternoon?"

"I told you. She didn't want to face Darren alone."

"He's her husband."

"She needed support." But as he said it, he wasn't so certain.

"Aren't their marital problems between the two of them? Where do you fit in?"

"I'm a buffer."

She raised her eyes. "How can they ever solve anything if a brotherly paragon like yourself is always standing between them?"

He threw back his head against the sofa. For a brief moment he wanted to get up and leave, but he couldn't because Darren's words, mumbled as he left the house late that afternoon, assaulted him. "Hell, Ben, why does Bess need me when she's got you? You know, much as I try, I'll never be you, but I gotta tell you— I love Bess and want to be worthy of her."

Was he part of the problem? That was the very question he'd been mulling over ever since this afternoon. Before he could frame a response to Laurel's question, she started in again, clearly on a roll.

"And Mike? You bail him out time after time—and each time he gets your attention. So maybe the stakes get bigger and bigger for him. He's a kid, Ben. How else is he going to learn except from experience? Why are you so determined to protect him from consequences?" She paused, holding his hand in a death grip. "And what about Brian? How come he gets off scot-free while you attend to everyone's needs? He's a responsible adult with a thriving business."

He couldn't take it anymore. He stood up and paced back and forth. She didn't understand. "Are you through yet? What about Terry?"

Her face flushed, she stood, too. "What *about* Terry? Hasn't he figured out yet that instead of coming to you for everything, he could cut back on his expenses? Show a little thoughtfulness?"

She approached him and put her hands on his shoulders. He looked away, furious with her, questioning himself.

"Look, I don't mean to sound so judgmental. I know there's a middle ground here somewhere. Part of why I love you is that you *do* care, that you *are* so responsible. But you have a life, too. Or should have."

"Whoa," he backed away. "What did you just say?" He couldn't believe it.

"You are entitled to a life, too."

He bit his lip, then said, "Not that part. Before that."

She stepped forward, slid her arms around his waist and looked up at him with the warmest brown eyes he'd ever seen. "I said—" she paused for emphasis "—I love you, Ben."

He reined in his emotions, not daring to loose them. "But?"

"I love your family more every day. They're wonderful, giving people. Here's the 'but.' If you care for me, too, if we're to think about a future, there's something I have to know. There might come a time when I'd be the one in crisis, when you might have to put me first, ahead of your family. Could you?''

Dad. The image was accompanied by a stab of pain. From the time he was a little boy, Ben had tried to make up for his father's handicaps. Fix everything. He remembered the charge his father had given him before he died, the responsibility for the family Ben had willingly assumed. But was his caring stifling his family instead of liberating them?

He could hardly bear to look into Laurel's face, it was suffused with such doubt and longing.

''Ben?'' Her lips parted, her eyes filled.

He crushed her to him, muffling his racing heart with her body. Finally he found his voice. ''You *are* important to me. I hope I can always be there for you, but you have to understand—''

She placed the pad of one finger on his lips. ''I'm trying. I didn't mean to come across so selfishly.''

''Never selfishly.'' He kissed her gently. ''You've given me lots to think about.'' He disengaged himself, then framed her face in his hands. He knew what she needed to hear him say, what he wanted to say, but the words wouldn't come. Instead, he finished inanely with ''Thanks for the beer and the sandwich.''

She clutched his arms, her eyes desperately searching his. ''Don't leave.'' The invitation in her voice, then the light caressing of her palms on his chest stirred a need too powerful to resist. ''I still feel like celebrating tonight,'' she whispered as her hands found his belt.

''Then I'm your man.'' He spanned her waist and drew her toward the bed, knowing he needed to love her so fiercely that his questions would be lost in the frenzy of their mating.

GRETA REMOVED the dessert plates, then refilled the coffee cups. Katherine sat at the head of the table, her daughter to her right, Laurel to her left. John had returned to Chicago earlier in the day, but Nan had decided to stay for the week. Much as she relished her solitude, Katherine had to admit the dinner with her special female guests had been a pleasant diversion. Laurel had told Nan all about her dream of opening The Gift Horse and the steps—and detours—she'd taken to achieve her goal. Laurel finished with a triumphant account of yesterday's opening.

"From what I saw," Nan commented, "you have some rare pieces. None of the cookie-cutter merchandise I so often see in gift shops."

"One of the great joys of this business is discovering local artisans, who often have no idea how unique their products are. I love being able to help them."

Nan stirred sugar into her coffee. "But how did you begin making such contacts?"

"That came naturally. My mother is a weaver and my father works in wood. The rocking horses are his. As a child, I began meeting other craftspersons at the shows where my parents exhibited. When I was asked to be the sales rep for their cooperative, it felt like the perfect job."

"My," Katherine interjected, "all that traveling must have been difficult."

"I admit to having seen the inside of more motels than I want to think about." Laurel smiled. "But otherwise, how would I have discovered Lake Michigan—and Belleporte?''

''We're glad you did,'' Katherine said quietly, wondering why this young woman had so captured her affection. From the beginning, Laurel had seemed like an old friend. And how very strange that she would have asked about the house. Why, very few current residents had any idea Summer Haven had once been white. Maybe this fall she'd consider having it repainted. After all, white had been the original color. But after that awful afternoon thirty years ago, Frank had insisted on the change, apparently hoping a coat of paint could blot out memories of what they had lost.

''...were your parents native West Virginians?''

Katherine perked up at Nan's question. ''No. My father was from Maryland, but he was orphaned as a young boy and grew up in foster families. I don't really know much about my mother's parents. Apparently they moved a lot. They're both dead now. Actually, I never knew any of my grandparents.''

''That's too bad,'' Katherine said. ''So it was just you and your parents?''

''Yes.'' Katherine couldn't help studying Laurel's hands as they circled her coffee cup. Tapering fingers, graceful. When she spoke, she often gestured with her hands in a way that reminded Katherine of someone. Ballerina-like, not distracting, but rather a joyful adjunct to communication. She studied Laurel's gestures as she filled Nan in on her girlhood—homeschooling, freedom to explore the mountains and hollows, fascination with nature.

A thought formed, and then, Katherine gasped, the

sharp intake of breath piercing her chest. Laurel and Nan were staring at her.

"Are you all right, Mother?" Nan rose and crouched beside her. Laurel reached for her hand.

The young woman's face swam in front of her. Darn it, she was fine. It was just the shock of the insight that had come to her like a bolt of lightning. Irrational. Ridiculous. Yet nothing in a long time had filled her with such certainty. "I'm fine. A touch of heartburn." *Heartburn.* She managed an ironic smile. *Heartache,* more likely. "Please, it's nothing."

Nan helped her into the easy chair in the living room. "You're doing too much. I knew it."

Laurel looked pale. "Maybe she overdid yesterday."

Katherine struggled to sit erect. "Nonsense. What do I have to do to convince you two I'm fine? Dance a jig?"

"Mother—" Nan started toward her.

"Calm down. I will sit right here like a good girl and tolerate being patronized by my youngers."

Laurel approached and perched on the arm of the chair, patting her shoulder. "'Youngers.' I like that." She tilted her head in a hauntingly familiar way. "That really should be the antonym for 'elders,' shouldn't it?"

"That or 'heed-me-nots.'"

Laurel chuckled. "We really must talk words one day soon."

"I'd like that. It would be—" she chuckled conspiratorially "—*vivifying.*"

Bending down, Laurel placed a fleeting kiss on her cheek. "Thanks for a lovely evening." She stood and faced Nan. "I really enjoyed meeting you. Please stop by the shop again soon."

While Nan escorted Laurel to the door, Katherine rested her head on the upholstered pillow and closed her eyes. Nan would call her a foolish old lady, lost in false hopes. Yet the sheer coincidence of it boggled the mind. If only she could slow the beat of her heart, which was relentlessly competing with her reason.

"Mother, you look so tired. Let me help you to bed."

Katherine waved her daughter away. "Not yet. I want to ask you something."

Unable to conceal her concern, Nan knelt at her feet and laid her cheek on her mother's knee. "What is it?"

Katherine licked her lips and struggled to keep emotion out of her voice. "Does Laurel remind you of anyone?"

Slowly Nan raised her head, her expression confused. "Whatever do you mean?"

"She asked me if Summer Haven had ever been painted white?"

"So?"

"It's been brown about as long as Laurel's been alive. Besides, she's never been to Belleporte before. So how would she know that?"

Nan stared at her mother for a long moment before her eyes widened in sudden comprehension. "Mother, you're not thinking…"

Katherine felt her mouth go dry. "Don't you see the resemblance?"

"Oh, Mama, don't torture yourself."

"I knew Laurel reminded me of someone."

"Mother, Jo's been gone for so long. We've never heard from her. Not once in all these years."

"Your father told us to forget about her," Katherine said, making no move to wipe away the tears gathering in her eyes. "But how could I forget my own daughter?"

Nan's arms went around her.

"Laurel's the right age." She couldn't bring herself to add, "to be my granddaughter."

Nan took her by the upper arms and held her firmly. "Stop it, Mother. You're trying to talk yourself into something. It will only end in pain. And you—we—have had more than enough of that."

Katherine laid her weary head on her daughter's shoulder. "But what if…what if I'm right?"

WHEN NOEL CAME through the door, Pat looked up from her loom, her lips forming a smile of greeting that slowly faded as she read the concern—and judgment—in his face. "What is it?" she asked, taking the shuttle to the end of the row.

Noel set the bag of groceries on the counter, then spread the mail on the kitchen table. "I think you'd better come take a look."

Pat ran a hand randomly over the piece she was working on, seeking comfort from the texture of the wool. Outside the window she could hear songbirds chirping, and from somewhere across the valley the insistent whir of a buzz saw. Noel mechanically sorted the groceries—cold stuffs on the counter near the refrigerator, canned goods by the pantry. The lines in his face were deep, his jaw tense.

She came up beside him and laid a hand on his shoulder. "What is it?"

"You're not going to like it." With a forefinger he pushed an envelope toward her. "It's from Laurel."

Her face lit up. "Why wouldn't I like it?"

"She's sent a newspaper clipping and photograph from the grand opening."

"Good, at last I'll be able to see the shop."

She barely heard his next words. "That's not all you'll see."

Something in his tone made her go weak in the knees. With bone-chilling dread, she pulled Laurel's letter from the envelope, along with the clipping. In large type the headline read "Gift Shop Opening Well Attended." Then her eyes fell to the photograph. Laurel standing beside a tea table with...with... "No!" She heard a shrill cry that sounded like her own voice just before the floor rose to meet her.

CHAPTER TEN

JOHN KELLEY SAT at the head of the table in the Sullivan Company boardroom beneath an imposing oil portrait of Frank Sullivan, company founder. Flanking him were Jay and the chief financial officer. At first Ben had been intimidated by the lush Oriental carpet, the highly polished conference table, the floor to ceiling windows overlooking the Chicago skyline. As the discussion proceeded, however, and it became clear his input was not only helpful but appreciated, he relaxed. He wanted this work not merely because he needed the money, but because others valued his expertise. It didn't hurt, though, that he now knew the source of his office rent for the next few months.

He studied the room, tailor-made for movers and shakers, knowing he, too, could've opted for this life. Recruiters had more than once laid down attractive alternatives to his one-man operation in Belleporte. Family considerations had put such opportunities beyond the realm of possibility, but he had to admit he thrived on the challenges Jay and John offered him.

John closed his folder, took off his glasses and smiled. "Ben, we appreciate the good work you've done so far, but this is only the tip of the iceberg. We'll look forward to your further input." He rose, extended his hand, then, closely followed by the CFO, left the room.

As soon as the door clicked shut behind them, Jay rounded the table. "Ben, my man, this is huge. Way to go!"

Grinning, Ben stood and shook hands. "I know I didn't get this work solely on the basis of my boyish charm. Thanks."

Jay clapped him on the back. "Forget it. Your objective viewpoint is genuinely helpful. I hope you have time for a late lunch before you head back to Belleporte."

"I'm starving," Ben said, recalling he'd been too uptight to eat breakfast.

The lunch crowd had come and gone from the nearby steak house, and Ben found the quiet, dim interior relaxing after his tension-filled morning. After they ordered, Jay unbuttoned his suit jacket and spread his arms across the back of the booth. "Sure there's no way we can convince you to join our legal department?"

It was not the first time the suggestion had been made. "Afraid not."

"Family keeping you busy?"

"If it's not one thing, it's another," Ben said. For the umpteenth time since his Saturday conversation with Laurel, he second-guessed himself. What was his obligation to the family, anyway? Just this week when Terry learned he was coming to Chicago, he had made another appeal for money, this time for sailing lessons offered through the university. Hell, Ben didn't even know how to sail. Terry had seemed baffled when Ben turned him down, suggesting he pay for them himself.

"With what?" was his brother's response. Ben had gritted his teeth. "The same way I pay for things— out of what I earn," he'd replied testily.

Jay leaned forward, a sly grin on his face. "And what about Miss Gift Horse?"

"Laurel?"

"Yeah, Laurel." Jay made a give-it-to-me gesture with his fingers. "Don't hold out on me."

"I've been spending some time with her," Ben said noncommittally.

"That would be putting it mildly from what I hear via the Belleporte grapevine. Just as I suspected earlier, she's the one, isn't she?"

Ben rested his elbows on the table and looked straight at Jay. "I think so."

"Tell me about her."

"Attractive, opinionated, energetic and, how can I put it...?"

"Sexy as hell?"

Ben grinned. "You got it."

"I'm coming to Belleporte this weekend. I'd like to meet her."

"Anytime but Saturday night. We have a big date."

"Celebrating?"

"The successful grand opening of her shop."

"Granny's sure high on her."

Ben chuckled. "They make quite a pair."

The waiter served their steak sandwiches and fries. Jay took a bite of his sandwich, chewed thoughtfully, then spoke. "Mom's worried about Granny."

Ben set down his fry. "Why? She seems full of energy."

"I don't know quite how to tell you this, but it has to do with your Laurel."

"Laurel?"

"I'm afraid I need to ask your help on a sensitive confidential matter."

"I have no idea what you're talking about, pal."

"Granny's gotten this crazy idea in her head. You may not even remember hearing about this, but my mother had a sister, Jo. Something happened the day before my parents' wedding. Jo was supposed to be the maid of honor, but she left without a word after an argument with my grandfather. It's like she just disappeared."

Ben was dumbfounded. "You mean she's never been heard from? Surely the family tried to locate her?"

"Grandfather wouldn't hear of it. Said Jo had made her bed and she could damn well lie in it. Essentially he turned his back on her, and the family was given little choice but to go along with him. He could be quite domineering," Jay said in classic understatement. "And, no, she's never been heard from."

"What does this have to do with Laurel?"

"Granny has this nutty notion that Laurel resembles Jo. And somehow Laurel knew that years ago Summer Haven had been painted white. But, hell, any old pictures of Belleporte cottages could've revealed that."

"What does Laurel have to say about it?"

"That's just it. Granny doesn't want to involve her until she knows something for sure. As she said, there's no point in upsetting Laurel needlessly. Mom has finally convinced my grandmother to hire someone to conduct a low-key investigation. Frankly, I think this is all wishful thinking on Granny's part. Any connection would be an extremely unlikely coincidence. We want to move quickly, though, before she gets any more worked up. We need to prove to her she's deluding herself. That's where you come in.''

''Me?'' Ben stared at Jay.

''Yeah. You lawyer types know investigators, right?''

''Yes, but—''

''We wouldn't trust anyone else with this, Ben. Any search has to be handled discreetly.''

''You realize the position you're putting me in? It's like a betrayal to go behind Laurel's back like this.''

''But look at it this way. There's probably nothing to it. Why get Laurel all worked up about it? Besides—'' Jay spread his hands in a gesture of appeal ''—you'd be doing us a tremendous favor.''

Ben stared at the cooled, congealing French fries and felt a lead ball forming in his stomach. In essence, he owed his career to the Kelleys and Katherine Sullivan. They asked for little in return. But this? ''I'll think about it and get back to you.''

''Fair enough. Just don't wait too long.'' With that, Jay dug into his meal with an enthusiasm Ben wished he could emulate. Instead, he sat there pushing cold potatoes around his plate, realizing he was smack dab in the middle of a moral bind.

''I'M SO GLAD you suggested this,'' Laurel said, spreading her towel beside Ellen's. They'd selected a spot on the beach just down from a group of cavorting children.

''We both needed a break.'' Ellen began coating her

thighs with sunscreen. "Have you even been swimming yet?"

Laurel laughed. "Come to think of it, no. If you hadn't dragged me out of the store and convinced me Megan could close, I'd still be there."

"There's usually not that much traffic late in the day."

"No. In fact, I've considered closing half an hour earlier."

Ellen squeezed more sunscreen into her palm and began applying it to her freckled shoulders. "But business is good?"

"The opening was fantastic, but I should've expected a lull after that, since most of the natives have made their initial sortie." Laurel settled back in the warm sand, relishing the feel of the sun on her face. "How's the real estate market these days?"

"Rentals are great. Sales are slow. They should pick up after the Fourth, but I still have time to help out at the store when you need me."

"You've been a godsend, but I don't want to impose."

"It's fun. I feel rather like a midwife to the enterprise."

Laurel spread her arms and traced angel wings in the sand. "It's just about perfect, Ellen. I love the town, the business is doing better than I'd hoped, and—"

"There's Ben," Ellen said with a teasing smile.

"Yes, there's Ben." Laurel had a brief misgiving. "You're sure you don't mind?"

"Honey babe, I'm long past whatever feelings I

imagined I had for Ben. Besides, it's fun to watch you two together. You're goners. Both of you.''

Laurel closed her eyes, a satisfied grin playing over her lips. Last night's celebration dinner had been special. Chateaubriand, champagne and Ben's approval. Heady stuff. She almost chuckled aloud, remembering how they had looked at one another and, without a word being spoken, risen from the table, returned to her apartment and fallen rapturously into bed. Her body tingled even now with the memory.

Ellen stretched out beside her, protecting her face with a large straw hat.

"I'm a lucky lady," Laurel murmured. "I once told Ben that, except for my marriage, I'd led a charmed life."

"No trouble spots these days?"

Laurel thought about Ellen's question. "Only the fact my parents couldn't come for the opening." She flopped over on her stomach. "We've always shared everything, and it didn't seem right not to have them here. But then I guess I have to realize they have their lives, too."

Basking in the sun, feeling every muscle and nerve melt into the earth beneath her, Laurel was about to doze off when she remembered something. "Ellen, did I tell you I finally met Jay Kelley? He stopped by the shop yesterday morning. If I hadn't seen Ben first, I'd have to think about Jay. He's a very good-looking man. And nice, too." She reared up and lifted Ellen's hat. "How about you? Jay's unattached. You're looking."

Ellen turned on her side and propped her head on

her hand. "Jay Kelley and me? Don't be ridiculous. We're from totally different worlds."

"Meaning?"

"Jay's family moves in the finest circles in Chicago. I'm strictly homegrown. I wouldn't fit in with his crowd, even though I have to agree with you, he's one good-looking guy."

"He seems really down to earth. And Katherine doesn't put on any airs."

"She doesn't need to. She's able to buy and sell us all and can tell most people to take a flying leap if she wants to."

"I could tell Jay adores her."

"They're a close family. I like all of them. But you can forget any little matchmaking schemes."

Laurel raised an eyebrow. "You're sure?"

Ellen lay back down and covered her face again. "Positive."

Still, the longer Laurel lay there, the more clearly she could see Jay and Ellen together. They'd be perfect.

Perfect. She considered the concept. Right now her own life was about as good as it could get. She smiled with satisfaction, then sat up, removed her watch and ran toward the water. A breaking wave hit her with a jolt that knocked the breath out of her and threw her back on her derriere.

She giggled. *Almost* everything was perfect, but no onlooker would ever confuse her with a sea nymph.

BEN WAS NO PLUMBER, but somehow he'd managed to get the downstairs toilet in his mother's house functioning again. Peering over his shoulder, she watched anxiously. "I couldn't get along without this."

As he eyed the row of potty chairs and low-hung towel racks, Ben wondered how anyone had the patience to run a day-care center. When he straightened, wiping his hands on the rag he'd been using, he took a good look at his mother. The worry lines in her forehead had deepened and her pale skin looked gray. "Are you okay?" he asked.

"Why wouldn't I be?"

He threw an arm around her shoulder and led her to the sofa, where he sat down beside her. "I can think of any number of reasons, starting with Bess and Mike." He paused. "It can't be easy having Bess and the kids move in."

"We're family," she said. "That's what matters."

"Your health matters. Dad wouldn't want you—"

She lifted her eyes to his. "Don't."

"Don't what?"

"Talk about him." She thrust a hand into her skirt pocket and pulled out a tissue. "Sorry. I'm just having a bad day." She blew her nose.

"You never talk about him, Mom." From upstairs came the strains of some female vocalist. A breeze from the open window stirred the garden flowers on the sofa table. "Wouldn't it help?"

"Help?" She rose to her feet and went to the book-case where his parents' wedding photograph was displayed. "Talk won't bring Matthew back. Neither will tears."

He watched her, aware that she was controlling her emotions only by a thread. He felt uncomfortable with his role here, but someone needed to ask the question. "Wouldn't it help to cry?"

She turned slowly to face him, a bitter laugh erupting. "Cry? Ben, I cried myself out in 1972 and 1973 when your father was imprisoned. Then I cried again after he came home and I realized the man I'd fallen in love with was gone." Her face turned red. "Those butchers altered the soul of my husband, and it took him years to create a new life for himself. For us."

Picking up the picture, she studied it, then ran her fingers over the surface of the glass. Finally she set it down and faced him again. "Don't talk to me about death and grief, Ben. I could write the book. When I need to cry, I'll cry. Understood?"

What could he say? Apparently his mother needed control more than release. "Understood."

Before she excused herself to go start dinner, she brought up one last subject. "If you want something to worry about, go talk to your brother Mike."

His stomach clenched. "Why?"

"He failed geometry," she said.

Just then Mike made a timely appearance in the doorway. Ben turned toward him. "I guess you heard," the boy said.

"Yes."

"You gotta get me out of summer school. Only geeks go to summer school."

"Geeks who fail courses."

"You could talk to Old Man Moberly and tell him I could double up next year. Take two maths."

"Think he's going to consider that when you couldn't pass one?"

"You gotta help me."

Ben felt a fuse burning in the neighborhood of his chest. Before it exploded, he turned to his brother, eyed him up and down and simply said, "No, I don't. I'm not the one who failed the course." Then, before Mike could say anything, Ben turned and left, not sure whether he was furious or triumphant.

Funny, he thought as he drove away from the house, *how harmony suffers from the truth.* He cursed under his breath. That little insight reminded him of the message from Jay on his voice mail requesting an answer about the investigation. The way Jay had put it was that they merely needed to prove Laurel *wasn't* related to Jo Sullivan. From what Ben knew, that ought to be simple enough to do. Laurel's parents were known entities, easy enough to trace, and if it would ease Katherine Sullivan's mind… Laurel would never have to know, and Katherine would be satisfied. Besides, he couldn't overlook his debt to the Sullivans and Kelleys. What could be the harm?

He picked up his cell phone and punched in the Summer Haven number. Jay answered. After a few minutes of small talk, including Jay's account of meeting Laurel at her shop, Ben drew a deep breath. "If your family is certain you want to proceed, I'll coordinate the investigation of Laurel's background."

"I appreciate it, buddy. I'm sorry for the awkwardness of the whole thing, but we wouldn't entrust something this important to anyone else."

After Ben hung up, he couldn't help wondering if he was wading into ethical quicksand.

ON A LATE JUNE EVENING, Laurel worked in the garden, stringing red, white and blue colored lights in the trees and shrubbery. Belleporte citizens took the Fourth of July seriously and there were planned activities ranging from a community picnic to water contests at the beach—all culminating in a fireworks display.

The past three weeks had been busy at The Gift Horse, so much so that Laurel had taken on Mrs. Arlo as part-time help. She had turned out to be a genius at arranging and rearranging the merchandise so that it looked fresh and appealing from week to week. One day she appeared with red-and-white ticking aprons with appliqued firecrackers to be worn by the staff. The next, she brought an Uncle Sam's hat for the outdoor rocking horse. Laurel filled the horse's oat bucket with small American flags and seasonal napkins and party favors. Daily the town filled with more and more tourists, lugging chairs to the beach, nursing sunburns and, thankfully, shopping.

Although Ben had been busy with some new work for the Sullivan Company, he'd been as attentive as his schedule would permit, often stopping by late in the afternoon to take her for a long walk on the beach. She sometimes wondered if she should have told him she loved him, but it wasn't in her nature to be coy. She knew she shouldn't expect a declaration from him. He'd made it clear from the beginning that he wasn't in a position to discuss the future. Yet. Everything was wonderful right now, so she could be patient, live each day as it came. She grinned wryly. Oh, yeah. Her philosophy of life was holding her in good stead.

Since that fateful night when she'd shot off her mouth about his family, he hadn't mentioned much about them, except to say Mike was enrolled in sum-

mer school. His silence on the subject made it hard to
tell whether he'd resented her opinions, which, she had
to admit, were based on no experience whatsoever.

She finished hanging one string of lights and continued with the next, hoping the extension cord would
reach. As she worked, she thought about Katherine's
plan to have an expanded tea in the garden on July 3,
complete with sandwiches, punch and Greta's specially decorated flag cake. Laurel hoped she wasn't
imposing on the woman's generosity.

There. She finished stringing the lights and, wonder
of wonders, when she went to plug in the cord, it
reached the outlet. The trees and bushes were spangled
with blinking lights. A spotlight installed under the
eaves shone on the flag flying from the new flagpole.

Sighing with satisfaction, she stepped into the street
to study the effect. The only thing she could think of
that promised to be more dazzling was her upcoming
date with Ben to watch the fireworks display. Of
course no fireworks would hold a candle to the explo-
sions in her body when he brought her home afterward
and touched her, kissed her.

She chuckled. No doubt about it. Ellen was right.
She was gone. Far gone.

WHEN BEN STOPPED by the house on the morning of
the Fourth, he found Bess and his mother in the
kitchen peeling potatoes. "Don't you know this is a
holiday?" he asked, pulling a chair up to the kitchen
table.

Bess shot her mother a knowing look. "Isn't that
just like a man? He must think all that food at the
picnic appears by magic."

"Would an appreciative word help? No one makes potato salad as good as Mom's."

His mother pointed her paring knife at him. "Listen to you. Full of flattery."

He held up his hands in the gesture of one falsely accused. "Just telling the truth, Mom, and nothing but." The house seemed unnaturally quiet—no stereo, no wrestling boys, no sounds of running showers. "Where is everybody?"

"Megan's at work," his mother said.

Bess carefully carried the pot of potatoes to the stove. "Mike took the boys to the beach. To say they're keyed up is putting it mildly." She salted the potatoes and turned up the burner. Then in a quiet voice she added, "Darren's coming to spend the day with us."

He noticed his mother tactfully busying herself with chopping onions. "How do you feel about that?"

Bess sat down across from him. "I'm not sure. It seems like he's really trying. But how can I be certain? I don't want to upset the boys by going home prematurely, but we'll have to reach a decision by the time school starts." She leaned forward. "What would you do if you were me?"

Ben, the Fix-It Guy, the big brother with all the answers. Well, he sure didn't have one for this. "I'm not you. I suppose the big question is do you love him enough to work with him, help him?" He studied her sad face, then added, "What price are you willing to pay?"

"It isn't easy making it on your own," his mother pointed out. Whether it was a result of the diced onions or something else, she ran the back of her hand across her eyes. The voice of experience, Ben thought. She'd been the backbone of the family now for thirty years.

In the awkward silence, he stood and crossed to the cookie jar. "Peanut butter, my favorite," he said with satisfaction, snagging a big one.

"Will you be at the picnic, son?"

"That's partly why I stopped by—to tell you I'm hip-deep in work. I can sure use this day to catch up."

"Aren't you seeing Laurel?" Bess asked.

"For the fireworks. Her shop will be open most of the day." He swallowed the last of the cookie, planted a kiss on his mother's cheek and headed out the back door.

"Ben?"

He turned and waited for his mother, who walked beside him to his car. He put an arm around her. "You okay?"

"I wanted to apologize. I was a little rough on you the other day." She hesitated. "I do my share of grieving, but I don't figure it does any good to inflict it on you kids."

"I'm here for you, you know."

"I know that. In fact, sometimes I think we lean on you way too much. Between work and this family, you don't have much time for yourself." She tilted his chin so he was looking down into her eyes. "Or for Laurel." Assessing his expression, she said, "She's special to you, isn't she?"

He swallowed. "Very."

His mother's face broke into a sunny smile. "Good." She nodded her head for emphasis. "Good. I like her, too. So do the kids."

Ben ran his knuckles over her cheek. "Is this sort of a blessing?"

"Faith and begorra," she teased, "the very best Irish kind."

He wrapped his arms around her, smelling the spicy-fresh scent he always associated with her. "Thanks, Mom," he whispered, grateful for her approval, but unsure whether anything had truly changed.

INCREDIBLY, next to the grand opening, the Fourth of July sales were the highest yet for The Gift Horse. Laurel couldn't believe the number of out-of-town customers, not to mention locals, who seemed to have an all-consuming need for items like the seasonal paper goods she'd recently begun to stock. Without Mrs. Arlo and Ellen, she and Megan would've been swamped. Laurel finally shooed out the last shoppers at six.

Emerging from a quick shower, she selected a pair of navy shorts and a boat-necked shirt, broadly striped in red, white and blue. Ben had called late this afternoon and asked if she minded walking to the office to meet him when she got squared around. They'd go to the fireworks from there. Since she needed to stop by the bank, anyway, to deposit today's income, that plan suited her fine.

She grabbed up a supersize beach towel and a cooler filled with cheese, fruit and beer. The fireworks display was due to start at dusk, but who knew when their personal fireworks would end? She shivered in anticipation. What could be better than being with Ben on a beach blanketed with stars of both the manmade and natural variety?

As she set off down the street, the faint, tinny sounds of "The Battle Hymn of the Republic" caught her ear. A hastily assembled band composed of local residents was holding forth in the park. Not great music, but appropriately homey and sentimental. Kids riding by on bikes streaming crepe paper waved at her. Pedestrians, most of whom she was delighted to realize she knew, greeted her. Even Arlo Bramwell smiled when she passed him.

The outer office door was locked, but Ben came quickly when she rapped on the glass. Sometimes, like now, he took her breath away. If he wasn't careful, he could get seduced right in his very own office.

He took the cooler and towel from her and set them on a chair in the reception area. "I'm almost through. Can you give me a few minutes?"

"Sure." Later she planned to give him much more than a few minutes. Like the long fuse of a Roman candle, sexual anticipation burned through her.

He gestured at a low table between two chairs. "Help yourself to the magazines. Oh, and there might be some new ones in the mail on Janet's desk." He walked back into his office and she could hear the low hum of his computer.

She walked around the room, studying the photographs of Michigan beach sites. Finally she sank into a chair and leafed through the stack of magazines. She didn't know quite how to tell him that *Golf Digest, Financial World* and dog-eared copies of outdated *Reader's Digests* left much to be desired as waiting-room entertainment.

She checked her watch. She'd been here five minutes, and from the other room, she could hear the continuing rat-a-tat of fingers on a keyboard. She stood and circled the photographs again. Still no Ben. Maybe she would check Janet's desk. With any luck at all, there would be a current issue of *Oprah* or *Midwest Living*. It wouldn't be snooping. He'd told her to help herself.

On top of the stack of mail was a tax quarterly, a guaranteed soporific, but underneath it, she struck pay dirt with a new *National Geographic*. She pulled it from the pile and was about to turn from the desk, when her eye fell on the memo pad beside the telephone.

What the…?

With a trembling hand, she pulled it toward her, reading and rereading the brief message, convinced that the letters absolutely could not be forming the words they did, could not be conveying the message that was causing her to shake with confusion and rage.

But there was no denying what was written in Janet's precise hand. *July 3, 5:10 p.m. Please call Roger Crandall regarding the Laurel Eden investigation.*

Investigation? Amid the chaos in her mind, Laurel tried to process the idea. Ben was investigating *her?* But why?

Then anger flooded her entire being—inchoate, numbing.

She picked up the pad and charged into his office, oblivious to the startled expression on his face. Slamming the pad down on his desk, she spoke in words so cold, so distant she was convinced they had to be coming from some other person.

"You have sixty seconds to explain yourself before fireworks the likes of which you've never imagined go off. Here. Now."

CHAPTER ELEVEN

BEN'S HEAD SNAPPED UP from the monitor. A Laurel he didn't recognize stood before him, her breath coming in short gasps, her cheeks flushed. But it was her flashing eyes that made it nearly impossible to speak. He rose to his feet. "What are you talking about?"

She said nothing. Just stuck out an index finger and pointed to the memo pad she'd slung onto his desk. Bewildered, he picked it up and studied it, his knees nearly buckling beneath him as the impact of the message set in. "Laurel, I—"

"I didn't know it was standard operating procedure for attorneys to run background checks on their..." She seemed to be having difficulty finishing her thought. "Lovers." She made it sound like a dirty word.

"It's not like that. It's not even a big deal."

She might have been seven feet tall the way she gathered herself to glare at him. "Not a big deal? Not to you maybe, but it's a very big deal to me." She made an elaborate show of checking her watch. "Ten seconds and counting. Make it good."

A punch to the stomach couldn't have made him feel any worse. "I—it's a matter of client confidentiality."

"So now you're your own client?"

"I'd never do that."

She edged around the desk, poking her finger at his chest. "Tell me, who is investigating me? And more importantly, why?"

He could smell her fragrance—the scent that made him wild for her. "Laurel, I can't." His anguished voice sounded impotent.

She continued to stare at him as if she'd never seen him before. Then her lips trembled and tears gathered in her eyes. He tried to put his arms around her, but she pushed him away and said brokenly, "I trusted you."

"Laurel—"

Her voice rose. "Stop Laurel-ing me. All I have to say to you, Ben Nolan, is that I'm glad I found out before it was too late. The last thing I need is another weasel in my life!" She wheeled around and marched to the door, then whirled to face him again. "One other thing. Is there a reason I need to hire my own attorney?"

He sank back into his desk chair, defeated. "No. It's not like that."

She stood rooted to the spot, disgust and hurt written all over her. "It better not be," she said, turning her back and marching through the reception area and out the door, closing it forcefully behind her.

Ben buried his head in his hands. He should have anticipated something like this. In his gut the investigation had never felt right. He loved Laurel and should have put her ahead of anything, anyone, no matter how obligated he felt toward Katherine Sullivan and Jay Kelley. Good old Ben, the responsible guy who always helped out, had betrayed the most important person in his life and it felt like crap.

His first instinct was to go after Laurel. But then reason kicked in. To say what? To explain himself how? God, she had every right to be pissed. The hell of it was, how was there any coming back from this?

He didn't know how long he sat there, sick at heart, in the eerie glare of the computer monitor. He roused himself only when he heard the thunder of the first booming sky rockets. Finally he clicked off the computer, locked the office and walked out to his car, never stopping to look up at the brilliant reds, greens, silvers and golds exploding over Belleporte.

Fireworks were nothing more than painful reminders that his future with Laurel had fizzled just like the dying sparks dissolving into the night sky.

LAUREL RACED DOWN the deserted street, ran up the darkened stairs of her apartment and threw herself on her bed. With giant hiccuping wheezes, the tears had commenced halfway home. Even now she couldn't get her breath. A pain, insistent and throbbing, robbed her of reason. All she could think was, "Is this what a broken heart feels like?"

Then the anger returned. She pounded her fists on the bed. The "Laurel Eden investigation." Investigation of what?

She'd been scrupulous in setting up her business. And as for her past, aside from her miserable four years with Curt Vanover, she had led a remarkably boring life, at least from an investigator's point of view.

Well, she wasn't going to waste energy grieving

over Ben Nolan. She reached for the bedside tissue and blew her nose so loudly it startled her. Determined not to lie in her bed like some wilting violet, she got to her feet and crossed to the window.

Over the treetops she could make out flashing traces of fire in the sky. The staccato bursts of sound reverberated in her skull.

She turned away from the window. *Perfect.* That's how she'd characterized her life to Ellen. To think that less than an hour ago she'd equated Ben Nolan with fireworks and hot sex. And even more than that, with love.

Damn it, she was not going to cry again.

Slowly she undressed in the dark, brushed her teeth and turned the air conditioner to maximum so she could snuggle beneath the quilt so lovingly stitched by her mother and seek some kind of comfort.

But tomorrow would not be about comfort. It would be about work, about excising Ben Nolan from her heart and, most important, about getting to the bottom of this ludicrous investigation.

"WHAT IN THE WORLD?" Janet Kerns gave Ben the once-over. "You look awful. Last night's fireworks too much for you?"

Uh, yeah. Way too much. "I didn't sleep well."

"Tell me about it. Your eyes look like a color map of the Red Sea, and did you think about brushing your hair this morning?"

Distractedly, Ben ran a hand over his head. "I had a lot on my mind."

She raised her eyebrows. "Apparently." She nodded toward one of the waiting room chairs. "What do you want me to do with those?"

Laurel's cooler and towel. Jeez. "Could you walk the stuff over to The Gift Horse later?"

"Sure, but—"

Before his secretary had further opportunity to cross-examine him, Ben said curtly, "Get me Roger Crandall on the phone." He brushed past her, closed his office door and sank into his chair. He had to get it over with. Follow through with the investigation. In the course of his sleepless night, he'd decided the only way he had any chance with Laurel was to prove to her that the investigation had resulted solely from Katherine's overactive imagination and, if he was truthful, his own innate desire to please people. All he could do, then, would be to cast himself on Laurel's mercy and hope he hadn't thrown away his best hope for happiness.

The staccato buzz of the phone line racked him. He picked up and, summoning calm, said evenly, "Ben Nolan."

"I think I've got something for you on the Eden case." The investigator hesitated. "I've found a link between Noel Eden and the Sullivans."

Ben sat forward, clenching the receiver. *This couldn't be happening.*

Crandall continued in his detached monotone. "I've been interviewing some of the Edens' neighbors, who, by the way, weren't terribly forthcoming."

"And?"

"They say Eden's a great fellow who doesn't talk much about his past. They do know he was a student activist in the late '60s and early '70s and that at some point he attended a Big Ten university.'' The man cleared his throat. ''Not much to go on, but I've been looking at old photo files from places that were hot-beds of student protest and I've found a coupla photos from the University of Wisconsin that sure look like Noel Eden. There's one major problem, though.''

''What's that?''

''The guy's name isn't Noel Eden.''

''What're you trying to tell me?''

With the patience of a teacher explaining a problem to a slow student, Crandall went on. ''If this proves out, Laurel Eden's father has to have changed his name.''

Ben made the next leap of logic. ''So...her mother, too, might have changed her name.''

''Seems like it. But I've saved the best for the last. Guess who else appears in one of the photos?'' He delivered his coup de grâce. ''A Jo Sullivan, who's a dead ringer for a younger version of Pat Eden.''

Ben wiped the film of perspiration from his fore-head. ''You're sure there's no mistake?''

''Not one hundred percent, but I'm gonna be work-ing on tracking down court records for a name change and asking some questions here in Madison. But, yeah, I think it's pretty much a lock that Laurel Eden could be your client's granddaughter.''

Battered by the ramifications of this news, Ben's brain barely functioned. ''I, uh, I'd like to defer any action on this end until I have your final report.''

''I'll be in touch.''

''Thanks.'' Ben let the phone slip into the cradle, then stared at it as if it were a time bomb. Katherine might be pleased, but Ben couldn't be concerned with that because another thought had taken possession of him. What would such news do to Laurel, so trusting and confident in her "charmed" life?

Then another ominous notion came to him. If, in fact, Jo Sullivan and Pat Eden were the same person, what had caused the young woman to turn her back on her family, assume a new identity and stay hidden for nearly thirty years?

It couldn't be good.

LAUREL BOLTED AWAKE. It was after nine. The store opened at ten. She never slept in. Then, crashing like a breaker over shoals, memory came—along with a pounding headache. *Investigation.* The ugly word soured her stomach. She struggled to her feet, reached the bathroom and splashed cold water on her face. Taking down the aspirin bottle, she shook two tablets in her hand, chasing them with a glass of water.

She braced herself on the basin and looked at her image. More than makeup would be needed to hide the ravaged look in her eyes. Besides, what kind of cosmetic bandage concealed a broken heart? She shook her head wearily. *Ben, how could you?*

But no matter her pain and disillusionment, the show must go on. Customers would be waiting. Sure enough, Megan and Mrs. Arlo were getting ready to open when she finally made her appearance. Fortunately, Megan was so involved in telling the older woman about her "yummy" date to the fireworks that neither of them noticed Laurel looked like a pathetic sea creature washed up on the sand. After greeting them, she hastily retreated to the rear of the shop to dust display shelves.

Because of the long Fourth of July weekend, the shop was busy all morning. Laurel did her best to avoid conversation, afraid someone would notice her normally cheerful disposition had been replaced by a bone-wrenching sadness, which hadn't been helped by Janet Kerns's delivery just before noon. The ice in the cooler had melted, floating the fruit and cheese and covering the untouched cans of beer. There was symbolism there somewhere.

In the afternoon Laurel buried herself in work, deciding which items to mark down for a post-holiday sale and preparing new price tags. Katherine arrived shortly before teatime, dressed in a bright yellow slack and sweater set. Perched on the chair by her tea table, her head cocked as she chatted with customers, she resembled nothing so much as a lively yellow finch.

Around four, Laurel looked out the window and saw clouds massing over the lake. Her American flag whipped with the sudden gusts. She hurried outside, smelling the approach of a storm in the air. Quickly she hauled in the rocking horse and the potted plants. Customers hastily completed their purchases in the desire to beat the rain home. Mrs. Arlo had already left, but Megan insisted she was staying to close, since her boyfriend was picking her up then.

"Do you have a ride?" Laurel asked Katherine, who was washing the tea dishes and putting them back in the cupboard.

"Greta brought me to town. I was planning to walk home."

"Have you checked outside lately?"

"Why?"

"It's getting ready to storm." Laurel looked around

the store. No customers. Megan knew how to close. "Let me drive you."

"But it's not five yet."

"I know. Megan can take care of everything." She mustered a grin. "It's the least I can do after all you've done for me this weekend."

Katherine studied Laurel. "You're sure it's not too much trouble?"

"I insist."

"Would you do an old lady a favor and stay for dinner? Nan, John and Jay left for Chicago this morning. I'd like the company."

It beat sitting in her empty apartment feeling sorry for herself. Besides, she enjoyed Katherine. "You've twisted my arm."

Laurel brought the car around front and helped Katherine in. Just as they pulled away, fat raindrops began peppering the hood.

Katherine craned her neck, peering at the sky. "Looks like we're in for one of our doozies of a lake storm. Maybe it will help clear the air."

Laurel said nothing. Clearing the air sounded like a darned good idea to her. But it wasn't the weather she was thinking of.

OUTSIDE, a furious wind howled and rain pelted Summer Haven, but inside everything was snug, a tribute, Katherine reflected, to her father's insistence on quality workmanship. Katherine and Laurel lingered at the dinner table over coffee and Greta's famous brownies. But throughout the meal, Katherine had felt vaguely disturbed. Something was wrong with Laurel. Oh, Katherine knew the young woman was trying her best to appear upbeat, but the smiles never reached her eyes, and in unguarded moments, she slumped with an air of defeat or sadness. Whatever could be the matter?

Just as she was getting ready to inquire, the lights flickered out, then came on again. Katherine shoved her chair back. "Let's move to the living room. There are candles there, just in case. Bring your coffee, why don't you?"

Through the French doors, they had a view of the roiling surface of the lake and the dramatic lightning display. "Almost better than fireworks," Katherine said as she settled in a chair adjacent to Laurel's.

"Infinitely better," Laurel said in a tone Katherine would normally identify as acerbic, which wasn't like sunny Laurel.

"I've always loved storms," Katherine said. "Ferocious, but cleansing. The ones that sweep across the lake are nothing short of majestic. Do you get storms like this in West Virginia?"

"Sometimes. But my favorites are the long, gentle rains that turn everything lush and green and leave swirls of mist on the mountains. It's like being lost in nature, in the very best way."

Katherine had found her opening. She studied Laurel closely. "You look rather lost tonight. Is everything all right?"

Laurel didn't answer right away. Instead, she set down her cup and stared out the window. "It's odd," she said, "how such a lovely, calm, peaceful scene can, in the blink of an eye, turn violent. You just never know."

Somehow Katherine didn't think she was referring

solely to the panorama before them. "Are we talking only about Lake Michigan, Laurel?"

"No."

The simple, forlorn syllable filled Katherine with concern. "Ben?" she asked, guessing the cause of Laurel's distress.

The young woman wove her fingers together and bowed her head. "Am I that transparent?"

A flash of lightning and the boom of a thunderclap echoing and reechoing over the water underscored Katherine's quiet "Yes." The electricity flickered again. "Could you use a sympathetic ear?"

Laurel turned slowly toward her, her cheeks pale, her eyes full of hurt. "Do you have any idea why Ben would have hired an investigator to check on me?"

Katherine's right hand went to her heart. *Oh, dear God, how had the girl found out?* What could she say? Just then came another ear-splitting crack of thunder. Once more the lights flickered, then went out. Katherine fumbled in the drawer of the little table by the chair and pulled out a box of matches. Trying to control her shaking fingers, she struck a match and lit the candle in the brass holder. The flame cast a shadow beyond Laurel and her.

"Let me help," Laurel said, taking the matches and lighting two more candles.

From the hallway a flickering light approached. Greta stood in the doorway, holding her own candle. "Are you all right, Mrs. Sullivan?"

How could she possibly be all right now that the truth—or what she believed was the truth—threatened to destroy Laurel's world but restore hers? "Yes, Greta. Thank you."

Greta retreated down the hall. Katherine licked her lips. "An investigation?"

Laurel gripped the arms of her chair. "I don't understand. Why would Ben be investigating me?"

"How did you find this out?"

"I saw a phone message on his secretary's desk last night. He was to call a Roger Crandall about—" she snorted pathetically "—the 'Laurel Eden investigation.' Look at me. Do I look like a...a...con artist or something?"

"No, dear, you don't."

"Then why?" Laurel's voice rose. "It makes no sense."

"You have a right to be angry." Katherine had to give her that. It had been a sneaky thing to do, going behind Laurel's back. Maybe it would have been better just to ask her outright. Katherine's chest tightened. Maybe that's exactly what she needed to do tonight. Now. Before her nerve failed.

The wind abated and the torrential rain fell in straight sheets. Except for the candles, they were shrouded in darkness. They sat in silence for a long time. Finally Katherine spoke. "Laurel," she said, her heart pounding, "I'd like to tell you a story."

"ONCE UPON A TIME..." Katherine began in a singsong, soothing tone.

Laurel frowned. Whatever did once-upon-a-time have to do with Ben's betrayal? As Katherine's soft voice continued, though, the familiar cadence sent Laurel's mind on a tangent, reminding her of the childhood stories her mother had woven for her, which had always begun with the ritual opening of every fairy tale. Laurel forced herself to concentrate. Something…a fragment of one of those stories… A memory too fleeting to catch passed through her mind. She strained to remember, but it flitted beyond her reach.

"…I was a well-intentioned but ignorant woman, believing I was fulfilled simply by going through the motions of making my family happy. Never standing up for myself. Always deferring, especially to my husband."

Laurel observed the older woman, hands folded quietly in her lap, her eyes fixed on some point out there in the impenetrable night. She was still not sure how Katherine's autobiographical tale was supposed to help her.

"I've made mistakes in my life, but none greater than this one. The one we never talked about in our family until now." When Katherine turned and looked at her, Laurel knew instinctively that she didn't want to hear what was coming.

"Please, Katherine, you don't have to—"

"Oh, but I do, my dear. Bear with me." The older woman took a deep cleansing breath and continued. "Frank and I had not one daughter, but two. Jo was two years younger than Nan, gentle and charming unless she took on a cause. Then she was nothing short of formidable. She could be every bit as hardheaded and stubborn as her father."

As Katherine outlined Jo's considerable academic and artistic achievements, Laurel found herself caught up in the story. An honors student at the University of Wisconsin, Jo, to her father's disappointment, had allied herself with a group of student protesters. "The late '60s were volatile times," Katherine said, "when parents often didn't understand their children. When young people labeled their parents 'the establishment' and rejected their values and politics. That's what happened with Jo.''

Remembering Katherine's use of the past tense earlier, Laurel laid a hand on the woman's arm. ''Is she dead?'' she asked softly.

''I—I don't know.'' The yellow finch of this afternoon looked decidedly more muted. ''I guess you could say to her family she has been.'' Laurel waited for her to continue. ''It's the only way you can carry on. But never a day passes that I don't wonder.''

''What happened?''

''Incredible as this sounds, I don't exactly know. Jo came here from graduate school in Madison for Nan and John's wedding. She was to be the maid of honor. Frank...'' Katherine's voice cracked. ''Frank nearly went berserk when he saw her. Nowadays it sounds like a cliché, but she was wearing sandals, love beads, a shapeless granny gown, and her hair—it was like a rat's nest. She and her father hadn't seen eye to eye on politics ever. But Jo seemed even more dogmatic and confrontational. It was almost as if she went out of her way to antagonize her father. She was as passionately anti-war as he was pro-war. Vietnam was a topic Nan and I desperately tried to avoid when those two were in the same room.'' Katherine shrugged her shoulders helplessly. ''And, of course, Frank made his fortune in Defense Department contracts.'' For a moment, Katherine seemed lost.

''The wedding?'' Laurel prompted.

''Oh, Lord. I can still see the whole affair, frame by frame, like some endlessly repeating film. The afternoon of the rehearsal, Nan and I were here—'' she gestured around the house ''—finishing the place cards for the rehearsal dinner, when Jo disappeared into the library with Frank. She said she had something to tell him.''

Laurel watched Katherine dig her nails into the upholstery of the chair. ''We could hear raised voices, then quiet, followed by the slam of a door. Jo went running toward her car, got in and roared off down the road, spraying gravel everywhere.'' Katherine looked at Laurel, her face etched with pain. ''That was the last time I ever saw my daughter.''

Laurel's heart raced unnaturally. It was a horrible story, yet she sensed the worst was still to come. ''But…?''

''Didn't we look for her?'' Katherine's laugh was bitter. ''Frank forbade it. He said Jo had cut her ties with us. Irrevocably. She had shamed him, shamed us. Clearly, he said, she'd put her own selfish needs ahead of everyone else's, including Nan's. The only way he'd take her back was if she crawled on her knees.'' She swallowed. ''And at Frank's order, the wedding went on with all of us playing our parts.''

Laurel swallowed back the bile gathering in her throat. ''That's…that's barbaric.''

Katherine eyed her. ''You didn't know my husband. He was not to be crossed. And I never did cross him. Nan, either. Except once. A year or so later, Nan and I went behind his back and hired an investigator, but the trail was cold. It was as if Jo had vanished. Then when we didn't hear from her… Anyway, Frank never knew what we'd done.'' Slowly she rose to her feet. ''Only in these past few months have I realized I could be my own person. I've acknowledged that what I did in giving in to Frank back then was wrong. Sinfully wrong.''

She made her way across the room until she stood motionless in front of a glass-fronted bookcase. ''I don't have a lot of time left on this earth,'' she said in a soft voice, ''but if I can make things right, I want to try.'' She opened the case and extracted a leather-bound volume, then returned to her seat. ''Frank wouldn't let us display photos of Jo or anything else that would remind him of her. But I always kept this picture here, where I could look at it whenever I wanted to.''

Mesmerized, Laurel watched as Katherine withdrew a five-by-seven photo, then studied it for endless seconds. Finally, she laid a hand on Laurel's knee. ''Laurel, dear, forgive me, but I have to ask you this.'' She held out the glossy photograph. ''Do you know this woman?''

In the candlelight Laurel studied the photo. Her jaw fell, her throat clogged. She didn't think she could bear to look up and acknowledge to Katherine the hideousness of the truth she held before her.

''Laurel?'' Katherine shook her knee.

Clutching the photo to her breast, Laurel rose from her chair and went to the window, where she stared sightlessly at the raindrops coursing down the panes of glass, wishing she could fling herself into the torrent. Anything to wash away the photographic image etched on her brain.

For a long time the only sounds were those of rain on the roof and the occasional distant rumble of thunder. Then at last Laurel turned. Katherine had risen to

her feet and stood in the shadows, looking diminished, old.

Laurel found her voice, though it sounded alien.
"Yes, I know her." She held out the photograph.
"This is my mother."

CHAPTER TWELVE

LAUREL STARED at Katherine, nausea welling within her. The hand holding the photograph trembled. "This...*this* is your daughter?" Her mouth turned to cotton. "No." She shook her head emphatically. "This can't be. My mother's parents are dead."

Katherine took a tentative step forward. "Laurel..."

As if the photo were tainted, Laurel laid it on the table, then turned to face the storm again, finding far more comfort in the deluge outside than in the drama unfolding around her.

Katherine's tone was placating. "That may have been what you were told. But this *is* a picture of Jo."

Neither of them flinched when, with startling suddenness, the lights came back on.

Laurel wrapped her arms around her waist in a futile attempt to salve the ache in her heart. No. There was no way her parents could have deceived her in this manner. They were gentle and honest...and...good. Pat Eden would never have turned her back on a mother like Katherine. She would never have lied to her own daughter. Slowly, she turned around, denial her only escape. "I'm sorry, Katherine, but there's been an awful mistake. It's merely a coincidental resemblance."

"No," Katherine said, leading Laurel back to the

sofa, where she eased her down, then sat beside her, clutching her hands. Katherine hesitated, apparently hoping her next words would remedy the situation. "Have you wondered why I am so drawn to you? Your mannerisms, your passion for life, the way you gesture, your coloring...it's all there. You are my granddaughter."

Laurel withdrew her hands. She didn't want to be rude to this woman she cared about, yet her mind couldn't take in the ramifications. "I can't believe it. My parents wouldn't... If you're my grandmother, they'd have told me. You'd have been in my life."

Katherine hung her head. "I have done an unspeakable thing. I let Frank influence me when my heart was screaming to run after my daughter." She looked up. "That's no excuse. But since Frank's death, I've become determined to try to set things right. If I can. If it's not too late."

"Wait." Laurel suddenly saw it all clearly. "The investigation—"

"Yes, I needed proof of my suspicions. It was a delicate mission. I asked Jay to solicit Ben's help."

Rising to her feet, Laurel slowly backed away from Katherine, her voice quavering. "Let me get this straight. The two people I most trusted in Belleporte— you've both been going behind my back, snooping into my past—"

Katherine stood and held Laurel lightly by the arms. "I can see how you might view it that way. Maybe I was wrong, but I didn't want to upset you needlessly. What if we hadn't found any proof?"

Laurel shook her head, desperately trying to make sense of what had transpired. "I love Ben. You are my friend. This hurts so much because it's as if you've both betrayed me."

"My dear, I know you need time…" Katherine faltered. "And I need my daughter," she said in a voice that under any other circumstances would have broken Laurel's heart. "And you."

Katherine's plea penetrated the haze of Laurel's confusion. "I…I don't want to hurt you. And if I could ever have imagined a grandmother, she would have been like you." Her throat thickened. "But this is a shock. I need time to think about everything. To hear my mother's explanation."

"I understand."

"Please, let me talk with my parents before you do anything."

"Certainly."

Laurel edged toward the door, barely controlling her emotions. "Right now, I need to be alone."

"Before you go, Laurel, there is one more thing. Please don't blame Ben. Blame me. He was only trying to help."

"Good old Ben," Laurel whispered under her breath as she stepped outside, oblivious to the rain cascading down her face and mingling with her tears.

HER HEART POUNDING with the swiftness of a panic attack, Katherine stared at the front door, then down at the youthful face gazing up at her from the photo on the table. Blood rushed to her head and she felt weak-kneed.

Her daughter was alive.

Relief, swift and steadying, rushed over her as she

sank into her chair. "Thanks be to God," she whispered. But now what?

Laurel had every right to be hurt and angry. To feel betrayed. Maybe it would have been better to let the investigation play out instead of confronting her tonight. Katherine shook her head. Too late now for second thoughts. Surely in time, Laurel would come around. Meanwhile, what was the next step? Contact the Edens... Jo?

Her mind racing, Katherine sat for several minutes before she reached for the phone. Each punch of a number had the finality of a rifle shot.

"Hello?"

"Did I wake you, Ben?"

"No, I, uh, I couldn't sleep. What can I do for you, Katherine?"

"You can call off the investigation. It's no longer necessary."

"But we've had a breakthrough. It seems your instincts may be right on target."

Katherine passed a hand over her eyes. "They are. Ben, Laurel knows. She identified a photo of Jo. Jo is her mother."

There was silence on the other end, followed by an anguished, "Dear God." And then, "Is Laurel all right?"

"She's in shock, naturally. And denial. Go to her, Ben."

"I—I don't think I'll be welcome. Yesterday, by accident, she found out about the investigation."

"I know."

"She thinks I betrayed her."

"We both did." Katherine felt as if she'd aged

twenty years in the last two hours. "You love her, don't you?"

"Yes, but—"

"Just go. She needs you, whether she knows it or not."

Katherine hung up, then went to her bedroom. Hidden for years beneath a stack of boxes in the back of her closet was a photo album. She took it out, settled on her chaise longue and began thumbing through the pages. Jo and Nan, little girls with skinny, tanned bodies, frolicking on the beach. Jo in Frank's lap, looking up at him with adoration. Jo and Nan raising the flag on the Fourth of July... Memories kept so long at bay inundated Katherine.

She closed the album, caressing the cover. Her eyes filled with tears. "Please, God, heal this broken family."

LAUREL STRIPPED OFF her rain-soaked shirt and removed her soggy shoes. Leaving the wet heap on the floor of her apartment, she headed to the shower like a sleepwalker. She lathered her hair, scrubbed her body and stood beneath the pounding spray, letting warmth replace the chill in her body. But there was no balm for her soul. Either her mother and father had kept a secret from her all her life, or Katherine was lying, or...something unthinkable had happened all those years ago. None of it made any sense.

Yet Laurel knew there was an explanation. One that had already spun her "perfect" world out of control.

She stepped from the shower, rubbing her body ferociously with the towel. The friction on her skin seemed to set a spark to the anger building in her. She threw the towel across the bathroom. Hell, she didn't even know who she was anymore.

Crossing to her dresser, she began frantically pulling clothes from the drawers. She'd go to West Virginia. She needed the comfort of home, of parents who would make this pain go away, who would tell her everything was all right.

Even as she began packing, reality set in. She couldn't go rushing off into the night. She still had The Gift Horse to run. She slumped onto the bed. The business was the one stable thing left in her suddenly chaotic existence. If she wanted to go to West Virginia, arrangements had to be made in the morning.

As she mechanically set the suitcase on the floor, her attention was arrested by the blinking light on her answering machine. She pushed Play.

"Laurel, please pick up if you're there. It's Ben. We need to talk…. Laurel, I'm coming over and—"

Pushing Rewind, Laurel glared at the machine. What was there to talk about? Ben had made his priorities clear.

She turned off the lights and slid beneath the sheets, knowing she was kidding herself. How could she possibly sleep? Jo…Pat…Mother. Katherine…Grandmother.

She balled a corner of the sheet in her fist and pulled it up to her chin, letting out a ragged sob.

Several minutes later she heard a car stop at the curb. Then a loud knock on the door of The Gift Horse. She drew the quilt over her head. She didn't want to listen to the voice shouting in the night.

"Laurel, let me in. *Please.*"

She clenched her teeth, stifling the wounded howl gathering in the pit of her stomach.

Again Ben's voice pierced the night. Then another loud knock.

Finally, silence. A car engine. The whine of tires on wet pavement.

Burying her face in her pillow, Laurel let the tears flow.

SUN DAPPLED the garden. Flowers rioted in the planters. Lush lawns were greener. The air smelled rainfresh. It should have been a beautiful new day, but all Laurel could see was the relentless gray of uncertainty. As if on autopilot, she went through her habitual motions of getting the store ready to open. She laid out the merchandise, cleared the register, restacked a display table.

Ellen was the first to arrive. "Laurel, what is the matter with you? You look as if you haven't slept in a week."

"That'll happen when a girl misses her beauty rest."

Ellen edged closer and took hold of her chin, searching her face. "No smart remarks, please. I'd say you're heartbroken. Ben?"

Laurel slid away and busied herself folding and refolding napkins. "That's not the half of it."

"What is it, sweetie?"

"I, uh, there are some family problems I need to deal with. Back home."

"Is somebody sick?"

Laurel could hardly bear her friend's concern. "It's nothing like that, but I have to leave. This afternoon."

"What about the shop?"

"I'm thinking of closing for a couple of days."

"Closing? Right now at the peak of the season? That doesn't sound like a very good idea."

"I don't have a choice, Ellen."

Brightening, Ellen said, "Oh, yes you do. Megan, Mrs. Arlo and I will help."

"But your real estate business—"

"My father's visiting this week from Florida. He'd love to get back in the harness. After all, he started the firm. He knows this place like the back of his hand and can show property better than I can. If there's some big sale pending, I'll leave long enough to handle it. We'll be fine."

"Who'll be fine?" Mrs. Arlo bustled through the door, trailed by Megan.

"You, Megan and I," Ellen said. "Laurel has to make a quick trip home to West Virginia."

Mrs. Arlo patted Laurel's shoulder. "Ellen's right. We'll handle everything." Megan nodded her agreement before she and Mrs. Arlo headed for the front to open the store.

Ellen turned to Laurel. "See? That was easily settled. You can be on your way."

"Not yet. I need to pay bills and place some orders before I head out. It'll be midafternoon before I get on the road."

"You're not thinking of driving all that way tonight?"

"I could get there around midnight."

Ellen marched Laurel to a small display mirror. "Look at yourself. Do you see what I see? One exhausted lady." She spun her around. "Don't be foolish. You need to stop for the night. Besides, you don't want to arrive exhausted and then have to face whatever it is that's waiting for you there.''

"I'm sorry. I...I can't talk about it yet.''

"No big deal. But I don't want to have to worry about you. Promise me you'll stop.''

Laurel knew she was defeated. And Ellen did make a certain kind of sense. Panicky as she was to get home, being totally strung out when she arrived wouldn't help anything. "I promise. There's a Hampton Inn in Norwalk, Ohio, where I've stayed before. I can reach it before dark. Okay?''

Ellen gathered Laurel in her arms. "Okay. And when you're ready to talk? I'll be right here.''

Laurel breathed in Ellen's comforting presence. "Thank you for being my friend.''

"It's easy,'' Ellen whispered.

Sitting at the computer later that morning, Laurel could barely concentrate on the numbers swimming in front of her eyes. She *was* tired. Concentrating was tough when all she could think about was the destruction of her world. Emotionally she ran the gamut from despair to anger to sadness to regret. More than anything, though, she felt rudderless.

Just before noon the phone rang. It was Katherine. Her grandmother? Laurel slumped back in her chair, shielding her bloodshot eyes with her hand.

Katherine sounded anxious. "Are you all right, Laurel?''

"I haven't done anything drastic, if that's what you mean.''

"I'm sorry about last night. I should have found a gentler way.''

"I'm not sure that would've been possible. You called into question the basis of my whole identity."

The older woman sighed audibly. "I know. I pray it will be worth it. I love you, Laurel. And I love your mother."

Laurel still couldn't fathom how Katherine could have let her daughter go...or how her own mother could have alienated herself from her family. "I don't know what to say," she said lamely.

"What are you going to do?"

"I'm going home. I need to get to the bottom of all this."

"Today?"

"Later this afternoon."

"I see." Katherine was quiet. "Could you...would you...tell your mother I never stopped loving her?"

Laurel wanted nothing more than to pretend all of this had never happened. Wanted to say, "*If* she is in fact your daughter." Instead, she said, "I'll try."

"I wish you God speed, dear girl."

"Thank you." Laurel threw her head back and stared at the ceiling. She was all cried out. Now remained only the bitter business of unravelling the past.

BEN SPENT THE MORNING tracking down Roger Crandall and asking him to fax the newspaper clippings to the office. He needed to see for himself the proof of the connection between Laurel's father and Jo Sullivan. He paced the floor of his office, impatiently waiting for the whir of the fax machine. Twice he'd called The Gift Horse and gotten Megan, who'd told him Laurel was holed up with the books and had left orders that if he called, she was not to be disturbed.

Hell, he'd made a mess of everything. Katherine might be relieved, but what had they done to Laurel, and the Edens, who undoubtedly were decent people? He had known nothing of the history. What had he been thinking? For all he knew, Jo Sullivan might have been justified in disappearing.

Laurel's silence, though understandable, was tearing him apart.

Shortly before two, he jumped as the fax machine began the excruciatingly slow process of printing. At last he grabbed up the sheets of paper. Though blurred, they showed a bearded radical holding a megaphone. He was standing on the steps of a university administration building, surrounded by a cadre of supporters bearing anti-war posters. The caption read, "Student Rally Features Michael Mays." Then, as if a spotlight had pinpointed the words, Jo Sullivan's name emerged from those identified as members of the campus group.

Ben studied the grainy photograph, trying to find the hint of a resemblance to Laurel. The man's beard and the co-ed's bushy hair obscured their facial features. Who were these people? What was their story?

He plucked up the fax sheets and headed out of the office toward Summer Haven. The sooner he put this assignment behind him, the better. Just thinking about it made him feel unclean.

An hour later, after Katherine had told him what she knew of her daughter's disappearance, she sat on the deck, staring out over the lake, the facsimiles in her lap. "So this is...Noel?" she asked. "I don't know for sure, but I think he's the reason Jo left. She must've loved him very much." She sighed. "I guess we'll know when Laurel gets back."

"Gets back?"

"What did you expect? She's going to West Virginia."

Ben hastily excused himself, raced to his car, then tore down the road. He knew what he needed to do. Knew it as clearly as he'd ever known anything. He couldn't let Laurel face this heartbreaking ordeal alone. Not if he loved her. And he did.

He screeched to a stop in front of The Gift Horse and startled two customers as he brushed past them into the store. Ellen looked up from the counter, where she was gift wrapping a box. "Ben?"

He was in no mood for pleasantries. "Where is she?"

Ellen laid aside the scissors. "Gone. She left about twenty minutes ago."

Placing both hands on the counter, he leaned closer. "You've got to tell me how to find her. She can't do this alone."

Ellen studied him. "I don't know what the *this* is, but it must be important."

"It is. Very."

"I don't know whether I'd be betraying a confidence."

Hell, he knew all about betrayal. He summoned his voice. "Please."

She fiddled nervously with the grosgrain ribbon she'd picked up. Finally, she sighed and said, "Okay. I talked her into stopping overnight and made her give me a number where she could be reached." She turned her eyes to him. "The Hampton Inn in Norwalk, Ohio."

He called "Thanks" over his shoulder as he ran

from the store, then broke speed records getting to his Lake City apartment. There he picked up his Dop kit and threw a few clothes in a bag. Just as he turned to leave, the phone rang. He wanted to ignore it, but Caller ID indicated it was his mother.

He picked up. "Mom? What is it? I'm in a hurry."

"Ben, you've got to come right over."

"What now?"

"Mike. The police." His mother's voice wavered. "He and some other kids went to the beach this afternoon. They, uh, had beer and marijuana with them."

Like an awful cliché, Ben saw his life pass in front of him with all its obligations and limitations...and losses. "Where are they?"

"At the police station. I'm tied up with the little ones. Can you go get Mike? Please." The last word was ragged.

Wonderful timing, kid. Ben didn't want to hear the whiny excuses, the you-don't-understand's. Didn't want to deal with Mike's rebellion or his half-assed judgment. Ben was damn sick of wearing the big red cape with the *S* on it.

Besides, he needed to get on the road. Katherine had been right on. Whether Laurel knew it or not, she needed him. He raked a hand through his hair. And, God, did he ever need her!

"Ben, are you there?"

"Uh, yeah, I'm here." Then with blinding clarity he knew what he had to do. "You may not like what I'm going to say, Mom. We've had all kinds of trouble with Mike since Dad died, and each time we've bailed him out, made excuses for him. I'm through."

"What are you saying?"

"That it's time he takes responsibility for his actions and suffers the consequences of his decisions. Somehow, I don't think it'll be the end of the world if he spends a few hours cooling his heels in jail. Might give him a whole new perspective on life."

"But—"

"When you called, I was on the way out the door. Laurel needs me, and right now she's my priority."

"What'll I do?"

If the subject hadn't been so serious, he might have laughed out loud when the answer came to him. "Call Brian. Let him deal with it." Then he added, "And when I get back, I'd like to straighten some things out with the family. Bottom line, Mom, I love you all, but I haven't been helping you, not the way I should have been."

"How long will you be gone?"

"As long as it takes to convince Laurel she's the most important thing in my life."

"Oh, son..."

"Yeah, Mom, I love her. Now, I need to prove it to her."

MILES OF INTERSTATE 80 had rolled beneath her tires, and she couldn't begin to say where she was. Numb, she tried to picture the cabin, the dogs, her parents— symbols of her security. And now? It was possible her entire life had been built on the lie that she had no grandparents, no aunts or uncles, no cousins. Then, as she passed a slow-moving semi, it dawned on her. Good God. Jay Kelley could be her first cousin. Nan, her aunt.

Her hands shook on the steering wheel, and even her small quota of adrenaline-driven energy deserted her. Spying a rest area, she exited and found a parking space. For a few minutes she simply sat, overcome with fatigue. Finally she roused herself, went inside, visited the rest room and bought a cup of coffee before getting on the road again.

Traffic picked up around Toledo. Not too much farther to Norwalk and the Hampton Inn. Ellen had been right. She was too tired, too emotionally drained to drive through the night, although she couldn't imagine how she'd ever sleep. Going round and round in her brain was the question of how to approach her parents. What to say? How would they react?

With sudden insight, a thought struck her. Was that why her mother had never come to Belleporte? Had she been afraid of being recognized? Laurel felt sick. Such duplicity would be so unlike the mother she knew…or thought she knew.

The beginning of Katherine's story thundered in her head. "Once upon a time, I was a well-intentioned, but ignorant woman…" *Once upon a time…* Perspiration broke out on Laurel's brow. Her eyes filled in recognition.

As if her mother sat right there in the car with her, Laurel heard the echo of her voice. "Once upon a time, there was a magic castle by the sea."

And she heard her toddler self urging, "Mommy, tell me 'bout the magic castle where the princess lives."

Mother. Cuddling her close. Closing her eyes. Smiling. Her dulcet voice spinning the tale. "A big white castle, with windows like surprised eyes and two chimneys so tall they scraped the clouds. Every morning, first thing, the princess would leap out of bed, spread her arms in joy and run across the dewy grass, past the swings and the flagpole, to the warm, sandy beach and the blue, blue water…''

How could she have forgotten? How could that scrap of memory have eluded her for these many months? All along, she *had* known Summer Haven, but in myth, not reality.

Her mother's myth. Her mother's connection to a special place that, in her heart, she had never given up.

WITH AN EYE on the rearview mirror for highway patrolmen, Ben kept his foot on the accelerator, stopping once for gas and coffee. Toledo passed in a blur just as the sun went down, its dying rays highlighting the flat countryside. He had no idea how Laurel would react when he arrived, but he couldn't worry about that. No matter how she felt about him, she needed somebody who cared about her at her side. He remembered how awful he'd felt when his father died, but at least he'd been surrounded by his family. Laurel had no one.

As he approached the Norwalk exit, a welcome calm settled over him, accompanied by a strong sense of purpose. Parking near the entrance of the Hampton Inn, he noted the No Vacancy sign, then approached the desk. ''Is a Laurel Eden registered?''

The pimply-faced clerk drew himself up. ''I'm sorry, sir. We cannot give out that information.''

Of course not. Ben glanced around the lobby, spotting a house phone. He crossed the room, picked up and dialed the operator. "Laurel Eden, please."

Then he heard Laurel's puzzled voice. "Ellen?"

He clutched the receiver in a death grip. "No. It's Ben."

"We have nothing to say to one another."

"That's where you're wrong. Please, Laurel. Listen to me. I made an awful mistake. I just hope I'm not too late."

"Do we have to do this now? I'm tired. Maybe when I get back."

He tried not to sound desperate. "I'm here, Laurel."

"What do you mean, 'here'?"

"In the motel."

She was quiet for a long time. Then she sighed. "Room 232. But you need to know—I'm not happy about this."

"I'll take my chances."

CHAPTER THIRTEEN

WHEN LAUREL OPENED the door of her room, she instinctively recoiled as if she thought he'd try to touch her. Ben winced and brushed past her, scanning the king-size bed with its peach and green quilt, the obligatory desk and upholstered side chair, the floral prints adorning the otherwise bare walls. She gestured to the desk chair, then stood leaning against the credenza, arms folded. Finally she spoke. "Why are you here?"

"You shouldn't be alone."

"Oh, great. Now you're playing Eagle Scout with me. What is it you *do,* Ben, when you're not taking care of the world? And who appointed you my keeper anyway?"

He flinched, her accusation hitting the bull's-eye, her bitter words revealing the extent of her hurt. "I guess I deserve that. Especially from you. I came to say I'm sorry. I blew it."

She shot him a mock thumbs-up. "Uh, yeah. But I have to understand you had a higher loyalty, right?"

No hot-boxed witness could feel any more uncomfortable. "I was wrong. I'd like to explain."

Laurel bowed, then gestured melodramatically about the room. "You're here now. I doubt I'll get rid of you until you have your say. After all—" her voice was icy "—you came all this way." She crossed to the bed, where she perched cross-legged, leaning against the headboard. "I'm beat, Ben. Make it short." She picked up a pillow and hugged it to her chest. The look on her face did not offer much hope.

Studying his clasped hands, Ben marshalled his thoughts for a closing argument. He looked up. "I'm not here to justify my actions. They were unpardonable. I'm here because I love you." He detected a flicker in her eyes. "Maybe, in a strange sort of way, it took something as monumental as my mistake to realize exactly what I'd jeopardized." He stopped, then struggled on. "I should have told you I love you a long time ago. I should have put you first, but I didn't."

Clutching the pillow, she avoided looking at him, but he noticed her chin tremble.

"I know that makes it difficult to trust me," he went on. "I put the needs of a client ahead of yours. It doesn't matter that I truly didn't think anything would come of the investigation. I should never have agreed to handle it."

"No, you shouldn't. Do you have any idea how it felt to read that phone message?"

"Like a betrayal."

"Exactly."

"I didn't set out to hurt you, Laurel."

"That's beside the point now, isn't it? My life as I knew it has pretty well come apart, thanks to you."

Her words roused him. "Has it? Are you sure something good isn't about to come out of all this?"

She tossed the pillow to the foot of the bed, jumped up and paced back and forth in front of him, every now and then jabbing a finger in his direction. He let her words roll over him. "Something good? Let's see. Let me tick off the benefits. For my entire life, I've apparently been living a lie. My parents aren't who they claim to be, and they've cut me off from the rest of my family. I've grown up in blissful ignorance believing I was someone I'm not. Oh, and there's more. All this time I had a grandmother, an aunt and a cousin who never bothered to confront the almighty Frank Sullivan. Tell me how much they could've cared." She halted in front of him. "There. Are you satisfied?"

He couldn't stand it. His eyes never leaving hers, he rose to his feet. "No. I'm not satisfied. And I won't be until you're whole." He put his arms around her and pulled her close. She resisted at first, then, as if all the air had left her body, she collapsed against him. "I love you," he whispered, rubbing his hands up and down her back. "Please don't turn me away."

He felt her muscles begin to relax. Then her shoulders convulsed and hot tears dampened his shirt front. He buried his face in her hair and continued holding her, caressing her. Still she'd said nothing. Her skin smelled of flowers and sunshine, her soft curls tickled his chin. He wanted the moment to go on indefinitely, because when it ended, she might send him away. Forever. One last time he needed to say it. "I love you." His voice shook with emotion.

He heard her draw a deep breath. She tilted her head back and searched his eyes for what seemed a very long time. He wanted to pour out excuses, rationalizations, apologies. Instead, he waited, mute, for her judgment.

She stepped out of his embrace and reached for his

hands. She looked small, defenseless. "We need to talk."

That was all she said, but it was enough.

LAUREL HAD TRIED her best not to listen to Ben. Not to accept his explanations. Not to believe he loved her. She might have been able to hold out...except for one indisputable fact. Despite everything, *she* loved *him.*

She led him to the bed, where he settled against the headboard, his legs stretched out, his feet crossed. Gathering up the discarded pillow, she sat facing him at the foot of the bed. In a small, dark corner of her mind, she acknowledged that she had made him the scapegoat for her problems. "You felt obligated to Katherine?"

"That's the reason I acted as I did, not an excuse. The Sullivans and Kelleys have been an important part of my life. Not just now. Always. And not just because of the help they've given me with the practice. I haven't said much about this, but our home wasn't a particularly happy place after Dad came back from Vietnam. We weren't prepared for the extent of the emotional damage. I was a clueless little kid, wondering why my father wasn't like other fathers. You know, easygoing, involved."

When Ben paused, Laurel tried to picture the little boy, so hopeful, so needful of a father's attention and love.

"Later, after therapy, Dad was better. He found a kind of peace with his new life. But for a while, there, I dreaded going home. That's where Jay and his family came in."

"They adopted you?"

"Something like that. Frank, for the most part, was a non-factor. But Katherine treated me like a grandson. Summer Haven was my refuge. Winters, when they were in Chicago, were tough times for me. I'll never forget their kindness and hospitality."

"So when Jay asked you to investigate—"

"I was in a bind. I knew whatever I decided, I'd be compromised."

"But you did it anyway." She was trying hard to understand, but his deceit still rankled.

"Honestly? Jay and I thought this whole business was wishful thinking on Katherine's part. She liked you and wanted you to fill that void in her life."

"Why couldn't you have told me?"

"And upset you with no cause?"

Reluctantly Laurel conceded his point. "Well, I guess we can talk this to death. What's done is done."

He sat forward and seized her hand. "I never meant to hurt you."

No, he probably hadn't. And maybe his decision about the investigation wasn't the biggest hurt. That was waiting for her tomorrow, when she got to West Virginia. "I know. But, Ben, I didn't need protecting. I was smothered once by a man convinced he knew what was best for me. I won't settle for that again."

"You won't have to."

When he drew her closer, then pulled her down so she was cuddled against his chest, she had to admit she was glad he was here. She listened to the steady beat of his heart, inhaled the starchy fragrance of his shirt, let her hand creep up and rest on his chest. She was so very tired. Lulled by the soft sound of his breathing, she felt her eyelids droop.

"Laurel, I want to go with you tomorrow."

Her first instinct was to refuse, but then she hesitated. He was trying to tell her something. Prove something. "Why?"

His eyes answered even before his words. "Because I love you."

She thought about what he'd said. If she let him stay…if she let him come with her to face her parents…that was commitment. She didn't doubt she could handle tomorrow's confrontation by herself. Handle the rest of her life by herself, if she had to. But did she want to? "Ben, like I said before, I don't need to be taken care of."

He turned her face so he could gaze into her eyes. "Maybe not." He wrapped her in his arms and covered her forehead with kisses. "But I do."

Do your parents know you're coming?" Ben asked as they pulled away from the motel the next morning after arranging with the management to leave Laurel's car in the lot.

"No. I didn't want to have to explain on the phone."

"Tell me about them." He already knew the basics, but he needed more.

Laurel pondered his question. "You're wondering what kind of people would have found it necessary to turn their backs on a family like the Sullivans?"

"Something like that."

"I've been asking myself the same thing. But, then, my parents have always been somewhat unconventional."

"How's that?"

"They have strong convictions. I suppose some people would call them tree huggers. Ecology is big with them. They were heavily involved in protesting Vietnam. In fact, I think my father in those days was like a union organizer, recruiting student protesters on university campuses."

Ben wondered what her reaction would be to the kind of clippings he'd seen. Michael Mays had been a high-profile activist.

"They've never talked much about that time. They tease sometimes, calling themselves grown-up hippie radicals." She turned her head to study Ben. "Will that bother you? Your family can't be very sympathetic with those who held anti-war views."

It was an important question and deserved an honest answer. "You're right. It was hard for men like my father—who believed in this country, in following orders, in honor—to differentiate between attacks against government policy and a lack of public support for the troops in Southeast Asia. The backlash was painful on many levels." He thought back to the days when, overcome with bitterness, his father had scarcely left the house. "For some vets like my father, it took a long time to make any peace with what happened on the home front." He sighed, and Laurel laid a hand on his knee. "But it was a long time ago."

"I always thought my parents were bigger-than-life," Laurel said. "They could do anything—build a cabin, grow amazing fruits and vegetables, work with wood, weave fabric, teach me all kinds of things from music to science to politics. I grew up thinking everyone was like us. Then I went to college."

Ben heard her voice fall. "What happened?"

"Peace, love, happiness—which I had always taken for granted—were regarded as empty watchwords of a long-gone social ideal. I remember a professor who even laughed at the notion. 'Can you imagine a student movement that actually espoused those principles as a basis for everyday reality?' I tried to argue with him. 'What else are we supposed to do? If we don't strive to live by our values and ideals, who are we?' I asked. I'll never forget the silence in the classroom. When I looked at my peers, I realized they hadn't the foggiest idea what I was talking about. That was the moment I realized that all my life, I'd been marching to the proverbial different drummer. The same one who guided my parents."

"Your professor was wrong."

"I know that now, just as I know that we each have to find our own path. For me that meant accommodating my idealistic notions to the real world, but never forsaking them."

He covered her hand with his. "For what it's worth, I love you for those very reasons. You fill me with peace, love and happiness."

By early afternoon, they wound through the West Virginia countryside. Laurel stared pensively out the window. It was a hot summer day, but the mountains, shaded by deep green trees and canopied by a brilliant blue sky, looked cool, inviting. He sensed her withdrawal the closer they came to her home. He couldn't imagine what she must be thinking, feeling, now that her whole world had been rocked to the core. Resting his arm on the seat back, he let his fingers play with the hair at the nape of her neck. "Scared?"

"Petrified." She swallowed, then gazed up at him. "I just want it over. Once and for all."

"I'm with you, Laurel. Every step of the way."

PAT KNELT in the garden plucking at the weeds. The dirt was warm, soothing to the touch. The earthy redolence and the scent of blooming flowers filled her with simple pleasure. Dylan lay on the front porch panting in the heat, but Fonda had darted off into the woods, no doubt chasing a trespassing squirrel or rabbit. Through the open door of his shop, she could see Noel hunched over two sawhorses, cutting some lengths of board. She sat back on her heels. Even now, after all these years, she enjoyed watching him when he didn't know he was being observed. He did everything with the intensity of a perfectionist. Although she couldn't hear him, his mouth was puckered in what she knew was a whistle.

He'd given up so much for her. Had he ever wished his life had been different? If so, she'd never know. Not once in thirty years had he ever suggested he had any regrets. She knew, though, that he worried about her—about her regrets. Early on, it had been difficult, but then she'd come to grips with the realities. Noel and Laurel were worth whatever sacrifice she'd had to make. Years had passed, and she had scarcely given her old life a thought.

Then came Laurel's bombshell. Belleporte. Despite her best intentions, Pat had been unable in the past few months to keep memory—or fear—at bay.

She chastised herself. It was too beautiful an afternoon to dwell on her personal clouds. She gathered the pile of weeds and walked toward the shop, where she tossed them in the trash bin. Noel looked up, then laid his saw aside, that lazy grin that still sent shivers through her creasing his face. "Hi, lady. Wanna lay across that big brass bed in the cabin?" He winked.

"I had in mind something more like a cold glass of lemonade." She crossed to him and slid her arm around his waist, then planted a kiss on his warm, tanned neck.

He chuckled. "Guess I'll have to settle for what I can get."

Feeling almost girlish, she pulled his arm around her waist and together they set off for the house. "That other option?" She smiled up at him. "Maybe later."

"Hope springs eternal."

Dylan made a show of rousing himself. They stopped to pet him, but he suddenly stiffened, his head cocked. Then he tore off down the steps, barking excitedly.

"What's that about?" Pat asked.

"Listen." Noel cupped his ear. "Hear it? Someone's coming."

Pat's smile faded. Few of their friends or neighbors were in the habit of dropping by in the middle of the afternoon and the mail had already come. A sudden cool wisp of air passed across the back of her neck, setting up gooseflesh.

"Know anybody who drives a Honda?"

"No." Pat watched the car pull into the yard. A man was driving and beside him was... "Noel, it's Laurel."

"Laurel?"

Pat had already started toward the vehicle. "Something must be wrong." Noel followed. Then, oblivious to Dylan's excited circling, they watched as Laurel and a nice-looking young man got out of the car.

"Mother, Dad. This is my friend Ben Nolan. Ben, my parents, Pat and Noel."

Ordinarily Pat would have suspected Laurel's visit had something to do with the fellow now shaking Noel's hand. But not this time. Her daughter had not stepped forward. Had not acknowledged Dylan. She remained standing there, studying Pat with an expression at once questioning and distant. Pat looked into Laurel's eyes and trembled. Her daughter was staring at her as if she were a stranger.

Behind her, Pat became aware that the men had stopped talking and were observing them. Pat took a step forward. "Laurel…"

Her daughter's next words stopped her cold. "Mother, I've come home for the truth. To find out who I really am."

LAUREL WATCHED the flush fade from her mother's face, saw her fingers pluck at the loose denim shirt she wore. For a brief second she regretted her abruptness, but she wasn't in the mood for polite formalities.

Her father looked from her to her mother and back. In an even tone he said, "Your mother and I were about to have a glass of lemonade. Why don't you and Ben freshen up and join us? Then we'll talk." As if accompanying a programmed robot, he took her mother by the arm and led her toward the house.

Laurel was grateful when Ben didn't say anything, but simply grasped her hand and followed her parents. Inside the house, he gave her fingers a comforting squeeze. Laurel went straight to the bathroom, closed the door and sank down on the commode, desperate to calm her fluttering nerves. Finally she rose, dashed cold water over her face, finger-combed her hair and went into the great room.

Ben sat in the rocker, holding a glass of lemonade. Her parents sat on the sofa, her mother's face pale and drawn. That left Laurel the worn but comfortable blue-and-white checked armchair. An untouched glass of lemonade was on the oak table beside it. The only cooling came from a ceiling fan. Broad patches of sun streaked through the windows, yellowing the wooden floor where the light fell. Home, which had never failed to offer her comfort, felt foreign. These people on the sofa—so familiar—were strangers.

Her father turned toward her, his eyes full of pain. "To answer your earlier question, posie, you are our daughter, whom we love very much."

Laurel couldn't afford the luxury of pity. "Oh, I know I'm your daughter. The more important question is who exactly are you?"

Her mother pulled her legs up under her and crossed her arms. "Don't be ridiculous, Laurel. We're Pat and Noel Eden. What's gotten into you, anyway?"

Laurel was suddenly glad Ben was there. Otherwise, she might have turned coward, opting to continue the elaborate game of make-believe. She ignored her mother's question. "I understand now why you wouldn't come to Belleporte, Mother."

"What do you mean? I didn't come to Belleporte because I was too busy."

"Too busy? Busy running from the past, I guess."

The room shrank, as if she and her mother were the

only persons on the planet. "Don't start, Laurel," Pat said.

"Well, when will it be time?" Laurel felt anger curdling her words. "I'm a grown woman. I can handle a little thing like the truth."

"Laurel..." Her father's voice stopped her. "You're upset. Justifiably so, I presume. But can't we talk about whatever's troubling you without rancor?" He turned to Pat. Laurel could barely hear him. "It's time," was all he said.

Instead of facing her, her mother turned her head and stared toward the window, her profile so implacable that Laurel was stupefied. Ben nodded at Laurel by way of encouragement. She took a deep breath, knowing that, like her father, she didn't want needless unpleasantness.

Deliberately she softened her tone. "Mother, do you remember when I was little, how you used to tell me stories? They always started the very same way—with the magic castle." Her mother continued gazing at the window, but when she bit her lip, Laurel knew she had her attention. "Remember? 'Once upon a time, there was a magic castle by the sea. A big white castle, with windows like surprised eyes and two chimneys so tall they scraped the clouds...' But the magic castle wasn't by the sea, was it, Mother? It was beside Lake Michigan and it was called Summer Haven."

Dylan's tail thumped against the floor, a wasp buzzed at the screen door. Noel reached for Pat's hand. Laurel watched as her mother slowly turned back to her. Her voice sounded like a scratchy recording. "What is it you want to know?"

Laurel searched for the words. The wasp's buzzing

seemed to be coming from inside her head, intensifying, battering her brain. "Are you Jo Sullivan?"

Her father's knuckles whitened in the effort to steady her mother. Ben, Laurel, Noel—all of them stared at Pat. Noel dropped her hand and put his arm around his wife, his eyes never leaving her face. "The truth, darlin'."

Looking for all the world like a trapped animal, her mother raised haunted, tear-filled eyes to Laurel. "Yes," she whispered.

"Katherine, then, is my grandmother?"

"Yes." Pat wiped a stray tear away with her fist. "She's...all right?"

"Better than all right," Laurel said. "She's wonderful."

"My father?"

"He died last year."

Pat nodded as if she'd expected that answer. "Nan?"

"Fine, too."

Again the silence came, broken only when Laurel mustered the most significant question of all. "Why, Mom? Why?"

Pat's eyes rounded. "Do we have to go into this?"

Laurel felt a tick of irritation return. "Yes, we do. I have a grandmother, an aunt, a cousin. I deserve to know who I am."

Noel cleared his throat. "Your mother and I never meant to hurt you. Far from it."

"You must have had a reason." Laurel sensed herself becoming desperate.

"We did. *I* did." Her mother's words hit Laurel with the force of hailstones. "There was an argument.

I was told I was not welcome at home. I left. End of story." Then, for the first time, her mother's tone became sarcastic. "Except for the fact I tried, repeatedly, to make contact. The phone numbers had been changed. Unlisted. Letters were returned. Let's just say that eventually I got the message. Loud and clear."

Before she was conscious she'd moved, Laurel found herself across the room at her mother's feet. "But *why?* I don't understand. Katherine's not like that."

"It wasn't Mother."

"Then *who?*"

"My father." Pat collapsed into her husband's arms.

Ben crossed the room and hunkered beside Laurel. "Maybe a break is in order. Your mother's had quite a shock."

Noel caught Laurel's eye. "He's right, posie. Later, okay? For now, why don't you take Ben for a walk, show him the place, get some air?"

Laurel didn't know whether she could stand, but with Ben's help, she found her feet. It was clear that her mother had had enough for the moment.

But Laurel wasn't finished. Not by a long shot.

BEN GRIPPED Laurel's hand tightly and led her outside, down the porch steps and toward a grove of trees at the back of the property. Dylan ran ahead of them and was soon joined by another dog.

"That's Fonda," Laurel explained, nodding toward the second dog.

"As in Henry, Jane, Peter or Bridget?" Ben knew

the joke was lame, but maybe it would lighten the mood.

"You have to ask? Only one of them made a trip to Hanoi."

So much for lightening the mood. Laurel knelt to greet Fonda. Hungry for attention, Dylan brushed against Ben's leg. Ben idly stroked the dog's head while gazing at the panorama before him. This was a spectacular setting, a clearing high on a ridge facing east. In the distance, chain after chain of mountains stretched to the horizon. Overhead a hawk circled lazily. From somewhere lower in the valley came the laughter of children. Being here gave him a whole new appreciation for Laurel—for her playfulness and joy. Now, though, as she petted Fonda, such emotions had been replaced by a heartbreaking wistfulness.

"Come," she said, taking his hand again. "I want to show you something." She led him about a quarter of a mile through the trees to a large rock outcropping at the edge of a cliff that sheltered a natural stone bench. She pulled him down beside her. "Look," she whispered.

He'd thought the previous view was spectacular, but this one made it pale by comparison. "Wow!"

She sat for a few moments, her eyes fixed on the vista. "This was always my special place. Where I'd come to daydream, to think." Her hands lay in her lap, her breathing light, her body still. A picture of repose, except for the tension in her shoulders, neck and face.

"How are you, Laurel?"

She looked up and ran her fingers gently across his cheek. "Numb. I want answers."

"I know, but your parents—especially your mother—needed time. They seem like fine people."

"I'm still scared. And angry."

Ben studied the wildflowers clinging to the cracks of the rocky precipice, blooming despite their precarious rooting. He plucked one and handed it to her. "See? Survival's what it's all about. Your parents must've had their reasons. Withhold your judgment until you've heard them out. Listen to them with an open heart." He put his arm around her. "Like you listened to me," he whispered.

She nestled against him for a long time, neither of them speaking. Finally she stood. "Thank you, Ben." She held out her hand. He got to his feet and let her lead him. On the way back, she spoke only once. "Like Dad said, 'It's time.'"

PAT STOOD at the window watching Laurel and Ben, knowing with a mother's intuition that Ben was much more than a friend. Ordinarily she'd have rejoiced. Now she merely gave thanks that Laurel had someone with her as the whole shameful story came to light. She prayed, too, that somehow her daughter would find a way to forgive her—them—for the lie they'd lived all these years.

Her husband came up behind her and put his arms around her, snugging her back against his chest. She sighed heavily. "Were we wrong, Noel?"

"At the time we did what we thought was best. For us, but especially for our baby."

She mulled over all the years—Laurel as a toddler discovering nature, as a twelve-year-old winning a ribbon at the county fair, as a teenager earning a scholarship to the university. "It's been a good life, hasn't it?"

"And it will be again. You have to believe that."

Pat nodded toward the window where she could see Ben and Laurel mounting the porch steps. "They're here."

"Tell it all, darlin'. Probe the wound. Let it heal."

Pat turned in his arms. "I can't lose her."

"Give her some credit. She loves you."

Fear raced up her spine. "I hope it's enough."

"Love always is."

Pat heard the screen door open and closed her eyes briefly before gathering herself and walking toward her daughter. "I'm ready, Laurel."

Ben placed his hands on Laurel's shoulders. "Perhaps I should excuse myself. This is really between you and Laurel."

"No," both women said at once.

"I want you here," Laurel said.

"This is a family matter," Pat said, "and I have the welcome sense that that includes you."

Laurel reached up and squeezed Ben's hand. "It does," she said in a firm voice.

Pat breathed a sigh of relief. No matter the outcome of this conversation, at least Laurel had someone standing by her. Pat found Noel's eyes, warm with encouragement. Someone standing by. Just as she had always had in her steadfast husband. It was more than many people ever knew.

THEY TOOK UP their same places—Ben in the rocker, Laurel in the armchair, her parents on the sofa. Laurel studied them, wondering in how many ways the next few minutes would change her life.

Noel began. "It's important for you to understand the context in which everything happened. The late '60s and early '70s were chaotic times. Culturally. Politically. Morally. Campuses were hotbeds of change, even revolution. Young people were challenging the norms of their elders—in dress, music, behavior and politics. Civil rights, women's lib, anti-war movements. It was both exhilarating and terrifying to be young and idealistic then."

Laurel leaned forward. "What does that have to do with you?"

"Everything," Noel said simply. "I dropped out of grad school to move from campus to campus organizing student anti-war protests." He shrugged. "I even gained a sort of minor celebrity. Had my picture in *Newsweek.*"

Her mother took up the story. "I was a frivolous sorority girl, going blithely about my life until a friend's fiancé was killed in Vietnam. Like so many, I got caught up in the cause, dropped out of the sorority, moved to a coed apartment I shared with other liberal-leaning students. I shucked my fancy wardrobe, wore sandals and granny dresses, let my hair grow. Even smoked my share of dope. For a time it was probably more a rebellion against conformity and my upbringing than it was a genuine conviction. Until I met your father." The hint of a smile played over her lips. "He was so clear in his views, so dedicated to his cause, and, frankly, so charismatic that I fell in love with him the first time I met him."

Noel picked up Pat's hand. "And here was your

mother—this beautiful, intelligent, passionate young woman who was genuinely grappling with these huge issues of the day. And who thought I was wonderful.''

''We were helplessly, hopelessly in love,'' Pat said. ''I left school and followed him, helping recruit. Of course my father was outraged, my mother baffled.'' She drew a hand to her chest as if holding in some heartache. ''This is where the truth becomes more painful.''

Laurel waited, trying to imagine the dichotomy between the Sullivans' views and those of her parents. Trying to picture the confusion of the Vietnam era.

''I hadn't been home since Christmas. My parents were beside themselves. Finally Nan called, begging me to come to Belleporte in May for her wedding. I loved my sister. How could I refuse? My parents didn't know about Noel. At my insistence, he waited at a motel in Lake City while I went to Summer Haven to break the news that I planned to marry him. I was scared. I knew how hard it would be for my family to accept him. Especially my father.'' Her mother's voice tightened as she got into the story. ''I thought I could soften them—him—up before they met Noel.''

Laurel sensed the worst was about to be revealed.

Pat slowly got to her feet and made a circle of the room, letting her fingertips graze over her loom, the back of Laurel's chair, the bowl of bittersweet on the table. She stopped next to the woodstove. ''I wasn't at Summer Haven even an hour.''

Observing her father's brow knit in pain, Laurel asked, ''What happened?''

''I knew I had to talk to my father first. The two of us went into his study.'' With an involuntary gesture,

Pat wrapped her arms protectively around her stomach. "We said horrible things."

No one in the room moved.

"Before I could open my mouth, Dad started in about my appearance. He called me a damned hippie whore. Reminded me I was there for Nan's wedding and accused me of being an embarrassment to the family. When he asked me what people would think, I was quick with my rebuttal. I told him the same thing they'd think if they knew his fortune had been bought with the blood of American soldiers."

Pat was so caught up in the moment that the others might as well not have been present. "He asked me what I meant. So I told him I wasn't so naive I didn't know about his war profiteering. How he was getting rich while others died in the rice paddies of Vietnam."

Agitated, she paced back and forth in front of the fireplace, as if reenacting the scene. "I'll never forget what he said next." She balled her fists. "'What damn commie is filling your head with this bullshit?'"

Her face contorted, Pat stopped pacing. "I told him about Noel. Not surprisingly, he blew a fuse. Told me I had a choice. To come home at once—by myself—or go live off radical hot air with my druggie boyfriend. All I could do was stare at my father—his face was crimson, his eyes were bulging. I suddenly wondered if I'd ever really known him at all. Finally I said, 'I love him.'"

Laurel noticed her father bow his head.

In a monotone, Pat continued. "I remember how his voice got low, with an edge like steel. How each word came out with the precision of a surgeon slicing

skin. 'Then…get…out…of…my…house. And…don't…
ever…come…back.'''

Pat crumpled to the stone hearth, her hands covering
her face. Laurel's instinct was to go to her, but she
sensed there was more.

Finally, her expression ravaged, Pat looked up. "I
didn't even get to tell him or my mother or my sister
that I was pregnant."

The word *pregnant* rolled around Laurel's brain,
echoing and reechoing. "Me?" she managed to say.

"You." Pat clutched her knees. "For your sake, I
tried later to make contact. But my father had delivered his judgment. With every blocked phone call,
every returned letter, I heard his ultimatum again. Before you were born, your father and I made a decision.
You were never to know about this. We didn't want
you to experience the kind of hurt and rejection I had.
It was a risk we simply weren't prepared to take."

In her mother's voice Laurel sensed the desperation
the young couple must have felt. "So?"

"We literally dropped out," Noel said with a rueful
smile. "I changed my name, your mother became Pat
instead of Jo, we married and moved here."

"Changed your name?" Laurel didn't know how
much more news she could take. "Who…who are
you?"

"I was born Michael Mays. I'd been an orphan a
long time, as you know, so it wasn't that big a deal
to me. Besides, it was important to protect you, and
Michael Mays was too well-known by the media.
Starting a new life seemed best."

"Eden," Laurel murmured. "Ironic."

"Hopeful," Pat said. "And it has been Edenesque...until now.'' She found Laurel's eyes. ''Can you forgive us?''

''Posie, please understand. We didn't want you hurt. You were our precious baby. You are our precious daughter.''

Laurel looked from one of them to the other, then found Ben's eyes. She longed to go to him, find refuge in his arms, blot out the revelations that were so difficult to assimilate. Instead, she faced her mother again. ''They tried to find you once. Why didn't you ever go to them?''

The blood drained from Pat's face. ''When? Who?''

''Grandmother. Nan. A long time ago. You'd vanished without a trace.''

''I never knew they tried to find me. I thought they didn't care. I—I wrote them off.''

Noticing Laurel's agitation, Ben picked up the thread. ''Katherine couldn't—or wouldn't—buck Frank again until after his death. Recently, though, she commissioned me to launch an investigation.''

''But Katherine had already guessed,'' Laurel said, swallowing hard. ''Somehow she suspected I was her granddaughter.'' Laurel went and sat on the floor at her mother's feet. ''She's never stopped loving you, Mom.'' A ragged sob caught in Pat's throat. ''Come home to Belleporte with me.''

Pat shook her head violently. ''No. I can't. *This* is my home. Here. I won't go back.''

''How will you heal?'' Noel asked her in an anguished tone.

She stood and turned her back. ''Please. Leave me alone. Some things are beyond healing.''

''Pat?'' Noel stood, but his wife was already running from the room. He looked helplessly at Laurel. "I'm sorry," he said, "for so much." Then, with a shrug, he followed his wife.

Ben pulled Laurel into his embrace. She stood there trembling, knowing that, at this moment, only within the circle of his arms could she find any peace.

CHAPTER FOURTEEN

KATHERINE GATHERED up her canvas tote, a folding chair and a wide-brimmed straw hat and started down the steps to the beach. She couldn't recall the last time she'd done this. Hooking the chair over her arm, she clung to the weathered railing and carefully began her descent. When had she started holing up in the house and not going to the lake? As a girl, she'd spent nearly every waking moment swimming or playing at the water's edge.

Locating a smooth area near the breaking waves, she set down her bag, planted her chair and settled into it, enjoying the caress of the moist breeze on her cheek and the sun toasting her legs.

It had been only twenty-four hours since Laurel left, yet the waiting was interminable. Here by the water, though, it didn't seem so bad.

Laurel should be back soon. It had taken every bit of Katherine's willpower not to call directory assistance for the number of an Eden family in West Virginia. She could have insisted she accompany Laurel. Yet she understood Laurel needed time alone with her parents before anything else happened. After all, Katherine rationalized, she'd waited all these many years for news. She could surely wait another day. For the moment she needed simply to content herself with offering thanks that her daughter was alive and her granddaughter would soon be back in Belleporte.

Fool, she remonstrated. *You want much more than that.* She wanted reconciliation. Forgiveness. And not just from Jo and Laurel. She would also have to find a way to forgive Frank. And, most of all, herself. She was increasingly convinced something awful had passed between Jo and Frank that day—something he'd never fully confessed. No matter what, though, he'd had no right to break up their family.

The fact they had been caught up in Nan's wedding was no excuse for her inaction, but Frank did nothing halfway, and when he had slammed the door on Jo, that was it. According to him, his daughter had disobeyed him, humiliated her sister and betrayed the family values. Always stubborn and prideful, Jo had stormed out when he'd confronted her. From that point on, Frank had said, they had to treat the schism as a death in the family. Katherine had pleaded, cried. To no avail. And when there had been no communication from her daughter after the unsuccessful investigation, she'd gradually accepted the fact she had two choices. Leave Frank or do as he said.

Their relationship had never been the same after that. She'd made the best of the situation, going through the motions, performing her role as society matron. But the Frank of her young womanhood—charming and irresistible—had ceased to exist.

A particularly large wave broke against the shore, causing her to look up. The broad expanse of the lake was the same as it had eternally been. The sand beneath her bare feet felt warm, soothing. She studied her wrinkled, blue-veined legs, then shut her eyes. Where had the years gone?

Clamping her hat to her head with one hand, she tiptoed toward the lake, squealing when a tongue of cool water washed over her feet. She waded in, knee-deep, then thigh-deep, smiling in wonder. This was the Katherine of those long ago summers—before Frank. Odd. Not until this very day, when she'd returned to the source of her childhood joy—the water—could she truly begin to let go of the past. To hope for the future.

She spread her arms and embraced the scene before her. Regardless of Laurel's report, Katherine knew that somehow, some way, her family would be whole again.

Then, without thinking and heedless of her hat, she plunged into a breaking wave and stroked through the water, barely able to contain her laughter.

BEN HAD SLEPT on the sofa bed in the great room, Dylan snoring by his side. He awakened early, longing to slip up to the loft and gather Laurel in his arms. Yesterday evening had been strained. They'd managed polite conversation during the simple supper, but Pat and Laurel were drained and had little to say. Laurel had excused herself early and gone up to bed. Pat and Noel soon followed.

Unable to sleep, Ben had sat on the front porch watching a huge moon rise over the mountains, pondering all he'd heard. On the one hand, he couldn't fathom how a father could so irrevocably shut out his daughter; on the other, knowing Frank, it was a no-brainer. The man had been a law unto himself. The mystery was how Katherine had stayed married to him. Maybe the same way his mother had stayed married to his father. By doing whatever it took, at whatever cost.

He'd worried, too, about Katherine's reaction when she learned that Pat…Jo…wasn't ready for a glorious family reunion. Most of all, he'd wondered how this would affect Laurel. She knew the truth now, but would it make her any happier? Change anything for the better?

Dylan stirred, then sat up and licked Ben's face. "Hey, mutt. Watch it." Ben sat up, scratched the dog behind his ears, then grabbed his Dop kit and overnight bag and disappeared into the bathroom.

When he came out, Noel stood at the stove sautéing onions and green peppers and Pat was beating eggs. Judging from their appearance, neither of them had slept any better than he had. Pat looked up. "Coffee?"

"I'd love a cup. Thank you." When the first jolt of caffeine hit, he rubbed his stomach in satisfaction.

"Are you going back today?" Noel asked.

"That was the plan. Laurel can't be away from the shop too long, and I have several out-of-town depositions this week."

"You're an attorney?" Pat asked.

"Yes, I have a practice in Belleporte." He chuckled in an attempt to lighten the mood. "Funny, I know all about you, but you're probably wondering who the heck this fellow is who brought your daughter home."

Noel smiled. "It had crossed our minds."

Ben had rarely met a man he'd taken to so instantly. Noel's steadiness, quiet humor and sensitivity were rare qualities. "Well, let me give you the short version." He launched into his personal and professional history and had just finished when Laurel came down the stairs from the loft. She wore a black T-shirt, which accentuated her pale skin and brought out the depths of her sad eyes. Whether she intended it or not, it made her look like a victim. "Good morning," she murmured, heading straight for the coffeepot.

Noel and Pat shot each other troubled glances. Ben moved to Laurel, put his arm around her and kissed her cheek. "I've just been giving your parents the life and times of Ben Nolan, attorney-at-law."

She smiled wanly. "Yeah, I guess I sort of sprung you on them."

An awkward silence followed. Then, both at once, Noel and Pat said, "Sit," and "Have some breakfast."

For a time there was no sound except that of toast being buttered and forks scraping on plates. Ben noticed that Pat hadn't touched her food. "Laurel," she finally said. "Please understand. I couldn't run the risk of taking you to my family and having them turn us...you...away. There'd been enough hurt. All we were trying to do was protect you."

Laurel shoved her plate toward the center of the table. "Or deprive me. Of grandparents. Of a history."

Ben's stomach knotted.

"Katherine is a warm, wonderful woman," Laurel continued. "How can you go on punishing her?"

"You don't know the meaning of punishment," Pat said dully. "Not a day has gone by that I haven't second-guessed myself. But you can't expect to wipe out the hurt and rejection of thirty years overnight."

"No, I suppose not." Laurel studied the tabletop,

then looked up. "Will you at least think about coming to Belleporte?"

"I can't."

"Please, Mom. Katherine's final words to me were, 'Tell Jo I never stopped loving her.' She's an old woman. Don't wait until it's too late."

Noel laid a hand on Pat's. "Couldn't you do as Laurel asks? Consider it?"

Ben watched relief ease Laurel's features when Pat said, "All right. I'll think about it. But don't expect too much."

Ben and Laurel packed up and left shortly after breakfast. They'd hardly reached the highway when Laurel flipped on a talk radio show and pretended to listen, though Ben knew she was lost in her own thoughts. It was enough, for the moment, simply to be with her.

As they approached the Cleveland metro area early in the afternoon, Laurel finally turned off the radio and gave Ben his first real opening. "How could he have done that?"

She'd clearly been brooding. "Who?"

"Frank Sullivan. Every time I think about him kicking my mother out, I get mad all over again. And not just at him. At all of them."

"I wasn't clear whether Frank kicked your mother out or whether she stormed out. Sounds as if they were both at fault."

"Are you defending him?"

Ben chose his words carefully. "Some pretty rough accusations were made."

"I guess. War profiteering and radicalism. But still. He was the adult in the situation."

"Do you think your mother would interpret it that way?"

"What do you mean?"

"She was adult enough to leave school, stand up for her convictions, live with a man, conceive a child." He adjusted his cruise control for the metropolitan speed limit. "She hit Frank right in his ego when she suggested he'd made his money illegally—and immorally."

Laurel squared around in her seat. "Surely you're not taking his side?"

"At the risk of sounding like an attorney, let me play devil's advocate. Put yourself in Frank's shoes. He was a self-made man who'd built Sullivan Company into a major player. So far as I know, he was never involved in any under-the-table kickbacks that sometimes taint government contracts. Somebody had to supply the needs of the Defense Department. Surely Frank can't be blamed for running his business to make a profit."

Ben glanced out of the corner of his eye. Laurel wasn't buying. "Besides," he continued, "he'd come from a humble background. It was a matter of pride to provide well for his family. Then along comes his beloved daughter, who seemingly throws it all up in his face."

"What's so damn wrong with being against war?"

This was not going well. "Nothing in the abstract. But there is a fine line between blindly sticking to your principles and destroying family relationships."

"So you're suggesting my mother was wrong for standing up to him?"

"Whoa. Devil's advocate, remember." He changed

lanes and speeded up. "I'm not knocking your parents or their views. But I've got to tell you, I'm glad somebody was supplying guys like my dad with the weapons and matériel they needed."

"I can't believe what I'm hearing! You think Vietnam was a just war?"

"I don't think we should have been involved in Southeast Asia in the first place, but once there, we damn well should have supported our troops."

"Why? So we could stand by and let the politicians get us in deeper and deeper? Somebody had to stop them. The war was senseless, immoral."

His hands tightened on the steering wheel. "Even if men like my dad who were imprisoned by the Viet Cong thought their cause was 'senseless' and 'immoral,' they would never have found the courage to survive the inhumane treatment they received without believing Americans stood behind them. How do you think they felt when they were liberated and discovered half the citizens of the country they'd fought for regarded them as warmongers?"

"You feel strongly about this, don't you?"

"You bet I do."

Her cheeks were flushed. "Well, so do I. I'm proud of what my parents did."

He didn't want to upset her further, but he couldn't let her remark pass. "And I'm proud of my father and what he and so many others did." Nor did he want the conversation to end on this note. "But that was all thirty years ago and—"

She interrupted him. "It doesn't feel like it right now. The truth I learned yesterday makes it all pretty darned immediate."

He fought for patience. "None of this is either-or, Laurel. Not the war, and not what happened between your mother and grandfather."

Reaching into her purse, she pulled out her sunglasses, put them on and effectively ended the discussion.

Ben concentrated on traffic, trying, with no success, to blot the conversation from his mind. Laurel had defended her mother, which, ultimately, didn't bode well for Katherine.

The truth was, Laurel had been spoiling for a fight, and he'd almost let her sucker him in. She was seeing everything that had happened as black and white, when there were layers upon layers of gray. Both Frank and Pat had been hotheaded, and each had let stubbornness and pride overrule common sense and love. The way they'd left things with Pat this morning, it didn't look as if she was going to mellow any time soon. Which put Laurel right in the middle between her mother and grandmother.

After several miles, Laurel turned on the radio again, this time to a classic rock station. After adjusting the seat back, she closed her eyes and appeared to go to sleep. But Ben knew better. Her body was rigid.

He brought himself up short. He'd hit her pretty hard with his arguments. She needed his support, not his rhetoric, and time to process it all. What she'd suffered was a devastating, life-altering blow. For now, he realized, all he could do was stand by patiently—and love her no matter what.

WHEN BEN TOUCHED her shoulder, Laurel opened her eyes. The Norwalk exit sign loomed in front of them. "Did you get some rest?" he asked.

"Mainly I dozed." And escaped. She knew she'd have to think about all of this, but right now it seemed overwhelming. So many emotions, so many questions. How did she feel about her parents' deception? About Katherine and Nan's caving in to her controlling grandfather? About the new relationships waiting to be explored back in Belleporte? Even about Ben. How could she offer him anything—much less love—until she had a grip on who she really was.

"Will you be okay to drive your car the rest of the way?"

"I'm probably in better shape than you are. At least I had a nap."

"I'll follow you," he said.

As they entered the parking lot, she dug in her purse for her keys. "Thanks for the moral support. I—I'm glad you were there." It was time to leave him. But there was something she needed to say and she had no idea how it would be received. "Ben, I have a lot on my mind. I need some time to sort things out, to get my bearings."

"You're saying you don't want to see me for a while?"

"Would you mind terribly?"

"What do you think?" As if memorizing her face, he traced her cheek with his forefinger. "Yes, I'll mind. In fact, I'll be miserable. But I understand. You need to handle this in your own way, in your own time." He leaned over and kissed her gently, fleetingly. Before she climbed out of the car, he took hold of her arm. "Could I offer one piece of advice?"

She nodded.

"You've joked about your *carpe diem* philosophy, but it may be your best defense in reacting to what's happened. Those old days are gone. You have only this day, then the next and the next. Your parents love you. Katherine loves you. Remember that, and seize the day."

She didn't have an answer for him. Instead, she squeezed his hand in acknowledgment, then stepped out of his car and retrieved her bag from the back seat. She left him then, started her car and pulled back on the highway, noting that he was, indeed, following her. Fortunately traffic was lighter than usual. She was tired in ways that went far deeper than mere sleep deprivation. Katherine would be waiting at Summer Haven for answers.

And right now, Laurel wasn't sure she had any.

BEN ARRIVED back in Belleporte shortly after seven, and instead of going straight to the office, he drove to his mother's. In his concern for Laurel and her family, he'd put the latest crisis with Mike on the back burner. During the drive from Norwalk he'd realized that unless he wanted a family schism of his own, it was time for a heart-to-heart with Mike. Laurel was seeing a side of Mike that Ben wasn't. Maybe he simply brought out the worst in the kid, or maybe he needed to give his brother a chance.

It was well and good to offer Laurel advice on how to handle things with her family, but he needed to practice what he preached. He loved his family, but they had to get some things squared around. Like Laurel, he, too, was having to redefine himself.

When Ben walked into the house, he found Bess, Brian and his mother huddled around the kitchen table. "I'm back," he said, dropping into the vacant chair.

"Can I get you some coffee?" his mother asked.

"Thanks, Mom."

While Maureen poured him a mug, Bess studied her nails and Brian stretched his legs beneath the table and leaned against his chair back.

"How was your trip?" Maureen asked as she set down his coffee.

"Necessary," Ben said. "I hated to leave you in the lurch with Mike, but Laurel needed me."

They waited, as if expecting him to fill them in, but instead, he said, "Where is Mike?"

Brian answered. "Downstairs."

"I'll talk to him later," Ben said, rubbing his forefinger around the rim of his mug. "Tell me what happened."

His brother folded his arms across his chest. "The short, sweet version is that he and his buddies got busted for possession. Mom finally got hold of me about ten-thirty and I sprung him out of the pokey. He claims he wasn't drinking and didn't know about the marijuana. A classic case of guilt by association, at least that's what he says."

Bess looked up then. "Go easy on him, Ben."

Ben continued staring at Brian. "You believe him?"

"I know he hasn't been a model kid, but about this? Yeah, I believe him."

As he drank slowly from his mug, Ben noticed the way his mother was gazing at him with a question in her eyes. Setting down the coffee, Ben steepled his fingers, resting his chin on them. "I need to talk to him." He looked at his sister. "And, Bess, I will listen to him."

She nodded.

"Before I go downstairs, though, there's something I want to say." He sensed tension in his mother. "I'm glad it's the three of you who are here, because I'm about to ask for your help."

"Help?" Bess echoed.

Ben straightened up, fighting to find the right words. "When Dad died, I promised him I'd take over as head of this family." Except for the squeak of Brian's chair leg on the tile floor, it was deathly quiet. "I realize now that isn't as easy as it might sound. The way I see it, the role of a family is to work together to solve problems. To be there for each other." He picked up his mug and cupped his hands around it. "I was trying to do it all on my own. I wasn't giving anyone else much of a chance."

"Ben…" His mother touched his arm and he set down his coffee. "You're being too hard on yourself."

"No, I'm not," he said thoughtfully. "I took everything on myself, and in the process, ended up resenting my responsibilities. Even, at times, resenting some of you. I'm not proud of that. Or of acting like I was the only one who had the answers." He turned to Bess and Brian. "I haven't been giving either of you much credit. We're all adults here. I'm not the father figure, I'm just one of you." He let his gaze sweep over all three. "And I need your help."

Brian eyed him intently. "What can we do?"

"Take me down a peg or two when I need it." Ben

chuckled sardonically. "I must've come across as overbearing a lot of the time."

"You do have a way about you," Brian said with a teasing grin.

"But we all need you," Bess murmured quietly. "*I* need you."

Ben corrected her. "We need each other."

"Son?" His mother caught his eye. "I think you're trying to tell us something more."

With a glance, Ben telegraphed her his gratitude. "What Mom's hinting at is that I've put my own life on hold these past few months, trying to be here for everybody. But I've realized martyrs don't win popularity contests. So I'm asking for us to work together to solve the problems, whether it's as monumental as Bess's marriage or as slight as Mom's plumbing. I can't do it by myself."

Nobody said anything for several ticks of the kitchen clock. Then Brian clamped a hand on Ben's shoulder. "I think maybe my brother is saying it's grow-up time for all of us." He grinned. "Deal me in, Ben."

"Me, too," Bess said, then added with a sheepish smile, "and I think you're implying that I have to face my feelings about Darren on my own instead of polling the delegation at every turn."

"Whoa," Ben said, spreading his hands. "I'm not going there."

Maureen inclined her head. "But I like the sound of it."

Ben looked around the table. "I love you guys," he said in a hoarse voice that didn't come out quite right. Hell, it had always been this easy, if only he'd given them a chance. He rose to his feet. "It's time for that chat with Mike."

Before he started for the stairs, Bess grabbed his hand. "We love you, too, Ben." Then with a meaningful glance at her mother, she added, "And we love Laurel, too."

A portion of the rock lodged in his stomach for so long broke off and dissolved. From the rec room he could hear the chipper voice of a sportscaster hyping the new outfielder the Tigers had recently brought up from the minors. Mike sprawled in the black vinyl recliner, a bag of pretzels lying in his lap. When he saw Ben, he froze. "You're back," he said, as if announcing the onset of Armageddon.

Ben hooked a hip over a bar stool. "Yeah."

Mike took his time folding the top of the pretzel bag, all the while watching the muscular ball player going through his arcane batting ritual.

"Could we talk?" Ben said just loudly enough to be heard over the TV.

Rolling his eyes, Mike reached for the remote and muted the sound. "I knew this was coming."

"What?"

"The big lecture."

"No lecture."

Mike looked at him with incredulity. "Right."

"Tell me what happened, Mike."

The boy wouldn't look at him. "The others have already told you about it."

"I want to hear your version."

Mike shrugged, but said nothing.

"Laurel tells me you're good help. She likes you.

Beyond that, she trusts you." He hesitated. "I think it's about time I got off your case and listened."

Slowly, Mike turned his head and studied Ben, skepticism and yearning warring in his eyes.

Ben cleared his throat. "I've been a horse's ass, Mike. Acting like I didn't trust you. Not being willing to hear what you were trying to tell me. I haven't been the big brother you needed. I've been more like a judge and executioner."

Mike remained silent, but a flush spread over his face.

"I pretty much nailed it, huh?"

With a nervous gesture, the boy cracked his knuckles. "Yeah. You've been on me big time ever since Dad died."

"And you've been doing some questionable stuff ever since then. Want to talk about why?"

"But I didn't do the marijuana on the beach. Swear to God."

"We'll talk about that later, but for what's it worth, I believe you." In front of him now was not the defiant teenager that drove Ben to distraction, but his hurting kid brother who had idolized their father. Ben moved to the sofa, which was set at right angles to the recliner. He leaned forward, elbows on his knees. "Mike, talk to me about Dad. You miss him, too, right?"

Mike clenched his hands in an effort to fight the tears filling his eyes. He nodded mutely.

"Are you angry about it?"

"Hell, yes. What's fair about dying like that? After all he'd been through. Dad was a hero. But did that count?" He jumped up from the recliner, leaving it rocking in his wake. "No way!" He walked several feet, then turned. "And you know what? Nobody in this family ever talks about it. About him. It's like, 'So, he's gone. Let's move on with our lives.' Well, I can't, see? So get off my case." Mike strode toward the punching bag suspended from a beam and threw a quick one-two.

Ben rose to his feet and approached his brother. "I loved him, too," he said quietly.

Mike whirled around. "Well, you have a weird way of showing it."

"Tell me how," Ben said, standing his ground.

"Talk about him, for God's sake. Don't act like you're him when you're not. Nobody's him. He's…he's gone."

Ben placed his hands on Mike's shoulders. "You're right. I'm not him. I could never be. I'm just Ben, your big brother who loves you."

Mike eyed him suspiciously. "Not lately. Not when I'm in trouble."

"Sorry, kid." Ben tried a smile. "Even then." He grabbed Mike in a bear hug.

At first his brother resisted, but then he threw his arms around Ben and whispered in a cracking voice, "I'm sorry for everything."

"Not half as sorry as I am," Ben said.

When he drew away, Mike wiped his nose on his sleeve. Then, with his eyes lowered, he spoke softly. "I'm ready to tell you about being arrested."

"Okay," Ben said, sitting back down. "I'm listening." And when he did, he discovered it made all the difference.

LATE THE NEXT AFTERNOON Laurel tied her running shoes around her neck and stepped off the boardwalk onto the beach. The sand was still warm between her toes. The lake was calm, the waves making a soothing shushing sound as they lapped at the shore. Just another peaceful Belleporte day.

Peaceful? It had been anything but that for her.

She'd been too tired last night to do much except check on the store, open a can of soup, shower and fall into bed, where all the ghosts of her newly discovered past haunted her until the wee hours when she finally lapsed into an exhausted sleep. After checking in with Megan and Mrs. Arlo this morning, she had called Katherine to set a time to talk, to get some answers to her questions.

Now, heading toward Summer Haven, Laurel wondered if it could ever again be the "magic castle" of her childhood. What would it become—a symbol of loss or of reconciliation?

A sudden breeze off the lake ruffled her hair, and for some reason, she was reminded of Ben's admonition. The past is gone. Seize this day. Could she overcome her resentment of the way the Sullivans had treated her mother—her? Would she be able to embrace the reality that she had a grandmother?

In some ways she longed for the blissful ignorance she'd enjoyed for so many years, but it was time to put away childish innocence. Time to face the present moment.

She stopped in her tracks and looked up. Exactly at that moment, shafts of gold from the setting sun fell on Summer Haven, bathing it in a luminous light. Laurel had always believed in signs. She wouldn't have come to Belleporte in the first place if she hadn't. But this?

Not stopping to put on her shoes, she started running toward the steps leading up to Summer Haven—and her grandmother.

KATHERINE CROSSED HER HANDS over her chest in a futile effort to control her emotions. She watched Laurel slowly, almost reluctantly, make her way toward Summer Haven. When she stopped, Katherine was seized by panic. What if Laurel changed her mind and didn't want to see her after all?

Replaying this morning's telephone conversation in her mind, Katherine knew she had no right to expect a happy outcome. Laurel had been polite but noncommittal. Upbraiding herself, Katherine went through a mental list of the reasons Laurel was entitled to be upset, praying her granddaughter would permit love to overcome her sense of betrayal. When Katherine again glanced at the beach, a tentative smile eased the tension in her jaw.

Laurel was running toward Summer Haven.

Heart pounding, Katherine went out onto the deck to greet her. Laurel paused at the top of the stairs, face flushed, bare feet encrusted with sand. The only sound was that of a flock of raucous gulls. Katherine waited, knowing instinctively that Laurel needed to set the tone.

Then with eyes full of yearning, Laurel approached and pulled Katherine into a warm, headily welcome embrace. "Grandmother, I'm home and I have so many questions," she whispered.

Grandmother. Dizzy with relief, Katherine studied

her granddaughter's face. "Then, darling girl, let's begin."

KATHERINE SAT in a wooden rocker facing the lake, and Laurel pulled a canvas beach chair close. Whether or not her mother and grandmother could mend their relationship remained to be seen, but there on the beach, gazing up at Summer Haven, Laurel had reached an irrevocable conclusion. Never again would circumstances rob her of family. She took a deep breath. "Did you know that after she left, Mother tried repeatedly to call and write to you?"

"Oh, dear God, how could that be?" Katherine turned ashen-gray. "I…we never received anything. And Jo knew our phone numbers."

Laurel shook her head. "No, she didn't. They'd been changed and were unlisted."

"How…?" Katherine buried her head in her hands. "Frank," she whispered. "I remember now. There'd been some threatening calls in the neighborhood. He changed the numbers. For security, he said, but…" She shrugged helplessly. "I wondered at the time about the wisdom of that, but Frank assured me that if Jo wanted to find us, she could. That she knew where we lived."

"The mail?" Laurel continued.

Katherine raised her head, her eyes pale marbles. "It had to be Stefan Mazerac."

"Who's that?"

"Our house man who was also Frank's driver. He always—" she struggled to go on "—sorted our mail. Frank must've…"

A welcome release of pent-up air left Laurel's lungs. "So you didn't ignore Mother's messages?"

"Ignore them? I was frantic with grief and worry. I would have given anything to hear from Jo, but I never did." Katherine studied Laurel with infinite sadness. "You must not think much of your grandfather."

Laurel tamped down the anger threatening to undo her. "Whatever he did, perhaps he had his reasons, but they are ones I will never understand. But that's in the past. What's important is what happens now."

"Will—" Katherine cleared her throat nervously. "Will she see me?"

"No." Laurel pictured her mother's ravaged, but obdurate expression. "Not yet."

"Ever?"

"I don't know."

Katherine hung her head, then spoke tentatively. "Did Jo say what happened between her and her father that day?"

As honestly as she could, Laurel told her about the accusations and Frank's ultimatum.

When she finished, Katherine nodded her head. "Both of them, stubborn to the end. I'll spend the rest of my life trying to forgive Frank."

An updraft hit the deck, and her grandmother shivered. "Let's go inside," Laurel suggested.

Katherine allowed herself to be led into the living room. When they settled on the sofa, Katherine said, "So Ben went with you?"

"How did you know?"

"Megan told me. You must be very important to him."

"Why do you say that?"

Then Katherine told her about Mike's arrest. "I understand Brian Nolan handled everything. According to Megan, Ben told his family he couldn't help, that he had to leave—that you were his priority."

Laurel shook her head wonderingly. "He never said a word about it."

"He wouldn't. He loves you."

And Laurel knew, beyond a doubt, that her grandmother spoke the truth.

Greta appeared at the door then. "Can I get either of you something?"

Katherine gave Laurel a questioning look, then said, "Two glasses of our finest wine, please."

Later, enjoying the rich bouquet of the vintage cabernet sauvignon, Laurel asked a final question. "Nan? Does she know?"

"She's coming this weekend, I'll tell her then. After I've phoned Jo."

Studying her grandmother, Laurel noticed the determined jut of her chin and the hint of a twinkle back in her eyes. "I don't know if—"

"She'll speak to me? I'll never know if I don't try, will I? And I've been waiting thirty years to try." Katherine set down her glass and picked up both of Laurel's hands. "But no matter what, I have a cherished granddaughter. No one can take that away from me. I love you, Laurel." A joyous smile illuminated her face. "And I love the beautiful music of that name, 'Grandmother.'"

CHAPTER FIFTEEN

PAT ROCKED back and forth in the porch swing, gazing out over the gray-green mountains, indistinct in the fading light. A bright evening star winked at her, daring her to make a wish, but it was too late for wishes. Too late for things to stay the same. And hurt, like a raw wound, was a constant reminder of a past she had spent years trying to overcome.

She closed her eyes, willing away the image of her mother and sister, giddy with excitement about preparations for Nan's wedding. Willing away the curiosity that had hounded her for years. How were they? Had they missed her?

And most painful—why hadn't they answered her letters?

She sighed, remembering how fierce her need had been to protect Laurel from the kind of rejection that bore into the very marrow of one's being. Innocent Laurel.

And now? Laurel was asking her to forget all those years. To reconnect with her family. But she couldn't do it for Laurel's sake alone. If she went to Belleporte, it would have to be because she could no longer live with the choice she had made over thirty years ago, and because her need was stronger than her guilt or the fear of rejection.

In the distance the plaintive cry of a mourning dove echoed the turmoil in her heart.

When the phone rang, she started, then resumed rocking. Noel would get it. She didn't feel like talking to anyone. But when she heard the creak of the screen door, she knew the call was for her. Noel said nothing, but merely held out the receiver. She raised her eyebrows in question, but he set the phone in her lap, lightly caressed her hair in passing and went back inside.

She stared at the device, sensing that when she picked it up, everything would change. Slowly she clamped it to her ear and said hello.

"Jo, darling, it's Mother."

With those words, Pat was swept into an eddy of colors, sounds, images, tastes, scents. As if drawing herself up from the depths of a bottomless sea, she found her voice. "I—I'm not sure I have anything to say except to thank you for your interest in Laurel."

"I have so much to explain, to tell you."

Pat licked her lips, stunned by the salty taste of tears.

"Jo...I've never stopped loving you."

She wanted to believe it. Desperately. But could she? "Mother, it's hard to put aside three decades of history."

"We can't get back those years, but I pray we have a future. If you'll just let me explain—"

"Please, I'm not sure I'm ready for this. Can we talk later?" Her heart threatened to explode out of her chest and her breath was coming in short pants. "I need some time," she whispered. Explanations? How could any of it be explained? Even her part. Pat didn't bother to wipe away the tears cascading down her cheeks.

"Very well," Katherine murmured, just before hanging up.

Why was she crying, anyway? Then it came to her. *Mother*. She'd called her "mother" without even thinking about it. Spontaneously.

Maybe it wasn't too late after all.

"MOTHER, WHAT are you doing?" The shrill voice carried over the sound of wind and waves.

Katherine turned toward shore, letting her feet sink into the sandy lake bottom. She shaded her eyes. Nan, looking out of place in her designer silk dress, waited at the water's edge, clutching her sling-back pumps, a horrified expression on her face. "What does it look like? I'm swimming." Though Katherine understood her daughter's reaction, she took perverse delight in shocking her.

In hose-clad feet, Nan waded in up to her ankles. "Please come out."

Windmilling her arms for balance in the chest-high water, Katherine approached Nan. "I hope you're not going to tell me I'm too old for this."

Her daughter had the decency to look embarrassed. "Actually, I was. You haven't been swimming in years."

"A waste," Katherine muttered as she crossed the sand to her towel. Looking up and down the beach at her neighbors, she added, "I don't come out by myself."

"I should hope not." Nan swiped at flecks of sand clinging to her skirt.

Katherine gathered up her tote bag. "Why don't we

change into something more comfortable and meet on the deck for iced tea. We need to talk.''

Nan eyed her sternly. "We certainly do."

Katherine took her time dressing. She wasn't sure how Nan would react to her news about Jo. Nan had adored her younger sister and been crushed when Jo walked out. Anger had been Nan's best defense against the loss, and only reluctantly had she financed the unproductive investigation the two of them launched without Frank's knowledge. Nan's stance had always been that her sister knew where to locate her family if she cared about finding them. The more years that passed, the less open Nan had been to the possibility of a reconciliation.

Katherine stepped into a pair of capri pants, pulled a loose knit shirt over her head, then, with difficulty, leaned over and strapped on her sandals. Ever since she'd told Nan her suspicions about Laurel, Nan had grown increasingly protective, worrying that Katherine was doomed to disappointment.

How would Nan take the news that her mother's suspicions about Laurel had proved true and that Jo was alive and well but so far unreceptive to a reconciliation? Katherine sighed, recalling her phone conversation with her recently found daughter. Please God, surely her hurt and stubbornness could be overcome.

With a quick glance at the strange old lady reflected in the mirror, Katherine left her bedroom, praying Nan's love for her sister would lead to understanding and forgiveness.

AFTER HER RETURN from West Virginia, Laurel had settled back into her routine at The Gift Horse out of necessity and as a means of keeping her confusing emotions at bay. Although she was pleased about her relationship with her grandmother, waiting for Nan's reaction was unsettling, as was the fact that, despite several phone conversations with her mother, Laurel had no sense whether or not Pat had made any decision. She understood her mother well enough to know heaven and earth couldn't move her until she was ready. *If* she ever was. Meanwhile, it was awkward and painful to be caught in the middle.

As she'd requested, Ben had kept his distance, calling only once. On that occasion, though, she'd found comfort in his words. "You need to focus on your family. I understand that. The thing is, families are not always easy or comfortable or even likable." He'd chuckled then. "I should know. And we sure don't get to pick the cast of characters. But, bottom line, they're all we've got, and we can't afford to lose them. Any of them."

Now, as she stood at the counter unpacking an order of spices, Laurel realized his words weren't entirely true. Sometimes you did get to pick. You picked your mate. The revelation drew a wondering smile from her because, more than anything, she wanted Ben Nolan for hers. After work she would march over to his office and put an end to this silly self-induced separation.

She was sidetracked, however, when, just before closing, Nan Kelley came into the store, her perfectly made-up face a mask. "Laurel, could we talk?"

She must know. "Of course." Nerves taut, Laurel directed her aunt outside to the garden bench.

"I understand you're my niece," Nan said without preface. "Frankly, I thought Mother was deluding herself. It appears I was mistaken."

"Yes, you were."

"Understand this, Laurel. I'm not unhappy with you. In fact—" her features relaxed, although her eyes remained wary "—I look forward to getting to know you better. But my first concern has to be Mother. I won't permit her to set herself up for further disappointment. Do you think Jo will see her?"

Laurel hung her head. "I don't know. She hasn't decided."

"That sounds like her."

The bitterness in Nan's voice stung Laurel. Neither her mother nor her aunt struck her as being vindictive. "She hurt you a great deal, didn't she?" Laurel ventured quietly.

Nan's cheeks reddened with something beyond a cosmetic blush. "I've never understood how she could leave like that and not once in all those years get in touch with us."

"As you must know by now, she tried. Put yourself in her position. She could never understand why her letters were returned, unopened. She thought she'd been disowned, not just by her father, but by you and her mother."

"How can I overlook thirty years of hurt?"

"That's exactly what Mother said." Laurel studied her fingers, then looked up. "Tell me, Nan, what's the alternative?"

"What do you mean?"

"Is misery so comfortable that neither of you can reach beyond it?"

"I won't have Mother hurt again."

"I don't want that, either. But surely you can try to forgive? Please."

Nan's perfectly manicured forefinger went to the corner of her eye. As if changing the subject, she cleared her throat and said, "I'm having a birthday party for Mother next Friday. It will be her seventy-fifth. I'm inviting most of Belleporte. I'd like you to be there and..." Her voice trailed off and she swallowed several times.

"You want me to ask my mother to come." Laurel sensed Nan could never have put her request into words, and, more importantly, that Nan was as afraid of rejection as Pat was.

Her aunt nodded mutely.

"I'll ask." Laurel embraced the older woman. "Mother has never forgotten Belleporte or you or Grandmother. Maybe, just maybe, love will do the trick."

A FEW MINUTES BEFORE SIX Laurel caught Janet Kerns locking up Ben's law office. "Too late, kiddo," Janet said, anticipating her question. "He waited for the mail, then left for Lansing a little past four. After that he's on to Detroit and Akron. Depositions."

"Oh." Even the one syllable couldn't conceal her disappointment.

Janet patted her shoulder encouragingly. "When are you going to cut my boss some slack?"

"What do you mean?"

"He hasn't been worth shooting around here. Dr. Kerns's diagnosis? He's been infected by the love bug."

Laurel managed a halfhearted smile. "I'd like to volunteer to help with his treatment. When will he be back?"

"Sometime Friday."

"In time for Katherine's birthday party?" Laurel's heart sank. Katherine planned to introduce Laurel as her granddaughter that evening. She had counted on Ben for support.

"He mentioned receiving the invitation, but he didn't say when he'd be back."

"If you talk to him before I do, please tell him...I miss him and can't wait to see him."

Janet dropped her key ring into her purse, then winked at Laurel. "That's one message I'll be delighted to deliver."

Laurel took her time walking back to her apartment, faintly aware of the smells of barbecuing meat and the sounds of laughter wafting from backyard patios. A shudder of loneliness passed through her. She didn't truly belong anywhere. She wasn't a Sullivan yet—not really. Edens were a figment of her parents' imagination. Ben had left without a word. But then, he didn't owe her an explanation. She'd asked for time apart.

Somehow, though, she hadn't anticipated it would weigh so heavy on her.

IT WAS NEARLY DUSK on Wednesday when Ben pulled alongside Noel Eden's workshop. He had no idea whether his trip here would make any difference, but for Laurel's sake, he had to give it his best shot. Acting on impulse after his final deposition in Akron, he'd phoned the Edens, and although they'd seemed puzzled by his request to visit them, they'd been gracious. So here he was. Drawing a deep breath, he got out of the car and, accompanied by a tail-wagging Dylan, headed for the house.

Noel greeted him, clamping a hand on his shoulder. "Welcome."

"You're sure I'm not intruding?"

Noel glanced surreptitiously toward the kitchen, where Pat was rolling out pie dough. "On the contrary," he said in a low voice. "I think you may be precisely what's needed."

Before Ben could explore that cryptic remark, Pat raised her head. "Good to see you again, Ben. I hope you like cherry pie."

"It's my favorite."

They made small talk over dinner, but when Ben had scraped the last crumb of the delicious pie from his plate, he sat back in his chair. "I'm sure you've guessed this isn't a purely social visit."

Pat set down her fork, but it was Noel who spoke. "What's on your mind?"

Ben marshalled his thoughts before wading into their family business. "I know how much you love Laurel. I hope it will come as no surprise when I say I love her, too. She needs her family." He hesitated, then went on. *"Whole."*

Noel nodded encouragingly. Pat averted her eyes, though Ben could tell every nerve in her body was on alert. "I've come to ask you both to accompany me back to Belleporte. Friday is Katherine's seventy-fifth birthday party at Summer Haven. I can think of no greater gift for her than your presence. Or for Laurel."

Noel gently clasped his wife's hand. For the first

time, Pat looked at Ben. "Laurel mentioned it on the phone. Is it so important to her?"

"You know it is." Ben found Pat's eyes, so like Laurel's. "But I'd venture to say it's even more important to you."

Pat gave a helpless little shrug, then glanced away.

"Don't wait too long," Ben said. "Since my father died last spring, I've thought of a thousand things I wish I had said and hundreds of questions I didn't ask. You've lost thirty years of family. So has Laurel. Let it come to an end. Live in the now. Enjoy your mother while you still can."

"Pat?" The longing on Noel's face tore Ben up.

She gripped her husband's hand before facing Ben. "I—I'm afraid," she whispered raggedly. "I should have gone back long ago."

"Your father's dead," Noel said. "Can you forgive Nan and your mother? Give up the hurt?"

One lone tear hung on Pat's lashes. She looked mutely from one to the other of the men.

"Katherine is a lovely person," Ben said. "She knows she was wrong to let your father dominate her. I think you'll like the woman she's become. Laurel does."

Noel caught Ben's eye in a silent thank-you. Then he spoke softly to his wife. "Pride and stubbornness or love and forgiveness? It's your call, darlin', and now's the time to make it. Once and for all."

Pat raised Noel's fingers to her lips. "I love you, Michael," she said, and Ben sensed it was the first time in many years she'd used her husband's birth name. Then she smiled shakily. "All right. We'll come with you, Ben. For everyone's sake."

After Pat excused herself to go to bed, the two men sat on the front porch steps, Fonda sleeping at her master's feet and Dylan with his head in Ben's lap. Noel, showing characteristic sensitivity, asked Ben about his father. For some reason, Ben found himself saying things he'd never shared with anyone. Even Laurel. He told Noel about the confusion he'd experienced as a boy when the handsome, self-assured pilot in the photograph came home a drained, haggard half man. About the tension of wondering when the next mood swing would occur. And about the love his father showered on his children when the demons were in retreat.

"So senseless," Noel said, almost as if to himself.

"Dad didn't think so," Ben said. "No matter how down he was, he never wavered in his conviction he'd served his country well."

"He must have been a very brave man."

"He was."

They sat in silence for several minutes. Then Noel spoke. "Isn't it hard for you to understand, then, why I opposed the war?"

"History has shown pretty clearly that there were two sides. Neither appears blameless."

"Some of my friends died in 'Nam, some went to Canada. I did what I thought was right under the circumstances. But it was a long time ago." He quieted, then laid a hand on Ben's shoulder. "I hope my actions then won't affect our relationship."

Ben turned and looked straight into the man's eyes. "Quite the contrary. I've been sitting here thinking now might be a good time to ask you for your daughter's hand. I love her a great deal." His voice thickened. ''Besides, I can't think of anyone I'd rather have as a father-in-law.''

Noel's eyes glittered in the moonlight. ''Thank you, son.''

MADDENINGLY, customers loitered in The Gift Horse right up until closing time the afternoon of the party. Maybe it was just as well, Laurel thought, as she closed the door behind the last straggler. She'd been too busy to dwell on the fact that she had heard from neither her mother nor Ben. Her mother's silence was a disappointment even though Laurel acknowledged she'd had a shock and needed time to process her feelings. No matter how much she hoped for a quick, easy resolution to the years of estrangement, given the complexities, that wasn't apt to happen.

She grabbed a quick shower, then put on dressy white slacks and a watermelon-pink soft V-necked blouse. Fumbling with her white hoop earrings, she realized her fingers were trembling. She needed Ben. Not for protection, but for support and love.

Please let him be there tonight.

KATHERINE GLANCED around the living room, which was festooned with crepe paper streamers. Nan was a born party giver, and her efforts were visible. Brilliant bouquets of summer flowers graced most of the tables. John had set up a bar in the far corner, and friends, too numerous to count, had been offering birthday greetings since their arrival. A local guitarist strummed background music, and a table bountifully laden with Greta's most delectable dishes was proving a popular attraction.

Laurel stood by the deck door in animated conversation with Jay. Studying her two grandchildren, Katherine swelled with pride. Handsome, productive, likable. She hoped they would become friends.

With a cocktail in one hand and a wineglass in the other, Quincy Axtell, Belleporte's most eligible widower, made his way through the crowd toward... Katherine gaped. Toward Maureen Nolan—so alone even when her husband was still alive. Studying the adoring smile on Maureen's face, Katherine chortled. Why hadn't she thought of that match before? They were perfect together.

That momentary delight, however, was tempered by the realization she hadn't seen Ben, even though he'd told her he would be here. Several times Katherine had noticed Laurel scanning the crowd when she thought she was unobserved, disappointment momentarily displacing her mask of gaiety. Where was that boy?

One thing about being seventy-five—Gawd, how could she be that old?—you could get away with outrageous behavior and chalk it up to eccentricity, and right now she didn't want to dwell on Ben Nolan's whereabouts or greet any more well-wishers. She had a mission, and it involved Jay and Laurel. She shouldered her way through the crowd. This would do her good and keep her mind off the fact—as if anything could—that she hadn't heard from Jo.

Deep inside, she'd harbored the hope that Jo would come for this party. She should have known better. What she had done to her daughter was unforgivable.

HOLDING HER BEER in a death grip, Laurel looked up at Jay. "You're sure you don't mind? I mean, it must be a shock to learn you have a cousin and...it's me."

He smiled warmly. "A shock, yes? But a pleasant one. Not just for me but for Granny. She's loving having you as a granddaughter."

"I'm very fond of her." Laurel smiled wistfully. "Wouldn't it be great if everybody could just forget the past and start fresh?"

"Ever the optimist, are you?" His eyes twinkled.

"I try, but this situation isn't easily remedied."

"Don't give up yet." He nodded toward the kitchen, where Nan was in conference with Greta. "Mom's starting to come around."

"I know it isn't easy for her." Several children, shepherded by Megan and Mike, jostled past them on their way outside. When Jay took Laurel's arm to steady her, waves of loneliness swept over her. "Do you know where Ben is?"

He studied her with concern. "Did he tell Granny he'd be here?"

She nodded.

"Then he'll be here. Trust me."

Jay's words should have been comforting. Live for the day, Laurel reminded herself. Celebrate her grandmother and their newfound bond. She could wait to think about Ben.

Just then Katherine swooped down on both of them, a triumphant smile wreathing her face. "There you are. It's time. Come with me." She left no room for argument as she ushered them out onto the deck. "Wait here," she said, positioning them by the railing overlooking the water.

A humid breeze rose from the lake, caressing Laurel's skin. Below, children frolicked on the swings and slide. Adults in casual resort wear mingled, smiling, laughing, sipping cocktails. Behind her, Summer Haven embraced her with a cooling shadow. Laurel's heart skipped a beat. This was exactly how she'd pictured it that windy November day when she'd first glimpsed the house. A family home.

Only part of her family was missing. Her mother. Her father. And Ben.

Clapping her hands, Katherine emerged again, trailed by her guests. "All right, everyone. I have an important announcement." Conversation died. "First, I want to express my gratitude for a lovely birthday celebration." She gazed fondly around. "Coming home to Belleporte was the best decision I've ever made. Thank you for making me feel so welcome."

Quincy Axtell raised his glass. "That was easy to do."

"Hear, hear," someone echoed.

Katherine beamed, then, holding up her hand, once more silenced the throng. "I want to tell you about the best birthday present a crotchety old woman could possibly receive. Laurel?" She gestured for Laurel to join her. "You old-timers know that I have another daughter, whom I have not seen for many years." Laurel heard a catch in her grandmother's voice. "I've always believed God has a sense of humor and that there is no such thing as coincidence. Laurel came to Belleporte to open a shop. I came here to start a new life. Little did we suspect that we would find so much more." When she linked her arm through Laurel's,

Laurel shivered in anticipation. "Friends, our precious Laurel is Jo's daughter, my granddaughter."

Those standing nearby erupted with exclamations of delight. Surrounded by love and good wishes, Laurel was aware of her eyes misting as she embraced her grandmother.

After the initial flurry of congratulations, Katherine produced a penknife from her pocket. "If Jay will do the honors, it's time to make Laurel an official family member."

Jay took the knife, chuckling as if he'd anticipated the punch line of a joke. "Where do you want them, Laurel?"

"Want what?" Laurel felt Katherine's hands resting lightly on her shoulders.

Jay ran his fingers along the surface of the deck railing. "Your initials, of course."

"You're a Sullivan," her grandmother whispered. "You're part of us and of Summer Haven."

Before she answered, Laurel looked out over the serene, blue-green surface of the vast lake, her heart expanding with a sense of belonging. "There," she said, pointing to the time-worn "JS" scratched into the wood. "Beside Mother's."

PAT FRESHENED UP at Ben's apartment, where Noel was leaving their truck. Now that she was here in Michigan, she didn't know if she could go through with the birthday party. All those people. And what if her mother couldn't explain the past? Worse, what if she couldn't understand about the awful argument? About Noel? Then there was Nan to face. She must've been furious. How could Pat sashay into Summer Haven as if nothing had ever happened?

Noel appeared at the bedroom door. "We'll be late."

"I'm ready," Pat told him, then tensed. That was a lie. She'd never be truly ready. This was just something she had to do. Probably should've done long ago.

Sitting between Ben and Noel on the short drive to Belleporte, she clutched Noel's hand, digging her fingernails into his flesh. All too soon, Ben turned off the highway and rounded a curve. There it was. Still. The wrought-iron sign with its curlicue letters spelling *Belleporte*. Lofty trees formed a canopy over the road, then the woods slowly gave way to the village itself. Pat's free hand moved instinctively to her chest. "It's...it's the same. There's the florist and—wait, the golf course is over there." Everywhere she looked were familiar landmarks, some with shadings of difference, but she'd never imagined it would be so like the place that had lived in her imagination all these years. Memories swept her away. The bank. Primrose House.

"Let's take a detour up Shore Lane," Ben said quietly.

Coming into view was the Mansfield cottage, transformed. "Oh," Pat crooned, at a loss for words. The Gift Horse. She brushed away tears of pride. "It's...it's beautiful."

"It is, isn't it?" Noel murmured.

"Laurel's made it happen," Ben added.

"I wish—"

"Another day, darlin'. Laurel will want to give you the grand tour."

Then, after a few more blocks, Pat spotted the gazebo and, in the distance, Lake Michigan. Something primal turned over inside her. She put a hand on Ben's arm. "Stop." Then realizing she'd sounded rude, she explained. "I...I need a few moments. By the lake. Alone."

Neither man said a word. When Ben parked near the gazebo, Noel stood aside and let her out of the car. Slowly, heart pounding in cadence with the breaking waves, she moved past the gazebo to the end of the boardwalk. Dune grass whispered, gulls shrieked their hungry cry, a bold sun balanced on the horizon between sky and lake, and in the west aimless clouds bled from amethyst to peach to crimson. She hunkered down and scooped up a handful of sand, slowly letting the warm grains sift through her fingers. She closed her eyes, touch and sound and smell restoring her to Belleporte, the place she'd never truly left.

Finally she stood, dusting the last grains of sand from her hands, and with a deep breath, turned toward Ben's car. Both men looked up as she approached. She gave them the first genuine smile of the entire trip. "I'm truly ready now."

The road to Summer Haven was as she remembered it, except now it was paved. A few new houses sprouted from clearings, but most of the cottages she recognized. Because they were late, Ben had to park at the foot of the hill. Noel put his arm around her shoulder as they started walking up the drive. Sounds of music and laughter carried on the air, reminding her of so many bygone parties and celebrations.

Then she saw the house, sitting majestically on the ridge of the dunes, its gabled windows and twin chimneys just as she remembered. But something was different. It was brown. Not the pristine white castle of make-believe. Not the Summer Haven of her youth. A new Summer Haven.

The front door opened and a tall, dark-haired, elegant woman came onto the porch. She waited, arms at her side, her body held in tight control.

Pat left Noel and walked rapidly forward, then stopped. "Nan?" Time fell away.

"Jo?" Nan took two steps toward her sister. "You're really here."

"I'm really here. Please, forgive—"

Before she could finish the sentence, Nan had crossed the space between them and embraced her. "I didn't know how much I'd missed you until I saw you," Nan whispered.

Pat clutched her sister, feeling again her thin shoulder blades beneath her fingers, inhaling the familiar lily-of-the-valley fragrance she always wore. The words spilled out. "I tried to make contact, but when I didn't get any answers, when my letters were returned, I thought, 'They don't want me. They won't want my baby.'"

"Shh." Nan rocked her. "We want you. I want you. Both of you."

Becoming aware of Noel and Ben, Pat slowly withdrew and turned her sister toward Noel. "If you're deeply in love with your John, you'll understand that my love for Noel was so great I risked Father's wrath rather than lose him."

Noel stepped forward and laid a hand on a shoulder

of each woman. "I am so happy this day has come at last."

"I am, too. Welcome, Noel."

Pat looked past Noel to Ben. "Thank you," she mouthed.

Nan tucked her sister's arm in hers. "Mother will be thrilled. This is the only gift she's ever wanted. Let's not keep her waiting any longer."

Steadied by Nan, Pat allowed herself to be led into the house, knowing with a mixture of regret and anticipation that thirty years had been too long to wait.

No MATTER HOW LONG she lived, Katherine knew she would never forget that moment, when, with the aching sweetness of a birth pang, she looked up and saw her daughters walking toward her, arm in arm. A space filled with light seemed to form around her as the crowd fell away and she walked, arms outspread in welcome, toward her prodigal child.

"Mother!"

Katherine heard only that one blissful sound before gathering Jo to her, becoming one with her again at last. "Oh, my baby, I've missed you so." Then she choked, her throat clogged with emotion.

"I'm sorry," she heard Jo whisper.

"Oh, darling, I'm the sorry one. Your father was wrong. I was wrong."

Jo drew back, her brown eyes swimming. "We have so much to say to one another. So much to undo."

At last Katherine became aware of a slender handsome man standing behind Jo, stroking his salt-and-pepper beard and studying them with a compassion that pierced her soul. She held out her arm to him. "This," she said, "must be your Noel."

Jo turned slowly, and Katherine was struck by the love on her daughter's face. "Yes. And despite the pain, I'd do it all again for him." She cleared her throat. "Noel, this is my mother."

No handshake for Jo's Noel. He stepped forward, his eyes glazed with tears, and embraced Katherine as if he'd known her forever. "It was time," he said huskily. "Long past time."

Jo looked around. "Where's Laurel?"

"Right here, Mother." Tears streaming down her face, Laurel stepped from the curve of Ben's arm and joined what had become a group hug. "Thank you," she murmured, "thank you all."

WITH SURPRISING TACT and despite their curiosity, the guests, except for those close to the family, began to depart soon after the initial celebration of welcome. Ellen, her green eyes glowing, left what Laurel had noticed was an animated conversation with Jay and pulled Laurel into her arms. "I feel like I'm in a fairy tale. Oh, girlfriend, I'm so happy for you."

"I was so afraid," Laurel admitted, "and I couldn't talk to you about it."

"Soon, though. I want to hear the whole story."

"You will. In great detail." Laurel smiled delightedly. "You know, you're right. This is a fairy-tale ending."

"Or beginning," her friend added wisely, before kissing her on the cheek and returning to Jay, who waited with an eager expression on his face.

Laurel liked the sound of that—a beginning. She

joined her parents, Nan and her grandmother on the
deck. Her mother was starting to explain, from her
viewpoint, what had happened that day so long ago.
Perched against the railing, Laurel listened without
comment, thankful that her family was coming together, and at the same time regretful for the years and
shared experiences that could never be reclaimed.
Such a waste. Yet would she be the person she was,
otherwise?

At one point in the conversation, her grandmother
caught her eye and with a slight nod indicated the
beach. Laurel looked down. At the bottom of the stairs
sat Ben, gazing pensively out over the lake. With the
silent communication that only those bound by love
enjoy, her grandmother winked and Laurel knew
where she belonged.

Quietly she slipped around the corner and started
down the steps, aware only of a warm, moist breeze,
the repetitious assurance of breaking waves and the
promise of Ben. Dear Ben, who had loved her enough
to go to West Virginia and bring her mother home.

BEN SENSED her presence before he heard her. She sat
down beside him, hugging her knees. Without a word,
he put his arm around her and pulled her close. She
rested her head on his shoulder, and he felt a deep
peace. As if, for once, the heavens were aligned perfectly.

"I've missed you," she whispered.

"Me, too."

"You left Mike in jail. You put me first."

He nodded.

"Then you went all that way to West Virginia for me."

"I love you, Laurel."

"I'm glad there's plenty of that to go around. Megan, Mike—I love them, too. And when I get to know the rest better…"

"Shh. I know. Your dad? For the first time in a long while, I feel as if I have a father."

"We're lucky, aren't we? We have families who care about us. Who let us care about them."

He tilted her chin. "And we have each other." He took a deep breath before continuing. "Laurel…" He hesitated a moment, quelling the thudding of his heart. "Please marry me."

"Oh, Ben." Her eyes widened and her mouth formed the most beatific smile he'd ever seen. But still she hadn't answered him. "Only if you'll promise me one thing."

"What?" Whatever it was, it was hers.

She stood, pulling him up with her, and curled herself into his arms. "Look."

He followed her gaze. Summer Haven. Then it registered. "You want to be married here."

"Where else?" she murmured before framing his face in her hands and looking at him with wonder. "I'll always love you, darling Ben. It doesn't get any better than this."

He felt neither the sand beneath his feet nor the glow of moonlight on his face, only the sensation of her body melting against him, her mouth cleaving to his in a belonging he'd been searching for his whole life.

When the kiss ended, he chuckled deep in his throat.

"Oh, I don't know about that. I think it's going to get better and better."

"I stand corrected," she said, taking his hand and leading him down the beach beyond the lights of Summer Haven. "Now—" she studied him with an impish look that was pure Laurel "—about that skinny-dipping…"